"Of all the rotten, underhanded tricks I've ever heard!"

Kelsey drew back her elbow and jabbed Clay in the belly. "Get off of me!"

A little *woof* slipped through his lips as he grabbed his stomach. "Quiet, Kelsey, the sheriff will be here—"

She pushed him away with both hands and sat up. "You must think I'm a fool, believing this trumped-up story of yours. Sheriff coming to arrest me. Stolen jewelry—my foot! Of all the men I've known, Clay Chandler, you are the lowest, filthiest, rottenest skunk I've ever met!"

He sat up and braced his arm against the pillow. "Look, Kelsey, you've got it all wrong—"

Kelsey scooted sideways in the bed and reared back against the wall. "Get out!" She kicked him with both feet.

Clay tumbled backward onto the floor. Springing to his feet, he glared down at her.

Kelsey's cheeks flamed. He was naked...!

Dear Reader,

Outlaw Love is the first Harlequin Historical novel by Judith Stacy, who writes for other houses under her real name, Dorothy Howell. We are delighted to bring you this heartwarming Western about a U.S. Marshal who comes to town to put an end to a series of payroll robberies, and inadvertently falls in love with the woman who is the leader of the gang responsible for the thefts.

Our titles for the month also include *Knights Divided* by Suzanne Barclay. In this medieval tale from one of our most popular authors, a young woman finds herself embroiled in a maelstrom of passion and deceit when she kidnaps the rogue whom she believes murdered her sister.

In *Bogus Bride,* by Australian author Emily French, a spirited young woman must convince her new husband that although he had intended to marry her sister, she is his true soul mate. And in Nina Beaumont's new book, *Surrender the Heart,* a gambler and a nobleman's daughter, haunted by their pasts, turn to each other for protection against falling in love.

Whatever your taste in reading, we hope you'll find a story written just for you between the covers of a Harlequin Historical book. Keep a lookout for all four titles wherever Harlequin Historicals are sold.

Sincerely,

Tracy Farrell,
Senior Editor

Please address questions and book requests to:
Harlequin Reader Service
U.S.: 3010 Walden Ave., P.O. Box 1325, Buffalo, NY 14269
Canadian: P.O. Box 609, Fort Erie, Ont. L2A 5X3

JUDITH STACY
OUTLAW LOVE

Harlequin Books

TORONTO • NEW YORK • LONDON
AMSTERDAM • PARIS • SYDNEY • HAMBURG
STOCKHOLM • ATHENS • TOKYO • MILAN
MADRID • WARSAW • BUDAPEST • AUCKLAND

ISBN 0-373-28960-X

OUTLAW LOVE

JUDITH STACY

Judith Stacy began writing as a personal challenge and found it a perfect outlet for all those thoughts and ideas bouncing around in her head. She chose romance because of the emotional involvement with the characters, and historicals because of her love of bygone days.

Judith has been married to her high school sweetheart for over two decades and has two daughters. When not writing, she haunts museums, historical homes and antique stores, gathering ideas for new adventures in the past.

To David, Judy and Stacy, as always,
for your inspiration, patience and love

Chapter One

Missouri, 1876

Hanging was a hell of a way to die.

Clay Chandler pulled against the ropes binding his hands behind him and swallowed hard. He'd gotten himself into a devil of a mess this time. He might even get himself killed.

"You boys better call this off before it goes too far." Clay dipped his chin toward the silver badge pinned to his vest. "You hang me, and every lawman in the state will be all over these parts."

Beneath the oak a few yards away, the two outlaws looked back at him. The tallest one gave him a wide grin.

"Well, they're gonna have to find you first, Marshal." He laughed and elbowed his partner. "Get the rope, Deuce."

Deuce glanced nervously at Clay. "I don't know, Luther. Maybe he's right. Maybe we ought to wait for Scully—"

"Just shut your face, Deuce, just shut it. Scully ain't

here now and I am, and what I say goes. Now do like
I tol' you and git that dang rope.''

Clay's gaze swept the area. Their campsite lay in a
meadow beneath two big oaks, the intertwined boughs
forming a leafy canopy that blocked out the bright afternoon sun. To the north and east stood more trees,
and to the south a rugged, rocky hillside. Good cover,
Clay thought, if he could make it that far. He doubted
Luther was above shooting him in the back if he made
a break for it. His gaze fell on his horse, tethered on
the far side of the oak these two intended to hang him
from—a long run, under the circumstances.

Clay shifted on the ground where Deuce and Luther
had shoved him over an hour ago and stretched out his
long legs. The ropes dug into his wrists. He glanced at
the empty holster strapped to his thigh and mumbled a
curse at the two outlaws, then one at himself.

Luther turned his way again. He was tall and lean,
and his face looked like dry, cracked leather. ''Yessi-
ree, Mister Federal Marshal, we're gonna show everybody what happens when some no-count lawman
comes poking around these parts looking for the Dade
gang.'' He rubbed his hands together and looked at
Deuce. ''String him up, boy.''

Sweat trickled down Clay's temple. He'd tracked the
Dade gang for three days, hoping to find their hideout
and bring Scully Dade in. But the gang had split up
yesterday, and on a hunch he'd followed these two.
Scully Dade, wanted in three states, had gotten away,
and Clay had stumbled into an ambush.

He dug the heels of his boots into the soft, damp
ground. He'd made a greenhorn's mistake. Now it
looked as though he'd pay for it with his life.

Deuce advanced on him, the length of rope coiled in

one hand, the noose dangling from the other. Young—
maybe sixteen, Clay guessed—dressed in clothes that
were most likely hand-me-downs. He seemed unsure
of himself.

Clay looked up at him, his gaze steady. "Do you
know what the penalty is for murdering a federal marshal, son?"

He stopped and turned back to Luther. "Maybe—"

"Git on with it," Luther yelled. "I ain't got all gol-
darn day to stand around here."

Deuce glanced at Clay once more. "But—"

Luther stomped over to them. "Are you tetched in
the head, or just plain stupid?"

He gestured at Clay with the rope. "But he says we
could get in big trouble—"

Luther yanked off his hat and slapped Deuce over
the head with it. "Would you just think for one gol-
darn minute! You're fixing to hang him—what do you
'spect he's gonna say?"

Deuce cowered, then straightened when Luther put
his hat on again. "Oh."

He nodded and walked away. "I'll git his horse."

Deuce looked at Clay, wary now, and grabbed his
arm. "Get on your feet."

With Luther's back to him, and time and options
running out, Clay took the only chance open to him.
He surged upward and drove his shoulder into Deuce's
belly, lifting the boy off his feet. He stepped back, and
Deuce fell to the ground, gasping for air. Clay dropped
to his knees, groping with his bound hands, and pulled
the pistol from Deuce's holster.

A shot rang out, and a bullet whistled past Clay's
ear. Luther, arm extended, ready to squeeze off another
shot, stood only yards away. In a split second, Clay

calculated the odds of getting off an accurate shot from behind his back and ducking for cover before Luther could fire. It didn't look good.

Luther pulled back the hammer. "Don't make me have to kill you before I get to hang you."

Clay rose to his full height, towering over both the outlaws. His broad chest and the star pinned to it made an easy target. Clay uttered a bitter oath and threw the gun aside.

"That's more like it." Luther walked closer, keeping a steady eye on Clay, and nudged Deuce with his boot. "Git up, boy. You are an embarrassment to outlaws everywhere. I am downright ashamed to be in the same gang with you."

Coughing, Deuce struggled to his feet. "We're not really in the gang, Luther. Scully just lets us ride along with him sometimes 'cause—"

"Shut up!" Luther waved the gun again. "Do like I tol' you to do."

Deuce's shoulders sagged. "Why don't we just let him go, Luther?"

"We can't let no lawman get away with hunting down Scully."

"Then can't we just shoot him in the leg, or something?"

"No! I've been wanting to hang me a lawman, and that's what I'm gonna do." Luther's eyes were bulging. "If I shoot anybody around here, it's gonna be you! Now shut up and get that dang rope!"

Deuce picked up his gun and straightened the rope. He slipped the noose over Clay's head, while Luther kept the gun trained on him.

Cold beads of perspiration broke out on Clay's forehead. His muscles tense, he looked for any opportunity to get the jump on Luther. He gave him no chance, just held the gun steadily upon him while Clay climbed into the saddle of the horse Deuce led over.

"You go through with this and the whole place will be crawling with marshals," Clay warned. "There won't be a rock anywhere Scully Dade can hide under."

"Scully's got hisself a new hideout so good nobody's never gonna find it. And you ain't nothing but some lowly marshal who don't amount to a wad of spit. Nobody's even gonna know you're gone." Luther waved the gun at Deuce. "String him up."

Deuce threw the rope over the oak's lowest limb and tied it off. "Ready."

A slow smile spread over Luther's face. "Any last words, Marshal?"

Clay's heart pounded in his chest. Thoughts of his thirty-two years spent on this earth raced through his head, but nothing he wanted to share with these two.

He looked down at Luther. "I'll see you in hell."

"You can—"

Gunshots sounded, and two riders broke from the trees to the east. Horses at a dead run, they charged the campsite, bullets flying.

Deuce's eyes widened. "What the—"

Clay's spirit soared. He turned in the saddle. He'd tracked the Dade gang alone. No one knew where he'd gone. No one expected him to return. No one would come to his rescue, or so he'd thought. Was this a last minute reprieve? Or was he caught in the cross fire of someone out for revenge against part of Scully Dade's gang?

The riders drew nearer, their faces hidden behind red

bandannas tied over their noses and mouths, and over-size hats pulled low on their foreheads.

"Gol-darn it!" Luther swore. "It's the Schoolyard Boys!"

"Huh?" Deuce looked dumbly at Luther.

"Bunch of snot-nose kids trying to make a name for themselves! I'd like to tan their hides. Take cover!"

Luther ran to the oak, with Deuce stumbling along behind. They crouched behind its huge trunk, leaving Clay on his horse, hands bound behind him, noose around his neck.

"Whoa, fella, take it easy." The saddle creaked beneath him as the horse pawed the ground. Clay kept his voice calm, trying to soothe the stallion as he frantically worked the ropes that bound his wrists. The riders kept coming. Luther returned fire, and punched Deuce in the shoulder until he did the same.

From the corner of his eye, Clay caught sight of another horse emerging from the pines to the north. It galloped toward the campsite, unnoticed by Deuce and Luther. The boy riding it wore the same shapeless clothing, red bandanna and oversize hat as the other two barreling in from the east.

Clay gritted his teeth. He was a sitting duck. If he didn't get hit by one of the flying bullets, and his horse didn't run out from under him, this outlaw would surely blow him to kingdom come with one easy shot. He held his breath, cursing himself, Deuce and Luther, and now these Schoolyard Boys.

The rider bore down on him. The horse beneath Clay stepped sideways, stretching the rope tighter around his neck.

"Whoa, fella, whoa."

The boy pulled alongside, his horse tossing its head

in protest. In a swift motion, he pulled a bowie knife from his trousers and swung it at Clay, cutting through the rope and sending tree bark flying.

Clay's horse lunged sideways. He squeezed his knees tighter to keep his seat. His head spun. Were the Schoolyard Boys trying to kill him, or rescue him?

Clay turned in the saddle for a glance at the boy who had cut him free, half expecting him to be gone, half expecting a bullet to explode in his face. The boy was beside him, knife in hand. Their gazes met for a split second. Amid the chaos of flying bullets and thundering hooves, that second lasted an eternity.

The boy nudged his horse closer, brandishing the knife. Clay felt the blade slide past his wrists and the ropes give way. Without giving Clay another look, he wheeled his horse around and crouched low as he raced back toward the pines.

"Gol-darn it!"

Luther let out a yelp and grabbed his shoulder as he dropped to his knees. "I've been hit! I've been hit by one of them dang fool boys!"

Deuce shrank back against the tree, watching blood spew from Luther's shoulder. "Oh, God..." He turned away and threw up.

Clay pulled the noose from around his neck and swung down from his horse. He picked up Luther's gun and disarmed Deuce, shoving the weapon into the waistband of his trousers.

The Schoolyard Boys stopped firing and turned north, toward the pines. The last rider's horse went down. The boy flew through the air and landed hard on his belly. The other rider, not seeing what had happened, disappeared into the trees.

"Good! Serves you right!" Luther called to the fallen rider.

Clay took a length of rope and tied Luther's wrists. Deuce sat up, his arms folded across his stomach, his face colorless. Clay thought he might cry.

He pointed his finger at him. "You stay put." Deuce nodded quickly and shrank back against the tree trunk.

Clay mounted and rode out to the fallen boy. The horse was up and walking, seemingly uninjured by the fall. The rider hadn't moved.

Clay slid from the saddle and knelt beside him as he lay facedown in the grass. The hat still covered his head, but the red bandanna had fallen below his chin exposing a gently curving jaw and the soft lines of a face that had never seen a razor. And never would.

Light footsteps brushed the grass behind him. Clay tensed and reached for his gun, then froze as cold metal pressed against his cheek.

"Eat dirt, lawman."

The raspy, croaking voice sent a chill down Clay's spine. He glanced up to find the barrel of a Winchester inches from his face. His gaze traveled upward and met with the large eyes of the rider who had cut him free, barely visible between the brim of the battered hat and the red bandanna. He'd looked bigger than life, charging into camp, wielding the bowie knife. Now Clay saw that he wasn't much more than five feet tall; he could only guess at the slender build hidden beneath the clothing. But at the moment the Winchester added significantly to the boy's stature.

Clay raised his hands. The third member of the Schoolyard Boys rode up, leading the horse that had gone down. The Winchester waved a silent instruction, and Clay turned his back and stretched out on the ground, facedown.

No one spoke, but he heard groans and whispers and finally horses galloping away. He turned in time to see the Schoolyard Boys disappear into the trees.

He mounted again and rode back to the campsite. Deuce was still sitting where he'd left him, while Luther moaned and cursed everything in sight.

"Gol-darn it, I can't believe I got shot by one of them scrawny Schoolyard Boys. They're not even dry behind the ears yet. I won't be able to show my face in these parts again."

"Don't lose any sleep over it." Clay climbed down from his horse. "You won't be showing your face anywhere but in a jail cell for a long time."

"Dang it." Luther moaned as he sat back against the tree trunk. "I hate them boys."

"I wonder where they're from." Deuce gazed off at the pines.

Luther kicked him. "Shut up, will you? They're just kids. That's how come they got the name Schoolyard Boys. Everybody's asking that same question. Don't nobody know nothing about them boys except how they've been making a nuisance of themselves robbing the stage."

Clay turned toward the pines. There was no sign of the riders or their horses. But he'd learned something about the Schoolyard Boys that apparently no one else knew.

One of the Schoolyard Boys was a girl.

Kelsey Rodgers pulled back on the reins, and the horse pranced nervously in the soft earth. Her gaze swept the tall trees and the shallow stream running through the narrow valley. "This looks like a good spot. We'll rest here for a while."

"We should have let him swing."

Kelsey slid from the saddle and gave her friend a scathing look. "I told you, Mallory, we had no choice. He was a lawman, for pity's sake. Do you know what happens when one of them gets killed?"

Mallory dismounted and dropped her reins, allowing her horse to drink from the stream. "Yeah, I know."

"Then you should know, too, that he could cause problems for us."

Mallory tossed her head indifferently and sat down on the grassy bank.

Kelsey pulled off her hat. The long braid of her light brown hair uncoiled and fell down her back. "The last thing we need is a bunch of federal marshals swarming the countryside, which is what would have happened when word got out that a lawman had been hanged. Besides, with what we've got planned today, we'd most likely be the ones blamed for it."

Mallory shrugged indifferently. "I still say we should have kept out of it and let the bastard hang."

A chill swept up Kelsey's spine. At times, Mallory's recklessness alarmed her.

"Make her stop talking that way, Kelsey."

Kelsey put her arm around Holly as she climbed down from her horse. "Are you feeling better? You took a hard fall."

"I'm all right." Holly patted the big bay mare and bit down on her bottom lip. "But what about her? What if she's hurt bad? What if somebody finds out we took her—"

"Nobody is going to find out." Kelsey glanced at

the horse's front leg. "Looks like she'll need another shoe. I'll take care of it when we get back to town."

"You don't think the marshal recognized me, do you?" Holly twisted her fingers together. "My bandanna came down. What if he knows who I am? What if he finds out? If I go to jail, I'll never get to see—"

"He only got a glimpse of your face, not enough to accuse you of anything." Kelsey patted her shoulder. "Don't worry. Everything will be fine."

Holly nodded. "All right. If you say so."

Kelsey sat down beside Mallory on the bank of the stream. The ground felt cool and damp beneath her. They'd ridden several miles into the hills, a safe distance from the campsite. She allowed herself to relax.

"Lucky for that marshal we happened by and saw what Luther and Deuce were up to." Holly shrugged out of her jacket and tugged at the waistband of the trousers that covered her plump figure. She plopped down on the bank.

Mallory rolled her eyes. "Yeah, real lucky."

Holly untied the bandanna from her neck and dipped it into the stream. "It was nice of him to come and see about me when I fell."

"But if it hadn't been for Kelsey and her Winchester, God knows what he might have done." Mallory scooped water into her hands and rubbed it onto her face.

Holly blushed. "My word, what are you suggesting?"

"If anybody knows what I'm suggesting, Holly Duncan, it surely is you."

"How dare you!" Holly's cheeks reddened, and tears pooled in her eyes. "That's a filthy thing to say, Mallory Morgan—even for you!"

Mallory's blue eyes flashed. "I don't know why you act so innocent. Everybody in the whole blessed town knows that when you supposedly went to visit your aunt last year, you were really—"

"All right, you two, stop it!" Kelsey got to her feet and stepped between them. "We've got enough problems without you two fighting all the time."

Mallory shrugged and turned away. Holly sniffled behind her bandanna.

A long moment passed before Kelsey sat down between the other girls again. "How do you suppose Deuce got hooked up with the likes of Luther and the Dade gang? He doesn't seem the type."

"One thing's for sure," Mallory said. "His pa is going to whip him good if he ever finds out."

Kelsey nodded, suddenly feeling much older than her twenty-two years. Mallory, the same age as she, and Holly, who was four years younger, seemed to have aged immeasurably in these past months, as well.

"Do you think Luther will be all right?" Holly's brown eyes looked hopeful. "I didn't mean to really shoot him."

"Luther is too ornery to die." Mallory scooped water from the stream again and trickled it down the front of her shirt.

"I've never shot anybody before—you know I haven't." Holly wrung her fingers together.

Kelsey patted her shoulder. "Just be more careful next time."

"Damn, it's hot." Mallory stood and stretched her long legs. She was the tallest of the three, and her limbs were lithe and supple.

"How do men stand wearing these heavy trousers

and big hats and thick shirts?'' Holly tied the bandanna around her neck. "Can we be girls next time?''

"I'll work on it.'' Kelsey pulled a pocket watch from inside her jacket. "We've got to go. Holly, do you feel up to this?''

She glanced at Mallory, then nodded. "Sure.''

The three climbed onto their horses.

"Do you think the stage will be on schedule?'' Holly shifted in the saddle.

"That old sissy Otis Bean would pop a stay if the stage didn't get out of town on time.'' Mallory fastened the buttons on her jacket. "It'll be on schedule.''

"And you're sure of what's on board?''

Mallory smiled knowingly. "I have it on the best authority.''

"Let's go.'' Kelsey led the way into the woods.

A devilish grin crept over Mallory's face as she eased her horse up beside Holly's. "Maybe when we're done we should double back and make sure Kelsey's lawman didn't get into trouble again.''

"Mallory, you're awful. Just awful.'' Holly pursed her lips. "He's probably very capable.''

A slow grin spread over Mallory's face. "Probably very capable, indeed. A man his size has got at least one thing in his favor.''

"Mallory!'' Holly blushed. "The things you say— Why, you leave me breathless.''

"I'll bet the good marshal could too.'' Mallory laughed a low, husky laugh. "What about it, Kelsey? You saw him up close. What did he look like?''

Eyes slate gray, like a spring thunderhead. A day's dark stubble covering a strong chin and square jaw. Even, white teeth set behind a full, expressive mouth. Broad, sturdy shoulders.

"I didn't notice."

Holly shrugged. "We've probably seen the last of him."

"I hope so." Mallory urged her horse to a faster pace. "A lawman is nothing but trouble."

"Cold and heartless," Holly added.

Kelsey felt the gazes of her friends upon her, but couldn't bring herself to agree with them. They hadn't seen the marshal the way she did. They hadn't felt his breath on her face when she cut the noose from around his neck, or sensed the raw power he possessed when she freed his hands. They hadn't seen the steel gray of his eyes melt into pools of blue when he realized she'd come to rescue him.

Kelsey touched her heels to the horse. "We'll have to hurry to make it to Flat Ridge in time."

She pushed the image of the marshal from her mind. The lives of too many people rested on her shoulders for her to waste time on such thoughts. She couldn't allow herself to think of him. Not now.

She had a stage to rob.

Chapter Two

Clay pulled off his black Stetson and sat down on the rickety chair across the desk from Deputy Billy Elder.

"So them two ambushed you, huh?" The deputy's amusement was thinly veiled, in the guise of taking down Clay's report. "They got the drop on you. Bushwhacked you. Then tried to string you up. Is that about it?"

The chair creaked under Clay. "Yeah, that's about it."

Seated under the gun rack across the room, Sheriff Roy Bottom rubbed a cleaning rag over the barrel of a Winchester. Gray hair bristling from beneath his hat, he appeared content to let his young deputy handle the paperwork.

Billy looked up from the report on his desk. "And it was only them two. Just Deuce and Luther. They were the ones who bested you."

Around twenty, Clay guessed his age to be, with the look of an arrogant kid who ought to be taken down a notch or two. Clay had disliked him on sight. "Yeah, just the two of them."

Billy consulted his report again. "And you're a

United States marshal, sent here on special assignment to clean up the gangs. Have I got that right?''

"You got it right." Clay lunged to his feet and threaded his fingers through the dark hair at his temple. He'd had enough of Deputy Elder. He headed for the door.

"Chandler... Clay Chandler." Sheriff Bottom stroked his chin and propped the rifle against the wall. "I heard about you. Brought in Cecil and Cyrus Reynolds, and the Fields gang, as I understand it, all on your own. You've got quite a reputation for yourself, marshal. Who are you trailing now?''

"Scully Dade."

Billy snorted. "Shoot, the Dade gang makes the Reynolds boys look like ladies at a quilting bee.''

Cold determination hardened in Clay's belly. "I'll bring him in.''

Sheriff Bottom nodded slowly. "If what I hear about you is right, I believe you'll do just that.''

Billy mumbled his disbelief and shuffled his reports into the desk drawer.

"Appreciate your help on this one." Sheriff Bottom nodded toward the cells down the hallway. "At least that's two less to worry about. Doc says Luther's shoulder will mend in a few weeks. I'll hold him here till the circuit judge gets around again. Deuce's pa will be by soon. He'll probably beat the tar out of the boy. You can be sure he'll stay in town till the judge gets here.''

"Who's riding the circuit around here?''

The sheriff shifted. "We lost Kingsley.''

Clay had crossed paths with Judge Kingsley a time or two in the past. "No loss. Most judges practice law from the bench. Kingsley did it from somebody's back pocket."

Sheriff Bottom shrugged indifferently. "We got a new judge now. Some fella name of Winthrope."

The name coiled a tight knot in Clay's belly. "Harlan Winthrope?"

He nodded. "Could be. I never met the man. He ain't been out this way yet. You know him?"

Clay's stomach churned. "I know him."

"You'll be gone before he gets here, huh?" Billy asked.

Clay nodded. He definitely intended to be gone from this town before Harlan Winthrope arrived. "I'll be here a few more days, that's all."

He opened the door, then turned back. "Do you know about a gang called the Schoolyard Boys?"

"I sure as hell do." Billy rose and swiped his blond hair back with his palm. "Them boys are making a name for themselves around here."

The sheriff nodded wisely. "They hit the stage at Flat Ridge just this afternoon."

"This afternoon? You sure it was today?"

"'Course I'm sure. Why?"

Clay nodded toward the cells. "Luther claimed it was the Schoolyard Boys that shot him."

Billy's brows drew together and he sucked his teeth. "Now let me be sure I got this straight, Marshal Chandler. You were tracking Scully Dade, but lost him and got ambushed by Deuce and Luther and nearly hung. Then you came across the Schoolyard Boys, but they slipped through your fingers and robbed the stage coach not an hour later. Is that about the size of it?"

Clay pulled his hat low on his forehead and gritted his teeth. "That about sums it up."

Billy nodded slowly. "Much obliged, Chandler. Good having you federal boys on the job."

Clay turned and left the office. He strode down the boardwalk of Eldon's Main Street, his gut churning.

He didn't like being made a fool of. It was one thing that Scully Dade—a hardened lifelong outlaw—had eluded him. And even the likes of Deuce and Luther getting the drop on him could be palated. But he couldn't abide being made a laughingstock by a bunch of kids—school-age kids, with a woman among them, at that.

Clay pushed his way through the swinging doors of the Watering Hole Saloon. He caught a few curious stares from the sparse afternoon clientele as he made his way to the bar. The badge on his chest always attracted attention.

"Beer." He tossed a coin on the bar and took the mug the bartender slid his way. Clay settled in at a table in the corner, his back to the wall. He took a long drink and ran his fingers across the rope burn on his neck.

Clay pushed his hat back and rested his boots on the rung of the chair beside him. Here under special appointment from the governor, he and dozens of other marshals spread out across the country had been directed to get rid of the outlaws terrorizing honest, law-abiding folks, and make it safe for families and businesses alike. He'd been on the trail for months.

Clay took a long drink and wiped his mouth with the back of his hand. He'd asked specifically for this assignment. He'd bring in the Dade gang himself, and not just because it was his job.

Kelsey hurried down the boardwalk, doing her best to conceal the carpet bag in the folds of her pale blue dress, and slipped into the kitchen of the Eldon Hotel.

"Well, I wondered if I was going to have to cook this whole meal myself."

Etta Mae Brown's disapproving gaze met her when she stepped through the door. Kelsey untied her bonnet and hung it on the peg. "Like you'd let me help cook even if I were here all day long?"

Etta Mae giggled and stirred the boiling pots on the cookstove. "Oh, Kelsey honey, you know me too well."

She smiled and darted into the small bedroom just off the kitchen. Quickly Kelsey dumped the contents of the carpetbag into the bottom drawer of her bureau and shoved it shut.

Kelsey hurried into the kitchen again. The large room held a massive cookstove, a pie safe, a sink, a sideboard and cupboards, with a worktable in the center. A pantry stood at one end, and a narrow service staircase to the second floor next to it. A small round table sat near the doorway to the bedroom Kelsey used when she stayed overnight at the hotel, which lately had been more than in her own bedroom at home.

"Smells delicious." Kelsey made her way to the sideboard, careful to avoid the bits of dough, squashed peas and flattened potatoes that littered the floor. Etta Mae was a wonderful cook, but as messy as the day was long. She was short and stout from years of tasting her own creations, and her gray hair was streaked with white and arranged neatly on top of her head. Etta Mae had worked at the hotel since her husband passed away, over a year ago.

"Anybody new check in today?" Kelsey took a

fresh apron from the drawer and tied it around her waist.

"Hmm?" Etta Mae looked up from the pots she tended. "Oh, no. No new guests."

Kelsey sighed and mentally calculated the number of guests already in the hotel and the amount of income they generated. She hoped the supper crowd would be good.

"How's things at the house today?" Etta Mae turned to Kelsey, water and greens dripping from her spoon.

"Everything's fine." Kelsey washed her hands at the kitchen pump, then took out a knife and sliced the apple pie cooling on the sideboard. She kept her head turned, avoiding Etta Mae's probing gaze.

"And your pa?" She leaned closer, her brows bobbing.

"Pa's fine, too."

It could be true, Kelsey told herself. In fact, it probably was true. She just hadn't actually been home today to know for sure. So it wasn't really like lying. Was it? After all this time covering up her whereabouts, Kelsey still wasn't used to it.

Etta Mae stirred the boiling potatoes, splashing water onto the cookstove. "Do you think your pa will be coming into town anytime soon?"

"No, Etta Mae, I don't expect so."

"He trusts you to run this place without him, hmm?"

She couldn't remember the last time her pa had come to town to check on his hotel or any of his other holdings. He didn't want to come, and Kelsey didn't encourage him. It served no purpose for the town to see what Emmet Rodgers had become; it would only anger Kelsey further.

"You poor dear." Etta Mae sighed wistfully. "I don't know how you keep up with it all. If only your brother—"

"Seth will be home soon enough." Kelsey pulled off her apron. "I'm going to check the dining room."

They took turns preparing the tables. Etta Mae had done it today, in her typical fashion. Kelsey hurried about the room, turning the white cloths so that the stains and mends weren't so readily apparent, straightening the silverware and refolding the napkins. The dining room faced the street, so Kelsey kept one eye on the boardwalk and one on the lobby, waiting and hoping for diners to appear. She desperately needed a large turnout tonight. Tonight and every night.

The supper crowd proved disappointing. The hotel guests were there, all four of them, and Bill and Virginia Braden, who owned the dry goods store down the street.

Kelsey stood by the door, fretting over the number of diners, mentally calculating the price of their meals and what it had cost her to prepare them.

"You mustn't frown so much, my dear. How will you ever catch a husband like that?"

A chill slid up Kelsey's spine as she turned to find Jack Morgan standing beside her. Dressed in a white linen shirt with a brocade vest and dark jacket, he looked every bit the most prosperous man in Eldon. His eyes were warm, his expression was compassionate, but Kelsey saw past the benevolent facade he presented. She knew the real Jack Morgan, and not just because he was her best friend's father.

"Catching a husband is not high on my list of priorities, Mr. Morgan." Kelsey struggled to sound pleasant.

"Whatever you say, my dear." He gave her a thin smile and slid his finger along the mustache above his lip. "What are we serving tonight?"

That he referred to the hotel as partly his rankled Kelsey no end. He didn't own the place. Not yet. And she intended to see to it that Jack Morgan never took another thing from the Rodgers family again.

"Roast turkey. I'll show you to a table."

He smiled indulgently and gazed at the room. "No need. I believe I'll have no difficulty in finding an empty seat."

Stomach churning, Kelsey returned to the kitchen.

By dusk, business at the Watering Hole had picked up and Clay ordered his third beer. He made it a policy not to drink too much. A federal marshal was a temptation to a young gunslinger out to make a name for himself, or a local looking to liven up a Saturday night. Clay had to keep himself ready.

But today had been a hell of a day, so he indulged himself. He questioned that decision a few minutes later, when Deuce walked through the swinging doors. Clay dropped his hand to his side and rested it on his Colt.

Deuce spotted Clay and walked to his table. He stared at the floor for a minute, then took a deep breath. "I came to tell you that I'm sorry for what happened today."

Clay rocked back in the chair. "Is that so?"

He nodded. "And I appreciate you telling Sheriff Bottom that it was mostly Luther that wanted to string you up."

"He threatened to shoot you if you didn't go through

with it," Clay pointed out. "I just told the sheriff the truth."

Deuce's cheeks grew red. "I appreciate you not mentioning to anybody that I threw up."

Maybe it was the beer, or maybe it was the flash of memory from when he'd been sixteen himself, but Clay took pity on him. He pushed out the chair beside him. "Sit down."

His gaze came up quickly. "No. No, I can't." Deuce glanced back over his shoulder, then looked at Clay again. "My pa was powerful mad at me when he got me out of jail. He whipped me good. I really can't...sit down."

Clay shook his head slowly. "I don't think you're cut out to be an outlaw, Deuce."

He lifted his thin shoulders. "No, sir. Me either."

"Did your folks give you that name, boy? Or was it just hung on you?" Clay took another sip of his beer.

"My name's Dennis, but everybody calls me Deuce 'cause I'm the second one. I got a twin brother." He looked at the floor again. "We're twins, but me and Jared don't look much alike. He's real big and strong, like my pa. That's my pa over there."

Clay peered around Deuce at the man standing by the swinging doors. Tall, with big, powerful arms and a full chest, a strong face set directly down on broad, muscular shoulders.

"He's the blacksmith."

"Holy Jesus..." Clay gulped down three swallows of his beer.

"Pa never let me work at the livery with him and Jared, 'cause I'm so small. But he says now I have to work there everyday so he can see to it I don't get into any trouble."

Clay let out a heavy sigh and sat back in his chair. "If that were my pa, Deuce, I'd see to it I never got into a minute's trouble again."

Deuce's father left his station by the door and crossed the saloon. He offered his hand to Clay. "I'm Ben Tucker."

Clay got to his feet and accepted his iron handshake, the grasp of a man who worked hard for a living. "Clay Chandler. Glad to know you."

"I wanted to tell you personal, Marshal, that I'm much obliged to you for putting in a good word for my boy with the sheriff."

"I only told him what really happened."

Ben nodded. "You can be sure Deuce here won't be hanging around with the likes of that Luther McGraw again. I put a stop to that today."

Deuce grimaced and shifted uncomfortably.

Clay nodded. "I think he got in with the wrong bunch."

"Well, it won't happen again." He gave Deuce a stern look. "That right, boy?"

He nodded quickly. "Yes, sir."

"I'm beholding to you, Marshal. You need anything from my livery stable, you just say the word. Is that your bay stallion outside the sheriff's office?"

Clay nodded.

"I'll bed him down at the livery. No charge. The boy here will take your gear over to the hotel."

They turned and headed out of the saloon. When they reached the door, Deuce ventured a glance at his father. Ben gave him a cold stare and walked out ahead of him. Deuce's shoulders sagged, and he followed along behind.

Clay fell back in his chair and took a long drink of

beer. Thoughts of his own father, his own family, floated through his mind, and for a moment he allowed himself to indulge in the memories. Happy times, filled with the love and closeness of a family. Times spent with…Rebecca.

Anger coiled in Clay's belly. He pushed his beer aside and surged to his feet, knocking the chair to the floor. The saloon quieted, and gazes turned his way. Clay pulled his hat low on his forehead and kicked the chair aside. He didn't like to remember. It always made him angry. But the anger was easier to endure than the guilt that ate at him. Guilt for his actions—and his actions alone—that forever guaranteed that those happy memories were a thing of the past.

The saloon patrons gave him a wide berth—and plenty of stares—as he made his way to the street again.

Dusk had fallen, and Clay felt tired. He'd seen the hotel when he rode into town this afternoon, so he headed down the street in that direction. Shops were closing for the night, merchants and customers hurrying home to their families. They paused long enough to give him and the star pinned to his vest a curious look. He ducked into the alley, unwilling to be the object of any more idle gossip today. At times, the badge was a heavy load to carry.

Kelsey swept the last of Etta Mae's meal preparations from the floor and dumped them into the bucket of dirty water waiting beside the back door. She straightened and groaned softly in the silent kitchen. The guests were all upstairs, and Etta Mae had gone home, leaving Kelsey to close up for the night. She didn't mind cleaning the kitchen alone. Tonight, fueled by thoughts of her encounter with Jack Morgan, the work had gone quickly.

Kelsey wiped her hands on the linen towel and draped it over her shoulder as she looked around the room. Spotless. She carried the bucket onto the back porch. In the fading light, she saw the small stable and paddock across the dirt alley and reminded herself to take the mare to the blacksmith first thing in the morning, before its owner was ready to check out. Early, before prying eyes noticed.

A cool breeze stirred and Kelsey shuddered, anxious to finish her chores and get into bed. She drew back the bucket and tossed the dirty water into the alley.

At that instant, a man turned the corner of the hotel, and the water hit him square in the belly.

"Jesus Christ!"

Clay roared like a wounded tiger as the water splashed up his shirt and down his trousers and soaked his boots.

Kelsey gasped and looked down in horror at the incriminating evidence in her hand. She tossed the bucket aside.

His gaze impaled her, blazing like hot embers in the dim light. "What the hell are you doing?"

Her eyes rounded. "I'm—I'm sorry."

A stream of filthy curses tumbled from his lips as he looked down at himself and flung water from his hands.

"It was an accident. I didn't mean to—"

His frown grew more fierce.

"Let me help you." Kelsey pulled the linen towel from her shoulder and hurried to him. Quickly she pressed the towel against his chest, mopping up the wetness.

"I didn't see you standing there," Kelsey explained

hurriedly. She dipped the towel lower and pressed it against his belly. "I'm terribly sorry—really I am."

Fire, more intense than his anger, suddenly ignited low in Clay's belly. Through the layers of clothing that separated his flesh from hers, the feel of her fingers moving over him, dipping lower and lower, sent a surge of desire through him, swift and strong. Its urgency overwhelmed him.

He felt the towel against his belt buckle, then against the front of his trousers. Clay gulped and jumped back.

"Stand still." She stepped closer. "I'm not finished."

If she kept this up, she'd have a finish she hadn't counted on. Clay pushed her hands away. "Keep to yourself."

Annoyed, Kelsey planted a fist on her hips. "Stop making such a fuss. I'm just cleaning you up."

Raging heat consumed him. He glared down at her. "Didn't your mama tell you that's no way for a lady to act?"

Kelsey rolled her eyes. "This is hardly the time for concern over proper decorum. Besides, I have brothers."

"Well, I'm not one of them." Clay yanked the towel from her hand and mopped the water from his trousers.

Heat flushed Kelsey's cheeks, and she felt them redden. She took a step back, needing to put some distance between herself and this man, and the feelings his words had evoked.

"I've had a hell of a greeting in this part of the state," Clay grumbled as he wiped his hands on the towel. "This tops off my day just dandy."

Kelsey's back stiffened. "You needn't stand there acting as if this were all my fault."

He looked down at her, his eyes narrow. "You're the one who threw the water, lady."

"Well, you're the one sneaking around the alley." She planted her fist on her hip.

He waded the towel in his big hand and pointed. "I'm going to the hotel."

Her nose went up a bit. "I don't know where you're from, but around here, guests use the front entrance."

He lowered his face, leveling his nose with hers. "And I can sure as hell see why."

They glared at each other for a moment before Kelsey stepped back and lifted one shoulder. "Well, anyway, I'm sorry."

He grumbled, then flung the towel over his shoulder. "No harm done," he finally said.

"Good. Now, give me your trousers."

His chest swelled. "What?"

Kelsey's cheeks flamed. She twisted her fingers together. "To have them laundered."

He drew in a long, ragged breath, then handed her the towel. "I need a room for the night. Where's the hotelkeeper?"

"That would be me. Kelsey Rodgers."

His brows inched upward, and then he touched the brim of his black Stetson. "Clay Chandler."

Noting that he hadn't said he was happy to make her acquaintance, Kelsey turned quickly on her toes and led the way into the back entrance of the hotel. She felt him behind her, his height and wide shoulders a force of their own. The man radiated a heat she'd never noticed in any of her brothers. His big, heavy steps sounded on the bare floors, drowning out the light scuff of her slippers.

She tossed the towel on the sideboard as they passed

through the kitchen and led the way down the hallway to the small lobby. Modestly furnished, it held the registration desk, a settee and two upholstered chairs. The dining room was located at one end of the room and the staircase to the second floor was situated at the other.

Clay took in the lobby in one sweep, then sauntered up to the desk. He pulled off his hat and ran his fingers through his black, wavy hair. Kelsey slipped behind the desk and turned up the wick on the wall lantern. Their first meeting notwithstanding, she desperately needed another guest in the hotel, and she would take this stranger's money gladly.

She put on her best hotelkeeper's smile and turned to welcome him to the Eldon Hotel. The words suddenly died on her lips. Pinned to his vest, shining in the lanternlight, was the badge of a United States federal marshal.

Raw terror ripped through her. A federal marshal! Right in her own hotel! Had he come for her? Did he suspect her involvement in today's stagecoach robbery? Would he arrest her on the spot? Kelsey gripped the edge of the desk.

"I'll be staying a couple of nights." Clay dropped his Stetson on the desk. "Give me a room facing the street."

Kelsey swallowed hard and forced her gaze from his badge to his face. Recognition coiled her stomach into a knot. This wasn't just any federal marshal, but the marshal she'd rescued from a hanging only hours earlier.

Her gaze dipped to his neck, and she saw the rope burns inside his collar. At once she felt overwhelmed by the desire to press her fingers against the marks and soothe them with her touch.

She gave herself a little shake. What was she thinking? The man was a federal marshal. If he knew who she was and what she'd done, he'd slap her into jail without a second thought. She had to get rid of him.

Kelsey perused the register and cleared her throat. "Sorry, but we're full up."

One thick, dark eyebrow crept upward, and he turned to gaze pointedly at the deserted lobby. Silence hung over the hotel. Clay eyed the cubbyholes on the wall behind the desk, the rows of keys to unrented rooms dangling there.

"You're full up?"

Kelsey pushed her chin a notch higher. "Yes, we are. I couldn't squeeze another guest in here with a shoehorn."

Clay rested his forearm on the desk and leaned closer, his voice low and measured. "Look, lady, I've had a hell of a day and I need a place to sleep. If I have to, I'll go from room to room until I find an empty bed, and when I find one—"

"Let me look again." Kelsey dipped her gaze to the register once more, her mind whirling. He didn't recognize her. He didn't connect her with the hanging incident this afternoon. To protest his stay further would only call attention to herself, make him suspicious. She had no choice.

Kelsey forced a bright smile. "Well, what do you know? It seems we do have a vacancy. And it faces the street. How about that! Just sign in, please."

Clay straightened and scrawled his name in the register she pushed toward him. "The livery was supposed to send over my gear."

On the floor near her feet, Kelsey found saddlebags and a rifle. She hoisted them onto the desk. "A new Winchester rifle? Nice."

His hand froze on the saddlebag. He eyed her suspiciously. "You know about guns?"

Kelsey swallowed hard. "I told you I had brothers. Remember?"

Warmth spread through him as he recalled the incident in the alley, when her hands had been all over him. "I remember."

She passed him the key. "Room four. Turn right at the top of the stairs. Good night." Kelsey forced a smile.

Clay pulled on his Stetson and flung his saddlebags over his shoulder. "Good night."

He picked up the rifle and climbed the steps. Halfway up, he turned back. "Don't forget to lock that back door."

Stunned, she simply nodded, then watched as he disappeared up the stairs. Kelsey sagged against the desk. A feeling of foreboding crept over her.

In her heart, she knew it would be a long time before she saw the last of Marshal Clay Chandler.

Chapter Three

The morning chill seeped through Kelsey's shawl as the sun peeped over the Ozarks, doing little as yet to warm the air. She tugged the thin wrap tighter around her shoulders and pulled back on the lead rope, stopping the mare in front of the livery stable. She'd left the hotel at first light and kept to the back alleys, but still, it was nearly impossible to hide something as big as a horse.

"Good morning?" She peered through the open double doors of the livery. "Mr. Tucker?"

A light brown head of hair popped up from one of the stalls. Deuce smiled when he saw her. "Morning, Miss Kelsey." He propped his pitchfork against the wall and walked out to meet her.

Deuce stood only a little taller than she, and probably didn't weigh much more, either—a sharp contrast to his twin brother. It seemed to Kelsey he had always looked as he did right now, frayed collar on a too-large shirt, suspenders trying to hold up trousers Jared had long ago outgrown.

"I didn't know you were working down here now."

Deuce shrugged. "Just since yesterday."

"How are your ma and the girls?" After giving birth to Deuce and his twin brother, the Tuckers had produced five daughters. Kelsey saw them occasionally in town.

"Okay, I reckon."

"Are you here by yourself this morning?" She needed the mare shod right away, and knew Deuce couldn't handle it.

"No." Deuce tilted his head toward the rear of the stable. "Pa and my brother are here."

Kelsey peered past him, to the back of the darkened barn, and saw Ben and Jared, evenly matched in size and build, having coffee together.

Deuce patted the mare. "Need something this morning?"

Kelsey took in a quick breath and gave him the speech she'd rehearsed. "She lost a shoe—I've no idea how—and it's a bit of a rush. Could your pa see to her right away?"

"What's the problem?" Ben Tucker walked out of the stable and gave Kelsey a welcoming nod before turning a stern look on Deuce. "You finished cleaning those stalls, boy?"

"No, sir, I just—"

Ben jerked his thumb toward the stable. "I'll tell you when you can come outside."

Deuce ducked his head and hurried into the stable.

Kelsey shuddered. She wouldn't want the wrath of Ben Tucker aimed at her.

"Now, what's the problem here?"

"No problem," Kelsey replied. "I'm just in a small hurry. I was hoping you could take care of her first thing."

Ben ran his hand down the horse's neck, studying

the animal. "I'll have the boy bring her back when I'm done."

"Thanks." With a sigh of relief, Kelsey hurried back to the hotel. Etta Mae would arrive soon, and she didn't want to explain why she was out so early. She couldn't be too careful. Not with a federal marshal living under her roof.

Clay bounded up the front steps of the hotel, feeling better than he had in a week, the night in a real bed and the bath he'd just had accounting largely for his good mood. The smell of food reminded him of his gnawing belly, since he'd elected to have a supper of beer at the Watering Hole last night.

In the dining room, morning sunlight filtered through the ruffled curtains, brightening the white linen and silverware laid out on the tables. Every eye in the crowded room turned Clay's way as he sauntered to a table at the rear and sat down with his back to the wall. He dropped his Stetson in the chair beside him and gazed out the window.

The town appeared prosperous, with a number of shops doing a brisk business already. Wagons, buggies and horses moved along the dirt street. Women with small children, miners, men wearing suits with guns strapped to their thighs all moved along the boardwalk. Eldon seemed like a good town, Clay thought, growing, clean. A place a man could settle in, raise a family in, grown old in.

Annoyed with his thoughts, Clay turned away from the window. He needed a cup of coffee.

The door from the kitchen swung open, and the serving girl swept into the room, balancing a tray of steaming food on one hand. It smelled delicious. Then another scent tickled his nose, and it took only a second for him to recall it from the night before. His breath caught in his throat as he recognized Kelsey Rodgers under that tray.

She'd seemed bigger last night, when she doused him with water, set his nerves on end mopping his trousers and tried to have him sleep in the street. Now, seeing her in the morning light, he realized she stood just a shave above his elbow. Her features were delicate. She was like a finely crafted china doll, with big, expressive green eyes and light brown hair. She bent to set the plates of food on the table beside him, and he saw the fullness of her breasts pressing against the tiny row of buttons up the front of her soft green dress. Clay's belly tightened. He hadn't realized last night how pretty she was, either.

He watched as she turned and her gaze swept the room with a critical eye, then came to rest on him. He saw the sharp intake of her breath, and his belly coiled again.

"Good morning, Marshal." Kelsey stopped beside his chair and put on a bright smile.

Certain she gave that smile to every diner who took a seat at one of her tables, Clay sat back in his chair and gazed up at her. "Let me guess—the kitchen just closed."

Her brows drew together. "No."

"The cook dropped dead?"

She shook her head. "The cook's fine."

"You ran out of eggs."

"No..." Kelsey realized he was teasing her for claiming the hotel was too full to accommodate him last night.

"Out of steak?"

"No."

"Ham?"

Kelsey looked pointedly at him. "Actually, it seems we have more ham than usual this morning."

He grinned, and to his surprise, she giggled. It was a sweet, melodious sound.

From her pocket, Kelsey took a small tablet and a nub of a pencil. "What can I get you this morning?"

"Two of everything."

She nodded and worked her way back to the kitchen, checking with the other diners as she went. Clay gazed out the window until the scent of Kelsey and the food brought his attention back indoors. Efficiently she placed a heaping plate of steak, eggs, potatoes and biscuits in front of him and poured steaming-hot coffee into his cup. She went about her business, but Clay found his gaze drawn to her as she moved about the room. Lord, she was a pretty little thing.

"Excuse me, young man."

Clay looked up from his plate to find a tiny gray-haired lady standing over him. "Yes, ma'am?" He moved to rise, but she waved him into his chair with her lace-gloved hand.

"Sit down, sit down. A young man your size needs a good morning meal." She smiled sweetly at him.

He swiped the napkin across his mouth. "Care to join me?"

She smiled again, her lips drawing into a tight bow, and squeezed her eyes closed for a second. "Why, thank you."

He'd noticed her when he came in, seated at the other end of the room, having a biscuit and a cup of tea; Clay made it his policy to notice everybody when he walked into a room.

The lady settled into the chair across from him, taking a few minutes to adjust her skirt and shuffle her big, open straw satchel onto her lap. It was crammed full of all sorts of items, Clay noted, as every old lady's satchel was.

"My name is Miss Matilda Wilder." She smiled at him and touched her hand to the tiny hat nestled atop her gray head.

"Pleasure to meet you, ma'am. I'm—"

She giggled softly and batted her lashes. "Oh, my, dear, I know who you are. Everyone in town knows. You're the federal marshal sent to root out those awful outlaw gangs."

Clay sipped at his coffee. "That's right, Miss Wilder."

She pulled a large flowered handkerchief from her satchel and waved it at him. "I just want to tell you how happy we are to have you in our town. It's about time somebody did something to make our streets safe again."

"I'll do my best."

Miss Wilder sat back in her chair and smiled proudly at him, as if he'd just recited a poem at the school play. She dropped her handkerchief on the table. "You're a fine young man. I know you'll do a good job."

Clay couldn't help smiling. "Thank you, ma'am."

Miss Wilder drew in a big breath. "Well, I'll be on my way now. I'm going to write to Sanford—he's my nephew in Memphis—and tell him all about you. He's been after me to move down with him, and he'll be pleased to know Eldon has a fine young man like you on the job."

"Nice meeting you, ma'am."

Clay rose as she got slowly to her feet, gathered up

her handkerchief and stuffed it inside her satchel. She waved and shuffled away. He took his seat again, wondering if everyone in town would be as glad to have him there as Miss Matilda Wilder seemed to be. He'd find out soon enough. A lot of questions needed to be asked in this town, and he intended to start on them this morning.

Absently he reached for the saltshaker as he mentally reviewed the list of things he had planned for today. His hand came up empty, and he looked across the table to see the pepper shaker sitting alone. Clay scratched his chin. He was certain he'd seen the salt there when he sat down.

Clay shrugged and turned back to his breakfast.

Peeping through the swinging door, Kelsey watched as Clay sat back in his chair and started eating again. She hadn't slept a wink all night, worrying about him in her hotel. She had to find out just how long he'd be in town. She had plans to make—plans that definitely did not include a federal marshal sleeping over her head.

Her best smile in place, Kelsey glided through the restaurant, refilling coffee cups, until she came to Clay's table. He looked different in the morning sunlight. Not cast in dim shadows, or ready to be strung up, he appeared strong and sturdy. Handsome.

"More coffee?"

He reached for his cup. The sleeve of his pale blue shirt pulled back, and Kelsey saw the rope burns on his wrists. She fought the overwhelming desire to run her fingers over the injuries and refilled his cup.

"Best meal I've had in weeks." He sipped the coffee.

"The Eldon Hotel has the best cook in town." Kelsey shifted. "Etta Mae packs a wonderful cold meal. Could I have her fix something for you today?"

He shook his head. "No need."

"Oh?" She shifted again. "I thought you were leaving."

He lifted one wide shoulder. "No. Not today."

"Then when?" Kelsey edged closer.

Suspicion crept over his features, and she saw his brows draw together. "In a while."

Kelsey shrugged. "Just let me know, and I'll be sure Etta Mae makes something special for you."

Clay nodded slowly. "I'll do that."

Kelsey turned away, then whirled back to face him. "And don't forget, I want your trousers."

Heads turned, and she felt questioning gazes upon her. The marshall glanced around, then looked at her; a little grin tugged at his lips.

Kelsey willed herself not to blush. "Since you soiled yourself on hotel property, it's my responsibility to pay for the cleaning."

Nosy gazes swung to Clay, and it was all Kelsey could do to contain the smirk that threatened. He surged to his feet and crammed on his Stetson, pulling it low on his forehead. Kelsey's gaze traveled upward. She didn't remember him being this tall last night.

"I'm flattered by your interest in my trousers, Miss Rodgers. I'll keep your generous offer in mind." He gave her a quick nod and left the dining room.

Kelsey plastered a smile on her face and wound her way through the tables and into the kitchen again.

The back door and windows stood open, the fresh air mingling with the smells of frying bacon and baking biscuits. Etta Mae hummed softly to herself as she flipped hotcakes on the stove.

"Kelsey honey, could you get me some more milk? We've got a hungry crowd this morning!"

"Yes, we do." And thank God, Kelsey thought to herself as she placed the coffeepot on the edge of the stove. She wiped her hands on her apron and darted out the back door.

"Pssst!"

Kelsey gasped and spun around, seeing her friend a few feet away. She splayed her hand over her chest. "Mallory, you scared me to death!"

Quickly she glanced up and down the alley. "We've got to talk."

"I'll say." Kelsey crossed the boardwalk and stood beside her. Mallory wore a dress of blue silk, with lace gloves and a matching hat—the height of fashion in New York, according to the dressmaker there who'd sent the fabric. Perhaps a bit out of place on the streets of Eldon, had it been worn by anyone but Jack Morgan's daughter. Mallory wore her father's wealth well.

Mallory unfurled her fan with a flick of her slender wrist. "Papa sent for the sheriff to come to the house early this morning, and I heard them talking in the study. Papa is fit to be tied over yesterday's robbery. Fit to be tied!" Mallory giggled and tossed her head. "Isn't it wonderful?"

Kelsey pressed her palms together to stave off their trembling. "Does he have any idea—"

"That we're the ones robbing his payroll? That you, Holly and I are the Schoolyard Boys—the thieves?"

"We're not thieves, Mallory." Kelsey's expression hardened. "We're taking back what belongs to us. Jack Morgan stole from us. If he hadn't interfered in our lives, there would be no need to take his payroll. If we were common thieves, we'd rob a bank or a train somewhere.''

Mallory tossed her head and giggled. ''Anyway, Papa has no idea we're doing the robberies.''

Kelsey let out a heavy breath. Thoughts of what Jack Morgan had done to her family, and Holly's, riled her no end. ''Then what did he and Sheriff Bottom talk about?''

''Papa is sending the payroll out again this afternoon.''

''Today?'' Her eyes rounded. ''After it was stolen just yesterday?''

Mallory nodded. ''Papa insisted. He thinks the stage won't be robbed because no one will expect the payroll to be on board so soon after yesterday's robbery.''

A bold move on Jack Morgan's part. Kelsey pressed her lips together. And totally unexpected. But she now had this inside information from Mallory.

''We've got another problem.'' Kelsey pushed a stray wisp of hair behind her ear. ''Remember the marshal we rescued yesterday? He's staying here at the hotel.''

''Damn...'' Mallory shook her head. ''I told you we should have let him hang.''

Kelsey waved away her comment. ''Well, it's done now, and we'll have to deal with it.''

Mallory snapped her fan closed. ''It must have been him Papa and the sheriff were talking about this morning. He's some big federal marshal, with quite a reputation. Sheriff says he's tracked down and brought in dozens of outlaws.''

Kelsey rolled her eyes. ''Oh, dear...''

''How long will he be here?''

"I'm trying to find out."

Mallory shrugged. "Maybe it's better he's staying at the hotel. At least that way you can keep an eye on him."

"That's true." Kelsey tapped her finger against her chin and paced the boardwalk. "We've got to do it. That payroll is too much money to let slip by. No one will expect another robbery this soon."

Mallory batted her lashes. "I'll pay a call on sweet young Ernie at the express office this morning, as usual."

"Good. Then drop by Duncan's and let Holly know—"

"Do I have to go talk to her?" Mallory's lip crept out in a pout. "You know she grates on my nerves sometimes."

"I won't set foot in Duncan's General Store, not after what Nate Duncan did to my brother. Holly and I can't speak in public, Mallory, and you know that."

"Oh, all right." Mallory fumed silently for a moment.

"Besides, if we get our way, Holly will be long gone from this town, which should make you very happy."

"Oh, to be gone from this place." Mallory sighed wistfully, but then her eyes danced with mischief. "But if I were gone, how could I annoy Papa?"

Kelsey drew in a deep breath. She couldn't blame Mallory for the way she felt about her father or her involvement with the Schoolyard Boys. After the despicable things Morgan had done to her mother, Mallory took great pleasure in irritating Jack Morgan at every turn.

"Find out when the stage is leaving. We'll stop it at Waterbow Curve."

"What if the driver won't stop this time?" Mallory asked. "We almost had to shoot at them yesterday. Remember?"

Kelsey paced, tapping her finger against her chin again. "I've got an idea. You'll need to pick up a few things, then you and Holly get out to Waterbow Curve as quick as you can."

"Where will you be?"

A little grin tugged at her lips. "I'm going to take a stagecoach ride today."

Clay hurried out of the hotel and strode down the boardwalk, heat radiating through him. If that woman mentioned his trousers one more time, he wouldn't be held responsible for what might happen. And the fact that she didn't understand the effect her comments had on him was all the more maddening. Was she really that innocent? Or did she just think of him the way she would her brother, as she'd claimed in the alley last night? Either way, Clay decided, he'd spent too much time on the trail lately to be having conversations like that.

"Hey, Chandler!" Billy Elder waved to him from the jail. "Sheriff wants to see you."

Clay crossed the street. Roy Bottom nodded when he entered the jail. "We've got a serious problem on our hands with those Schoolyard Boys. We're recruiting you for the job."

"Hold on a minute, Sheriff. I'm here on federal business, not local problems." The Dade gang were his prey, not a bunch of kids who needed a good spanking.

"I don't give a damn what you're here for." Jack Morgan rose from behind the sheriff's desk, his face drawn in tight, angry lines.

"Who the hell are you?"

Sheriff Bottom cleared his throat. "This is Jack Morgan, one of Eldon's biggest businessmen."

"Eldon's biggest," he corrected. "It was my payroll that got taken when that stage was hit yesterday, Chandler—the fourth robbery in the last six weeks."

"Darnedest thing," the sheriff mused. "Every time that stage gets hit, Morgan's payroll for the mines is on board."

"I built this town, Chandler. I own it." Morgan curled his hands into fists at his sides. "The governor is a personal friend of mine. I've got eastern investors coming out in a few days, men who've got a lot of cash to invest and can make something of this town. Sheriff Bottoms here tells me you're some big-shot marshal. I'm sending my payroll out again today. I want it protected."

Clay's back stiffened. "What's that got to do with me?"

Morgan pointed a finger at him. "I want you on that stage this afternoon."

Chapter Four

Ben Tucker stood at the doorway of the livery when Clay walked up. "Leaving town so soon?"

Clay shook his head. Though he'd like nothing better than to be on Scully Dade's trail again, he'd gotten roped into riding shotgun for Jack Morgan's payroll on the afternoon stage, delaying his own work for a while.

"No, Ben. I'll be staying on here for a few more days." Clay glanced back into the stable. "Is Deuce around?"

Ben's brows pulled together. "What's that boy done now?"

"I need to talk to him."

"If he's caused any more trouble, I'll take a strap to him this time."

The image Ben's words conjured up didn't sit well with Clay. "He didn't do anything. I'm after the Dade gang, and I think Deuce might have some information on their hideout."

"That boy," Ben said, fuming. "I don't know what's gotten into him. When Miss Chalmers wouldn't let him come to school anymore, I told his ma she had to keep him busy at home, but she couldn't do anything with him. I never thought he'd end up in trouble with the law."

"I think he's learned his lesson. Besides, working here with you ought to keep him busy enough."

"Maybe I should have done that from the start. But the boy's so scrawny. If he hadn't come into the world at the same time as my Jared, I might have doubted his ma's virtue." Ben shook his head. "I guess every litter has a runt."

"Is it all right if I talk with him?"

"Sure thing, Marshal." Ben led the way through the stable, past rows of stalls. The horses chewed quietly on grain, occasionally pawing the soft earth or uttering a nicker, content in the barn's cool interior.

Ben stopped at the open door to the feed room. Barrels and sacks of grain lined one wall. A rickety desk sat against the other; papers peeked from the half-open drawers, and ledgers littered the top.

"Deuce! Get out here, boy!"

A second later, he appeared at the door. Perspiration dampened his forehead, shafts of straw clung to his clothes and stuck out of his hair, dirt smudged his face. His breathing was heavy and labored.

Deuce glanced at Clay, then his father. His eyes widened. "I didn't do nothing. I swear, Pa, I didn't."

"The marshal just wants to talk to you, boy. And as soon as you get done, I want you to take that mare back over to the hotel. Understand? Then come straight back. You've got a lot more chores to get done before the afternoon."

Clay thought the boy might fall over any minute, from fear and exhaustion. "I don't want to keep Deuce from his chores. I'll walk along with him while he takes the horse to the hotel and we'll talk then."

"All right. But you tell the marshal whatever he wants to know. You hear me, boy?" Ben turned to Clay. "You let me know if he gives you any trouble. I'll take care of it."

From the looks of Deuce, Clay doubted he had the strength to give anybody trouble at the moment.

Deuce led the mare from the stall. They walked in silence until they reached Main Street. Clay took the reins and tied the horse off at the hitching post outside Connie's Cookie Emporium. "I'm pretty thirsty. How about you?"

Deuce wiped his sweaty brow with his sleeve and nodded.

"I'll be back. You stay put."

Inside the store, dozens of colorful candies sat in glass containers along the counter, and the display cases teemed with cookies, pies and cakes. The scents of vanilla, cinnamon and apples mingled in the air. Behind the counter stood a robust woman who appeared to have perfected her recipes by years of sampling her own confections. She eyed Clay up and down.

"You must be that new marshal I heard about. Welcome to Eldon. I'm Connie. I just took some oatmeal cookies from the oven. How about it?" Clay nodded, and she twittered, her cheeks going as round as ripe apples as she fetched a cookie from the display case behind her.

He tasted and nodded quickly. "Give me a handful of those."

"Well, hello again, young man."

Clay turned to see Miss Matilda Wilder at his elbow. He touched the brim of his Stetson. "Good day, Miss Wilder."

She shuffled her big satchel onto the counter, waving

her flowered handkerchief. "Looks as though you have quite a sweet tooth."

Clay grinned. "I sure do."

"Well, good for you. Keep up your strength. You've got a big job to do, and we're all very proud of you, dear." Miss Wilder gathered her handkerchief and satchel and made her way out of the store.

Connie wrapped the cookies in waxed paper. "How about some cider to go along with these?"

"Sure. Make it two."

She poured the drinks and picked up her tablet to tally Clay's purchase. Absently she reached in her pockets, then felt behind both ears and patted her neatly coiled hair.

"I swear to goodness, where is my pencil? It was here just a second ago." Connie searched the counter, lifting the cookies and cups. "Where did it go?"

Clay dug coins from his pocket and dropped them on the counter, more than enough to cover his purchase. He thanked her, but she didn't notice as she searched for her pencil.

Deuce was waiting on the bench outside, where he'd left him. He'd washed up at the water trough; his shirt was damp.

Clay plucked a piece of straw from Deuce's shaggy hair. "You need a haircut, son."

He swiped his hand across his forehead, pushing back his bangs. "Pa takes Jared and me to the barber at the same time. Jared doesn't need a haircut yet."

Clay sat beside him and passed him the apple cider. "How's it going with your pa?"

Deuce gulped down half the cider and grimaced. "He's powerful mad at me still."

"Maybe you'd be better off working at home instead," Clay suggested. Ben Tucker had been right about one thing. Deuce was too small to do manual labor.

Indignation and a hint of anger showed in Deuce's eyes. "I've got five sisters at home. You think I should stay there? With all those girls? And do women's work?"

"No, I guess not." Clay bit into a cookie.

Obviously, Deuce's options were limited, and Clay could see how the boy, unable to attend school anymore, not wanted by his father and too prideful to help his mother, had been easy prey for the likes of Luther McGraw and the Dade gang.

"Your pa will come around, once you show him you've no intention of getting into trouble again."

"He don't need me. He's got Jared." He turned away.

Clay swallowed the last of the cookie. "How did you get mixed up with Luther and the Dade gang, anyway?"

His shoulders slumped. "I wasn't really part of the gang," he said. "I met Luther here in town, and he claimed he had a mine somewhere up in the hills, so I signed on to help him. Luther knew Scully, but he wasn't in the gang, either."

"Luther sure acted like he was." Clay touched his finger to the burns on his neck. "He seemed dead set on protecting Scully and his hideout."

"Scully just let Luther ride with the gang 'cause Luther could cook so good." Deuce bit into a cookie. "It's hard to find a good trail cook."

"Were you ever at Scully's hideout?"

"No. I only met up with the gang that one time, a couple of days before me and Luther—" Deuce glanced at Clay's throat and quickly averted his eyes. "Well, you know."

Clay ran his finger around the inside of his shirt collar. "Yeah, I know."

Deuce chanced a look at Clay again. "I'm real sorry. I didn't want any part of hanging you, but Luther kept going on about it. I didn't know what to do."

"Decisions in life keep getting harder, Deuce. You need to learn how to handle them. It's part of becoming a man."

Deuce's mulled that over for a moment, then nodded. "I guess you're right."

"Nobody ever said it would be easy." Clay chucked him softly on the shoulder. "But I can see you learned a lesson this time. I'd say that means you're on your way."

Deuce looked up at him again, and the tiniest grin tugged at his lips. "Do you think so?"

Shouts from across the street drew their attention to Duncan's General store. After a moment, the raucous noise stopped, a door slammed, and a young woman left the store. Head high, shoulders straight, she marched determinedly down the street.

Deuce popped another cookie in his mouth. "Don't give it no mind. It's just Nate and Estelle Duncan. They fight all the time."

Clay's gaze followed the young woman along the crowded boardwalk. She looked vaguely familiar, but he'd only met a few women in town, and none so young. "Who is she?"

"That's Holly, their daughter." He finished the last of his cider. "She's the reason they're always fighting."

From what he could see, she was a pleasant-looking

girl, fuller around the hips and waist than her corset could disguise. "Is she too willful to suit her ma?"

"More like her ma's the willful one. Holly's nice. She just got into a fix, I guess you'd say."

Clay looked down at him. "What sort of fix?"

Deuce's cheeks reddened. "She got in the family way."

"She had a baby?"

Deuce shrugged his slim shoulders. "I heard my mama telling my sisters about it, warning them about…you know. All of a sudden Holly's ma sent her to visit her aunt, and she was gone for a long time. Her ma made her give the baby away—that's what my mama said—because when she came back she didn't have it with her."

"What about the baby's father? He wouldn't marry her?"

"He couldn't. He got caught stealing from Mr. Morgan's hardware store and got sent to prison." Deuce gazed across the street. "I don't think Mr. Duncan liked him much, anyway."

Clay blew out a heavy breath. Maybe Eldon wasn't as quiet as he had originally thought.

He turned to Deuce again. "Tell me about Luther. Does he know where Scully's new hideout is?"

Deuce waved away the notion. "I don't think Luther knows anything. I think he just talks like he does."

"I'd say you're right about that. And I'm glad to see you realize it." Clay rose from the bench. "If you hear anything from the Dade gang, let me know."

Deuce nodded with less enthusiasm than Clay had hoped for, then rose and untied the mare from the hitching post.

"I've got to get over to Miss Kelsey's."

Clay's stomach twisted into a knot at the sound of that name. "Kelsey Rodgers at the hotel?"

"Pa put a shoe on her mare this morning." Deuce patted the horse, and it nuzzled his shirt, knocking him back a step.

Clay patted the big mare. "What about Kelsey? Has she been out of town having babies?"

"Kelsey? Shoot, no. She's nothing like Holly. Fact is, she and Holly don't even speak."

He didn't know why he'd asked about her in the first place, but now he had to know more. "Why's that?"

The mare pulled back. Deuce grabbed the halter with both hands. "Bad blood between their families. Emmet Rodgers—that's Kelsey's father—founded the town, along with Mr. Morgan. They've been partners since they were both young. They got rich together. The way I hear it, Nate Duncan thought Mr. Rodgers had done him wrong in a business deal, and they've been feuding ever since."

Clay took hold of the mare to keep it from dragging Deuce across the street. "So Kelsey's family is wealthy? Why is she running the hotel?"

"Her pa's busy running other businesses, or something. I can't remember the last time he even came into town." He shrugged. "I expect that suits the Duncans just fine. Too bad, though. Kelsey and Holly used to be good friends. But since her brother—"

The mare tossed its head, pulling Deuce off his feet. Clay held the horse with a firm grip until Deuce got a hand on the halter again.

Deuce gave the horse a wary look. "I've got to go."

"You'd better get back to the livery before your pa comes after both of us."

Deuce's stomach turned over, and headed off down

the street leading the mare. It seemed nervous with the other horses around, so Deuce cut through the alley.

"Hey, boy! Deuce! Get yourself over here!"

He turned and saw Luther's face wedged between the bars of the jailhouse window. He froze in place.

"What's the gol-darn matter, boy? You think you're too good to talk to me now?" Luther taunted him.

Reluctantly Deuce led the mare to the window. He glanced up and down the alley. "I could get in big trouble for talking to you again."

Luther's eyes bulged. "Well, what about me? I'm sitting here in the gol-darn jail cell, fixin' to go to prison. How's that for trouble?"

"I know, but—"

"And you don't even have a howdy-do to say to me? After all I done for you? After the way I took you in when your own pa wouldn't even pay you no mind whatsoever?"

Deuce's shoulders sagged. "Yeah, I guess you're right."

"'Course I'm right." Luther pressed his face closer to the bars. "What have you been up to?"

Deuce jangled the lead rope. "Helping at the livery."

Luther squinted, then pointed and snapped his fingers. "Where'd you get that horse, boy?"

"I'm taking it back to Miss Kelsey at the hotel."

His eyes widened. "Kelsey? That Rodgers girl at the hotel? Is it hers?"

"I guess."

"Don't you know where that there horse come from, boy? It's the one that went down with them dang-fool Schoolyard Boys. Don't you recognize it?"

Deuce looked at the mare, then at Luther. "No. I

guess with all the commotion, I didn't pay much attention.''

"That's 'cause you were puking your guts out while I was getting shot up," Luther barked. He stroked his chin. "Now why would a nice little lady like that Rodgers gal have a horse that was used by a bunch of outlaws?''

"I don't know.''

Luther's brows drew together. "I'll have to study on that a spell.''

"Look, Luther, I've got to go. If my pa finds out—''

"I'm stuck in this hole until the circuit judge gets around again, and all you're worried about is your pa.'' Luther waved him closer. "Get over here, boy.''

He glanced up and down the alley again, then ventured closer to the window. "What?''

"I'm getting powerful thirsty in this here cell," Luther whispered. "How 'bout you bring me a bottle?''

"No. I can't do that." Deuce backed up a step.

"You owe me, boy." Luther pointed an accusing finger at him. "On account of you, I got shot, arrested and thrown in this here jail. I coulda got you in with the biggest gang in the state. Scully would have taught you everything he knowed about outlawing. You'd have been somebody, boy. And look at you now, shoveling up after horses in your pa's livery. What kind of life is that?''

Deuce shifted from one foot to the other. "I don't know, Luther.''

"Come back here after dark and bring me a bottle.''

"I've got to go." Deuce pulled the mare down the alley.

"You better be back here! You owe me!''

He didn't answer, didn't even look back, just hurried

through the alley and over to the Eldon Hotel. Deuce put the mare in the small paddock, then stuck his head inside the open kitchen door. It smelled of freshly baked bread.

Etta Mae turned from the stove, dripping water. "Hmm? Yes? What is it, dear?"

Aware now of how long he'd been away from the livery, Deuce bounced anxiously on his toes. "Is Miss Kelsey here?"

"Oh, no, dear." Etta Mae turned back to the stove. "She went out to visit her pa this afternoon. Seems he's not feeling well. And she was just out there yesterday, too."

"When will she be back?"

"Hmm? Oh, I don't expect her back. She took her carpetbag with her. Left some time ago."

"Just tell her the mare is in the paddock."

Deuce went down the alley, but in the opposite direction, away from the jail. He ran all the way back to the livery.

Clay ducked into the express office and walked up to the counter. The sheriff had told him—three times—when the stage would be through Eldon, but he wanted to check the schedule himself, as well as some other facts.

Otis Bean, the senior agent, looked up from his neatly arranged desk. A green visor crowned his bald head, and black armbands fit loosely around his crisp white shirtsleeves. In the corner, at a much smaller desk, sat a young man, his dark head bend forward, diligently shuffling through several stacks of papers; junior agents worked hard on their way up.

Otis Bean peered over the top of his spectacles. "Yes?"

Clay braced his hands against the counter. "I'm Marshal Chandler. I need to talk to you about the stage robberies."

Otis looked Clay up and down, and his expression soured. "Well, you can be sure it had nothing to do with my stagecoaches—I don't care what Jack Morgan says. He might own everything in this town, but he doesn't own this office."

"Seems a mite peculiar, don't you think?" Clay hung his thumbs in his gun belt. "The only time the stage is robbed, Jack Morgan's payroll is on it."

"Hoodlums." Otis tossed his head. "Don't blame me if you law people can't keep the stage lines safe for decent folk to travel."

Clay inclined his head. "Makes me wonder who else knew the payroll would be on the stage. Morgan says he never sends it out on a regular schedule, just to keep anybody from learning the routine."

Otis's body went rigid. "Now you listen here, Marshal, I'm senior agent of this office, and I know my job. And so does Ernie." He jerked his thumb toward the young man seated in the corner. "If somebody is shooting their mouth off about Jack Morgan's payroll going out, it's not coming from this office."

The man had worked himself into such a snit, Clay felt inclined to believe him. "I'd like to see the journals for the days the Morgan payroll was stolen."

Otis's spine stiffened. "That is private information meant only for the stage lines."

Clay straightened and squared his shoulders. He tapped the badge on his chest. "Not anymore."

His eyes narrowed, and then he slapped his palms against the desktop and rose. "Ernie!"

The young man jumped from his chair. "Yes, Mr. Bean?"

"Get the records for the days of the last four stage robberies. Give the marshal whatever he wants." Otis turned and glared at Clay. "And I should hope this will actually result in an arrest."

Ernie gathered the ledgers and brought them to the counter for Clay, then hurried back to his desk. Otis stood watching Clay as he leafed through the pages showing the routes, schedules, passenger rosters, and cargo manifests.

The bell jangled and the door opened. Clay glanced up to see a tall young woman in pale blue step inside. Her brown hair was carefully coiffed, and she looked like an easterner. Her eyes flashed as her gaze swept the three men.

"Well, good morning, gentlemen."

She purred the words, like a cunning cat on the prowl, and sauntered over to Clay. She tapped the badge on his chest with her fan and smiled lazily up at him. "I do believe you must be that marshal I've heard so much about." She tossed an impatient glance at Otis Bean. "Introduce us."

Otis's lips curled downward. "I'd like to present Mallory Morgan. This is Marshall Chandler. Mallory is Jack Morgan's daughter."

He touched the brim of his hat politely. "Pleasure to meet you."

Mallory uttered a deep, throaty laugh and eased closer, holding her gaze steady on Clay's. "Yes, Marshal, quite a pleasure."

The young woman exuded a sensuality that permeated everything around her. All done up as she was, in that proper dress with the tight fitted bodice and the bustle that swayed provocatively, he sensed a recklessness about her, the kind that in his younger days he would have sniffed after like a dog on point; the kind he now knew could cause a man a world of trouble. Especially when packaged as the daughter of the town's richest man. Clay eased back a step.

Mallory smiled sweetly and touched Clay's chest with her fan again. "Well, I don't want to keep you men from your work. I'll just have a word with Ernie."

Her gaze turned to Otis, and her brows arched, as if she were daring him to object. He didn't, and she giggled softly and wound her way back to Ernie's desk, her bustle swaying.

Clay turned back to the ledgers, talking quietly with Otis. After a moment, he glanced up. Ernie, flushed and breathless, was on his feet. Mallory stood inches away, purring softly to him. She gestured with her fan and smiled seductively. He nodded and grinned like a babbling idiot, totally captivated by the spell she cast.

Clay turned back to the ledgers. He knew he'd worn the same dumb look as Ernie many times himself. What man hadn't?

Mallory stayed only a moment longer, then leisurely left the express office, offering a goodbye from behind her fan. Ernie sank down in his chair, heaved a heavy sigh and wiped his forehead with his shirtsleeve.

Another hour passed, while Clay examined the stage records, before Jack Morgan and Sheriff Bottom arrived.

"Do you always put the payroll on the stage?" Clay asked.

"No reason not to," Morgan told him. "I've sent it

that way for years, with never a problem. Why should I go to the expense of paying my own guards, when the stage line will do it for the freight cost? I'm not throwing money around like that.''

Otis Bean lifted a pocket watch from its pedestal on his desk. "Stage is due to arrive in six minutes."

Clay led the way onto the boardwalk. One passenger, a man in a yellow plaid vest, waited outside.

Otis paced the boardwalk, studying his pocket watch. "Five minutes! Stage in five minutes!"

"Anybody else taking the stage today?" Clay asked.

Otis consulted his schedule, clutched in his other hand. "No. Only whoever boarded in Whittakers Ferry."

Clay gazed down the street. "Where's that?"

"Ten or so miles east of here. Four minutes!"

"And the next stop is Harmonville?"

"That's right." Otis consulted his schedule once more. "After leaving here, the stage stops at the swing station for fresh horses—that's where the mine foreman picks up the payroll—then goes straight through."

Thundering hooves pounding the soft dirt street preceded the stage.

"Stage arriving!" Otis clutched his pocket watch.

The driver atop the big coach braced his feet and pulled back on the reins, stopping the team in front of the express office. The horses pawed the ground and tossed their heads. Leather creaked and the stage groaned, settling in a cloud of brown dust. The shotgun rider stood and stretched.

Clay's gaze swept the stage with a critical eye, the men up top, the baggage tied on, the sturdy horses out front. He stepped off the boardwalk and opened the coach door. Inside sat an elderly man with a white beard, dressed in a bright green suit—the perfect complement to the next passenger boarding. Neither man would be a help in a shoot-out, but neither would try to be a hero and get someone else shot.

Clay gave only a cursory glance to the widow seated in the far corner. No one liked to look at a widow. A bonnet and a thick black veil shielded her face. Black gloves covered her hands and the heavy gown draped the rest of her. In her lap she clutched her reticule and a small Bible.

A heaviness rose in Clay's chest. Rebecca…

Determinedly he pushed the thought from his mind and replaced it with preparation for the task at hand.

Otis consulted his pocket watch. "Three minutes! Stage leaving in three minutes!"

Clay watched as the strongbox was hoisted up top, then took the rifle Sheriff Bottom had brought for him and climbed up beside the driver. He paid no attention to the anxious look on Jack Morgan's face or the sheriff's attempt at advice.

Nor did he give any thought to the little widow in the coach beneath him. For all the memories the sight of her widow's weeds caused, she meant nothing to him. Just a passenger on the stage. Nobody important.

He was sure of it.

Chapter Five

"Name's Buck, Marshal. Better grab hold of something."

The driver shouted to the team, and the stagecoach lurched forward. Clay closed one hand over the edge of the seat and kept the other on the Winchester resting on his lap.

"That back there is Mick." Buck nodded toward the shotgun rider seated behind them with the baggage.

Clay turned and nodded, and Mick did the same. The man looked to be near thirty, Clay judged; he handled the rifle in his hand as if he knew what to do with it, and Clay was glad for that.

"Keep a sharp eye out behind for us," Clay called. Mick nodded and turned to face the rear.

"Expecting trouble today?" Buck shouted above the noise of the horses' hooves, the straining of the coach and the rushing wind.

"Always expecting it." Clay glanced at Buck seated to his right. He held the reins in powerful, callused hands, telegraphing his instructions to the team with expert care. A battered hat rode low on his forehead, and a gray-and-white beard covered his face.

"Morgan's trying it again? Just got robbed yesterday."

Clay looked back at the strongbox. "He's determined to send it out again today."

"That's Morgan." Buck shook his head. "Gets what he wants."

"Comes with having money," Clay commented.

"Maybe so. But you don't have to lie and cheat and walk over everybody in your path to get where you want to be."

Clay hadn't heard anyone speak out against the man before. "I take it you don't think much of Jack Morgan."

"Nobody does," Buck grumbled. "But nobody can afford to say it out loud."

The man who owned most of the town carried a lot of weight, and after what he'd seen of Jack Morgan, nothing Buck said surprised him.

"'Course after every one of them robberies, Morgan has to shut down the mine for a day while all his men come to town and get their pay in person. Morgan don't like that." Buck grunted. "Serves him right, if you ask me."

The stagecoach pressed farther away from town, bobbing and swaying with the dirt road cut through the hills. Dense trees lined both sides of the route, then gave way to meadows, an occasional farmhouse, hills and valleys. The afternoon sun had reached its peak and was dipping toward the horizon. Clay kept a keen eye on the road, assessing likely spots for an ambush.

"Coming up on a bad spot." Buck nodded ahead. "Benette's Bottom. We got hit there a couple of weeks back."

"By the Schoolyard Boys?"

"Yeah, that's what people call them, I reckon."

"Anybody hurt?"

"Shoot, no." Buck chuckled. "Everybody's making them boys out to be bad criminals, but they never even fired a shot. The way I hear it, they never once fired on anybody."

Clay gazed at the road up ahead, where it dipped into a narrow valley for a few hundred yards, then climbed through the hills again. Buck was right. It looked like a prime location to stop the stage. Clay pulled his Stetson low on his forehead and tightened his grip on the Winchester.

They passed through Benette's Bottom with no trouble, but Clay didn't relax. He kept a steady eye on the landscape ahead.

"Swing station is up ahead, just a couple of miles other side of Waterbow Curve." Buck shoved his chin in that direction. "Looks like we're going to make it."

Clay shifted on the seat. "Maybe so."

The horses pulled the big coach up the next hill, and Buck tightened up on the reins as they headed into a long, slow curve. On the left rose a dense wooded hillside, and to the right a meadow dotted with elms.

"What the hell? Whoa!" Buck pulled back hard on the reins. The stage came to a halt.

Clay braced his boot against the footboard and pushed his hat back on his head. "Holy…"

From the branches of the elms dangled women's undergarments. Lacy corsets, embroidered stockings, taffeta petticoats, chemises with tiny bows, all hung from the limbs, waving gently in the breeze. Across the ground, ruffled, delicate clothing lay piled in mounds. A saddled horse grazed near the elm, the reins dragging as it walked.

Buck and Clay looked at each other, then at Mick. Stunned, the three men turned back to the meadow.

"I never—" Mick's voice cracked. "I never saw so many unmentionables in one spot in my whole entire life."

"Look at all them ruffles and lacy things." Buck shook his head in awe.

Clay swallowed hard and shifted on the seat. He'd been on the trail way too long.

"I'll see what's going on." Mick climbed down from the coach.

"Watch yourself," Clay called. His gaze swept the wooded hills to the left, then settled on Mick as he picked his way around the silks and linens. "Check behind that—"

"Drop 'em, lawman."

Clay froze as cold, hard steel pressed against the base of his neck. He tensed and lifted the Winchester. Buck turned toward him and his eyes widened. "What—"

The gun barrel pressed harder against Clay's neck, a silent command. He lowered the rifle onto his lap again and chanced a glimpse behind him. Black lace ruffled in the breeze. Clay's stomach knotted. The widow.

A boy stepped from behind an elm, wearing a red bandanna and an oversize hat. He pointed a rifle at Mick, who dropped his gun.

The Schoolyard Boys. Clay mumbled a curse.

A low, raspy voice spoke from behind him once more. "I said drop them, lawman."

The gun barrel jabbed his neck. Clay cursed and threw down his rifle and pistol. Buck did the same.

A horse emerged from the trees on the left, and the

third Schoolyard Boy lifted a rifle and aimed it at the stage. Positioned in their cross fire, with no weapon and two passengers in the stage to consider, Clay could do nothing.

From the corner of his eye, Clay saw the pistol at his back wave at Buck, and he mumbled and cursed, too, but tossed down the strongbox. It landed with a thud in the soft earth. The boy under the elm poked Mick in the ribs, and he headed back to the stage. He climbed up top while the widow made her way to the ground on the other side.

Clay looked down at the widow below him. Both arms extended, she held the pistol on him. If a boy was under that dress, it was a hell of a good disguise. For an instant, he considered jumping her, to see if she would shoot. But the sound of her voice rang loud and clear in his memory. Hard, gritty determination. He wouldn't chance it.

Buck picked up the reins and shouted to the team, and the stagecoach pulled away. Clay watched as the third rider followed them through the hills for several hundred yards, until they reached the crest of the next hill. The boy pulled up and waited, keeping an eye on the stage, making sure no one got off and doubled back.

"Damn it to hell..." Anger coiled in Clay's belly. He was going to get those Schoolyard Boys.

Clay left the stage at the swing station, got a horse from the stationmaster and rode back to the scene of the robbery. He'd questioned both passengers before leaving, but neither could tell him anything about the little widow. Like Clay himself, the men had hardly noticed her, feeling uncomfortable in her presence.

She'd kept to herself. Then she'd done her talking with the pistol she took from her reticule and made the men draw the shades on the stage windows. The last they'd seen of her was her dress flapping in the breeze as she climbed up the side of the coach.

He'd tracked the Schoolyard Boys through the hills after finding the empty strongbox under the elms, then lost them after they rode into a creek. Whoever they were, they knew the countryside. Local boys. They'd be harder to catch than outlaws like Scully Dade, who kept on the move.

Dusk had settled over Eldon by the time Clay returned. Morgan and the sheriff had gotten the telegram he dispatched from the swing station. They were waiting at the jail.

"Did you find it, Chandler?" Jack Morgan came to his feet as Clay stepped through the door. The sheriff and Billy Elder rose and glared at him.

"No. They got away clean." Clay pulled off his hat and ran his fingers through his hair.

"Damn it…" Morgan pointed a finger at him. "I'm holding you personally responsible for this, Chandler. Those eastern investors will be here in a few days, and if I lose their backing, the governor is going to hear about it. You get my meaning, Chandler?"

Clay's eyes narrowed, and he stepped closer to Morgan. "Don't you threaten me."

"You're responsible for my payroll," Morgan hissed through clenched teeth.

Clay pulled on his hat again. "You expect me to work a goddamned miracle? Everybody in the whole town knows you send the payroll out on the stage, everybody at the mine knows, everybody at the swing station knows. You said yourself you've sent it that way for years. And suddenly it comes as such a big surprise to you that it's been stolen?''

"Stolen by boys!" Morgan shouted. "A bunch of kids!''

"Kids with guns." Clay nodded down the hallway to the cells where Luther sat. "And they know how to pull the trigger."

"And so should you!"

Anger roiled in Clay's belly. "And if you weren't so damn greedy, you'd send your payroll out on your own wagon, with your own guards, and not sit back and expect somebody else to handle the problem for you!''

"Listen here, Chandler—"

"Hold on now, hold on." Sheriff Bottom stepped between them. "This isn't getting us anywhere."

Clay and Morgan glared at each other.

Billy turned to the sheriff. "I told you to send me out with the stage. This never would have happened if I'd—"

Clay grabbed the front of his shirt and yanked him off his feet. He pulled back his fist, wanting nothing more than to bury it in the young deputy's big mouth, but the sheriff laid a hand on his arm.

"Take it easy now!"

Clay gave Billy a contemptuous look, then pushed him away. Stunned, he staggered, staring wide-eyed at Clay.

"Billy, you just shut your face and go sit down." Sheriff Bottom pointed to the chair beside his desk. He turned to Morgan. "Look, Mr. Morgan, Chandler here is a good man. He knows what he's doing. I've done some checking on him like you asked, and I know for a fact he's one of the best. And if he says nothing could have stopped that robbery today, I believe him.''

Morgan glared at Clay, then turned away.

"Good." The sheriff sighed. "Now, let's get down to business. What happened out there?"

Clay drew in a deep breath. "They stopped the stage at Waterbow Curve. Mick got out to—"

"How'd they stop it?" the sheriff asked.

He shifted uncomfortably. "Ladies' underwear."

"Huh?" Billy stared up at him.

"It was everywhere." Clay gestured with his hands. "Hanging from the trees, the bushes, piled on the ground. More ruffles and bows than most men—hell, most women—ever see in their lives."

Sheriff Bottom scratched his jaw. "What do you make of that?"

Clay shrugged. "Mick got down to investigate, and the widow inside the coach climbed up and got the drop on me and Buck. Then one of the Schoolyard Boys came from behind a tree and got Mick. A third one was in the hills on the other side of the road, holding us in a cross fire."

Billy shot to his feet. "A widow? One of them boys was disguised as a girl?"

"Pretty clever." The sheriff nodded. "I seen that little widow inside the stage, but it never occurred to me it was really a boy inside that dress."

Clay shook his head. "No, it was no disguise."

Billy leaned closer. "Are you saying…"

"Yes, that's right." Clay nodded. "One of the Schoolyard Boys is a girl. I'm sure of it."

Kelsey turned up the wick of the lantern on the bureau and picked up her hairbrush, studying herself in the mirror. An eye for an eye, she reminded herself. The Lord helps those who help themselves. And she was certainly helping herself. Surely she wouldn't go to hell for it.

She brushed her thick brown hair, then tossed the brush aside and pushed her hair over her shoulder. Stagecoach robbery left her stomach in such knots it took several hours before she could eat. Now, at nearly midnight, she was starved.

Bare feet silent on the hardwood floor, she pulled the sash of her wrapper tighter around her and slipped into the kitchen. Etta Mae had fixed roast beef and potatoes for the supper crowd tonight, and judging from the leftovers, there had been few diners, and that meant little income. Kelsey's shoulders sagged.

"What were you thinking, Papa, when you mortgaged everything we owned?" She whispered the words into the silent room, words that she wanted to scream at her father, but couldn't. "Damn you, Jack Morgan..."

On impulse, Kelsey scooted a chair to the cupboard and climbed up. Stretching on her tiptoes, she reached the bottle tucked away on the top shelf. A little smile pulled at her lips as she eyed the brandy.

And why not? she decided as her feet touched the floor again. She deserved it, after having the scare of her life today. Her heart had nearly stopped when Clay Chandler opened the door of the stage and found her sitting there in her widow's weeds. And when he climbed up top beside the driver, she'd been tempted to run for it. But with Mallory and Holly already in place, and no way to warn them of the marshal's presence, there was nothing she could do.

Nothing but rob the stage.

Kelsey took a glass from the cupboard and poured herself a shot of brandy. She tossed it back. The smooth heat trickled down her throat and pooled in her belly.

"Did you learn that from your brothers, too?"

Kelsey whipped around and saw Clay Chandler standing on the bottom step of the service staircase to the second floor. Her hand brushed against the bottle, sending it to the floor. It landed with a thud on the thickly braided rag rug, but didn't break.

Clay crossed the room and knelt to pick it up. His gaze settled on her. "Well?"

He rose before her until she had to tilt her head back to see him. His broad chest and wide shoulders overwhelmed her. A clean masculine scent wafted from him, bringing with it a heat that bathed her like a humid spring morning.

Clay inclined the bottle toward her. "Did your brothers teach you to drink like that?"

Heat surged upward from her belly, consuming her. Kelsey didn't know if the brandy caused it, or Clay standing so close, or the fact that she wore only her gown and wrapper. She swallowed hard. Maybe the sight of the black hair curling out the top of Clay's half-open shirt, the fabric of his long johns, his sleeves turned back, exposing the hard lines of his forearms, brought on those feelings. Maybe the unseen force that pulled her toward him caused it.

Kelsey backed up and bumped into the sideboard, jarring her sensibilities. She gazed up at him and the bottle and pushed her chin a notch higher. "I learned it on my own."

His eyebrow crept upward. "That doesn't surprise

me. Are you going to offer me some of this? Or do you prefer to drink alone?"

"I don't drink alone. I just... Oh, never mind." Kelsey whirled around and opened the cupboard door. Clay reached over her head for a glass, poured a drink for himself, then one for her. Kelsey hesitated as he held it out.

"I've had a hell of a day, and I don't like to drink alone, either."

He wasn't the only one whose day had been hell, but she couldn't tell him that, so she accepted the glass and followed him to the table. They sat on opposite sides, the lantern in the center giving off a soft pink light.

"What are you doing down here in the middle of the night?" Kelsey traced her finger down the side of the glass.

He sipped the brandy. "I was hungry for... something."

Even seated across the table, she felt his presence all around her. "You should have been here for supper."

He snorted a short laugh and nodded. "Yeah, I should have. It would have saved me a hell of a lot of headaches."

"Outlaws not cooperating today?"

"Nope." Clay gulped down another swallow of the brandy. "Looks like I'll be here a lot longer than I had intended."

Kelsey's stomach flipped over. "Why is that?"

He only shrugged. "Business."

"You must be anxious to get home. Where are you from?"

"St. Louis. My family has a place near there." Clay rolled the glass between his palms.

"Your wife?"

"No wife. No children."

She nodded. "You're married to your badge, is that it?"

Clay shrugged. "For the time being."

"Don't you miss your family?"

"I haven't seen them in years."

Kelsey's eyes widened. "Why not?"

He studied the brandy inside the glass and shook his head. "I've got work to do."

"But still, they—"

"I've got work to do."

His words weren't harsh, just firm, but they closed the subject. She dipped her finger into the brandy and swished it around. "Does that work include the Dade gang?"

No such thing as keeping a secret in this town. "I've been trailing them."

"I hear they've got a new hideout near here." Kelsey touched her finger to her lips and licked off the brandy.

Clay's insides flamed as he watched her delicate finger glide across her lips. A strong, powerful yearning took hold deep within him, a foreign sensation he'd never felt before. Or maybe just not in a long time, he thought. It had been a while since he felt much of anything.

Clay dragged his gaze up to her eyes again. "I've got a couple of leads on the location of the hideout."

He'd never find the Dade hideout. No one would. For a moment, temptation nearly got the best of her, but Kelsey held her tongue. She smiled and raised her glass. "Here's to the quick demise of the Dade gang."

Clay clinked his glass against hers, and they both

drank the brandy straight down. The rush of heat down his throat pushed his internal fire higher.

Kelsey drew in a deep breath and smacked her lips. She giggled and sat the glass down. "Etta Mae made roast and potatoes tonight. Still hungry?"

"Starved." Clay came out of the chair and rounded the table. Life on the trail had pushed his manners to the far recesses of his mind, but he dusted them off enough to remember one of the things his mother had made him practice so diligently.

He pulled back Kelsey's chair, intending only to assist her to her feet. She stood, but swayed, and he caught her in his arms.

"Oh, dear..." Kelsey touched her fingertips to her temple. "Too much brandy, I—"

He kissed her. Heat, urgency, desire, flamed inside him, and he wrapped both arms around her and snuggled her against his chest. His mouth covered hers, drinking in her warmth and sweetness. Her soft breasts pressed fully to his chest. Clay groaned at the exquisite pleasure.

She didn't pull away, but she didn't return his kiss, either. For an instant, Clay knew he should stop, but couldn't bring himself to pull away. Then she moaned softly and leaned her head back. Her lips parted ever so slightly. He accepted her invitation and pressed farther into the sweet recesses of her mouth, acquainting himself thoroughly. She responded, touching her tongue to his, matching his movements in kind.

Clay slid one hand up her neck and plowed his fingers through her luxurious hair. Desire pumped his heated blood furiously. He wanted her.

Thoughts spun through Kelsey's head, too quickly to be recognized. She could only feel. The rock-hard chest against her, the strength in the powerful arms around her, the taste, the intimacy, overwhelmed her. No man had ever held her like Clay. No man had ever kissed her like this.

Then, suddenly, he pulled away and loosened his arms around her. She gripped the chair to steady herself. His breathing was heavy, she saw, as was hers.

"I don't think we ought to have supper together tonight." He spoke in a ragged, croaking voice.

Dumbly she looked at him. "Aren't you hungry?"

Intensity burned in his eyes, changing them from blue to deep gray. "My God, Kelsey, I'm so damn hungry...."

He turned away abruptly and took the stairs two at a time, up to the second floor. Kelsey sank into the chair. A long moment passed before she realized it wasn't Etta Mae's roast and potatoes Clay was hungry for. And it wasn't what she was hungry for, either.

Chapter Six

Sunlight muted by a hazy sky pierced Clay's eyes when he stepped onto the boardwalk outside the hotel. He rubbed his palms over his face, wondering how he could feel this bad on a morning when he hadn't even been drunk the night before.

Dreams, he realized. The images floated back to him and seemed as real as they had during the night. He hadn't dreamed of anything that left him so randy in years. Or anything so absurd. Kelsey Rodgers wearing nothing but a gun belt, pouring him brandy, then the two of them rolling around in the mounds of lace and silk at Waterbow Curve.

Clay felt his body react to the vision again, just as it had during the long night. Annoyed with his wandering mind and his mutinous body, Clay headed off down the boardwalk. He'd skipped breakfast this morning, afraid of what he might do when he saw Kelsey's bustle bobbing around the hotel dining room. He had business to take care of. Scully Dade was out there somewhere. Clay needed to be on his trail.

He'd only gone a short distance when he spotted Matilda Wilder on the boardwalk. He considered crossing the street to avoid her, but she saw him and smiled sweetly. Maybe it was for the best, he thought. Spending a few minutes with this elderly, graying woman was just the thing to drive thoughts of the young, supple Kelsey Rodgers from his mind.

"Morning, Miss Wilder." He touched the brim of his hat.

"And a good morning to you, Marshal." She gazed up at him and shifted her satchel from one arm to the other. "Looks like we may get some rain today."

Clay leaned his head back. Gray clouds hovered on the horizon to the east. "You might be right."

Miss Wilder pulled her shawl closer around her. "I wonder if I might have a few minutes of your time, Marshal? I'm writing to Sanford—you remember, my nephew in Memphis? There's a matter I'd like to discuss."

"Yes, ma'am."

She glanced around and hugged her shawl tighter. "It's chilly this morning. Do you mind if we step inside to talk?"

Chilly? Clay though he would burst into flames any minute. He shifted uncomfortably. "Whatever you want."

Clay opened the shop door behind them and followed her inside. He froze in place. It was a dressmaker's shop.

Bolts of colorful fabric lay neatly stacked on shelves and tables, silks, muslins and linens prominently featured. Laces and ribbons abounded. A pattern book lay open, displaying drawings of the latest styles in petticoats. The aura and mystique of femininity closed over Clay like a heavy mantle. He mumbled a curse to himself. This was the last place he needed to be this morning.

Miss Wilder walked deeper into the store and stopped beside the potbellied stove; the last of the early-morning fire smoldered. Clay wound his big frame between the tables and the displays of feminine apparel. He pulled at the tight muscles of his neck, praying she would be brief.

"Thank you so very much for hearing me out, Marshal." She set her satchel on a table displaying jars of buttons.

He forced his gaze onto the tiny woman. "What can I do for you?"

Miss Wilder spoke, but Clay's attention darted to the curtain that opened a few feet behind her. A neatly attired women holding a pincushion stepped from the dressing room and spoke to whoever was inside.

"I'll get that other fabric. But try to talk her into this one, Mallory. It looks marvelous on her." She disappeared into the back room.

Even without his current condition, Clay wasn't one to go peeping into a private ladies' dressing room, but the mention of Jack Morgan's daughter caught his attention. Just as the curtain swung shut, he saw her reflection in the mirror. Beside her stood Kelsey Rodgers. She wore some blue something. Wisps of her hair had fallen and curved softly at her neck. Clay's insides clenched.

Miss Wilder gazed up at him, imparting some long story, but Clay didn't hear a word she said. His attention was riveted on the dressing room and the conversation he overheard.

Kelsey spoke, her voice hesitant. "I don't know, Mallory, it's awfully daring. Don't you think?"

"For the hundredth time—no! Kelsey, you're coming to my party. Papa's important friends from back east will be there. You don't want to look like a bumpkin, do you?"

"But this gown—it's so...so...."

"So, what? Tight-fitting?" Mallory asked.

"No."

"Elegant?"

"No."

The images the conversation conjured up sent Clay's thoughts reeling and his body churning.

"I had Miss Patterson make up this gown for you because I thought it would be perfect. I wanted to surprise you. Why don't you like it? What's wrong with the gown?"

"It's cut so low," Kelsey exclaimed. "My nipples are almost showing!"

Clay sucked in a quick breath as fingers of fire clawed at him. Reaction to the vision of Kelsey came swift and urgent.

"Miss Wilder, I've got to go." He had to get out of the store before he disgraced himself in front of this sweet little old lady.

Concern creased her brow. "Is something wrong, dear?"

"No, no." Clay backed into a table of fabric, upsetting the display of satins. He grabbed it with both hands and piled it on the table again, the soft fabric burning his palms. "We'll talk again later. I promise."

"Well, all right, dear." She waved her handkerchief.

Clay rushed from the store and drew in deep breaths of air. What was that woman doing to him? She had him imagining things, and dreaming things, and feeling things that he hadn't felt since—

Since before Rebecca's death. Clay shuddered at the memory. The day he held his sister in his arms and watched her life drain out of her in a rush of blood that covered them both had been the day he stopped feeling most everything. Except guilt.

Maybe it was better that way. Clay strode away from the dressmaker's shop and didn't look back.

Billy Elder sat behind the sheriff's desk when Clay walked inside the jail. Reared back in the chair, feet up, he frowned when he saw Clay. "What do you want?"

Clay crossed the room and shoved the deputy's feet off the desk; his boots hit the floor with a thud. Billy tensed and glared at Clay, but didn't say anything. Clay almost hoped he would.

"I'm here to question Luther."

Billy snorted a laugh. "Luther's got nothing to say to nobody this morning."

"We'll see about that." Clay took the large ring of keys from a peg behind the sheriff's desk.

Billy rose and followed Clay down the hallway. "You're wasting your time. Luther got all drunked up last night."

"Got drunk? How?" Clay demanded.

"The sheriff went to get him up this morning, to take him out to the privy, and he found a bottle under the mattress."

"How'd he get it?"

Billy shrugged. "Don't know. Luther didn't have any visitors yesterday. Me or the sheriff was always with him."

Clay looked in at Luther, sprawled on the cot against the far wall of the cell. Tangled in the blanket, his mouth hung open, snorting and gasping with each snore.

"If someone could get a bottle in to him, they could get a gun in, just as easily." Clay unlocked the cell door.

Billy edged closer. "You think the Dade gang is in town? You think they're planning to bust Luther out of here?"

"I doubt it." Clay walked to the cot and grabbed Luther by the shoulders. He pulled him into a sitting position and propped him against the wall; his left arm, where he'd taken the bullet, hung in a sling. "Wake up!"

Luther jumped and snorted and batted at Clay with his open hand. "Dang it! What in the name of the Lord in heaven—" He stared, bleary-eyed, up at Clay. "Oh. It's you."

"Who gave you the liquor, Luther?"

He yawned and rubbed his eyes. "It was Scully Dade hisself that walked his big ass right down here to the jailhouse and give it to me, under the very noses of all you lawmen." Luther laughed and slapped his thigh. "He's bringing me supper tonight."

"Scully Dade doesn't give two hoots about you, Luther. Why are you trying to protect him?"

"'Cause of people like you, fencing us in, chasing us down, telling us all the time what we can't do. A man's got no freedom no more. It ain't right, it just ain't right." Luther gazed up at Clay and chuckled. "I see them rope burns on your neck are healing real nice, Marshal."

Clay set the toe of his boot on the cot and leaned closer. "I'm going to see to it you have a few rope burns on your own neck, Luther, only yours won't ever heal. Dead men don't get well."

Luther's eyes narrowed, but he didn't say anything.

"I want to know where Scully's hideout is."

"I ain't saying." Luther crossed his good arm over the other. "'Less, of course, you could make it worth my while."

Clay glared at him. "I don't bargain with outlaws."

"You must think I'm too dumb to find my own butt with a stick and a map." Luther pressed his lips together. "I ain't telling you nothing. You hear me? Nothing."

"We'll see how badly you want to talk when Judge Winthrope gets finished with you." Clay turned and left the cell. He brushed past the deputy without a word.

"Mighty uppity." Luther rose and walked to the cell door as Billy closed it. He strained to look down the hallway until he saw Clay leave the jailhouse. "What you doing letting some high-and-mighty federal man waltz into your town and take it over?"

Billy turned the key in the lock. "It doesn't set too good with me, I can tell you that."

"Then don't just stand there with your fingers up your nose—do something about it. The sooner that marshal leaves here, the better off we'll all be." Luther stroked his whiskered chin. "You know, Deputy, you could be the one to put away them outlaws right under his nose, and embarrass him so bad he'd leave town for good."

"I'd like nothing better." Billy turned away, then stopped and looked at Luther again. "You know something you're not telling the marshal?"

A sly grin pulled at his mouth. "Maybe I do and maybe I don't."

Billy moved closer to the cell door. "You tell me what you know, and I'll make sure the sheriff knows it came from you, Luther. He'll talk to the circuit judge. Things will go easier for you."

Luther pulled on his chin. "A lot of things could happen 'fore that judge gets here. I was thinking of something a little quicker. Like maybe a decent meal instead of that slop I've been getting. A steak would taste mighty good."

"Sure, Luther. I'll get it for you tonight." Billy glanced back down the hallway, then grasped the cell bars. "Now, tell me what you know."

Luther edged closer. "I seen that horse them School-yard Boys used when they busted up my lynching party the other day, the one they used when they robbed the stage."

Billy licked his lips. "Yeah? Where was it?"

"Right outside this here window. Seems it belongs to that little gal over at the hotel."

"Kelsey Rodgers?" Billy's eyes widened. "It was her horse you saw with the Schoolyard Boys the day they robbed the stage?"

"Damn right."

Billy turned and headed back down the hallway. Kelsey's horse had been used by one of the Schoolyard Boys, and the marshal had said one of those boys was actually a girl. It could only mean that Kelsey was in the gang.

Billy paced the jail. He couldn't wait until the sheriff got back and found out what he'd learned. He'd solved the crime, and he'd never even left the jail.

* * *

The breeze picked up as Clay headed toward Lincoln's Laundry. Chances were, Luther knew nothing of the Dade hideout. If Scully thought the man might expose its whereabouts, he'd have given him a bullet instead of the whiskey the sheriff had found in his cell. Still, it nagged at Clay that someone was offering aid to Luther. He'd have to keep a closer eye on him.

Polly Lincoln was sweeping the boardwalk in front of the laundry, but stopped when Clay asked about his trousers.

"Kelsey picked them up earlier today."

He should have known. "Thanks."

Returning to the hotel, he found Etta Mae changing the tablecloths in the dining room. "Where's Kelsey?"

"Hmm?" Etta Mae turned and smiled. "Oh, she's gone."

"When will she be back?"

"Hmm? Oh, well, probably not for a day or so. Sue Ellen Parker and I are looking after the place, like we always do when Kelsey goes home."

"Home? I thought she lived here."

"Oh, my, no. Emmet has a big, beautiful house just east of town. Is something wrong?"

"No. I'll take care of it myself."

Clay left the dining room and walked down the hallway to the kitchen. He wasn't about to wait around until Kelsey got back into town to get his trousers. He needed them now.

The kitchen smelled of the apple pies warming on the sideboard when he walked in, but Clay hardly noticed. Visions of the night before, when he'd kissed Kelsey in this same room, flooded back. It was probably a good thing she'd be gone for a few days, he decided. Coming downstairs again, seeking another midnight meal, was mighty tempting.

He glanced around the room for his trousers, but didn't see them, so he went into her bedroom. It smelled like Kelsey. Not giving himself time to dwell on that, Clay spotted a package wrapped in brown paper lying on the bed. He ripped open the corner and saw his trousers inside. Relieved, he took them and hurried toward the door.

Something in the bureau caught his eye. He knelt and examined the fabric sticking out from the bottom drawer. His stomach turned. Black lace.

Clay pulled open the drawer and saw a black dress. Beside it lay a bonnet, a veil and lace gloves. Widow's weeds.

His brows drew together as he pushed the drawer closed and stood. Most every woman owned a black mourning dress, but usually it hung in the armoire, not crammed into a bottom drawer. Clay glanced around the room and saw everything neat and tidy. Odd that Kelsey would be so careless with this dress, especially when she might be expected to wear it on a moment's notice.

And odd, too, he thought, that only yesterday the stage had been robbed by a woman wearing this same type of dress. No doubt existed in his mind that one of the Schoolyard Boys was a woman, but he knew it wasn't Kelsey. When he saw the rider fall in the meadow and went to help, he'd glimpsed enough of her face to know it couldn't be Kelsey.

Clay paced the room, stroking his chin. He wanted to get on with his search for Scully Dade, but he had to clear up this matter with the Schoolyard Boys first. Slim as it was, the widow's weeds offered his only lead. He'd pay a call on Kelsey at her house, he decided, and strode out of the room.

Clay got directions to the Rodgers home from Ben when he picked up his horse at the livery. A few miles out of town, he followed a curving, tree-lined drive to a huge white house with a wide front portico, massive columns rising to the roof and beveled glass in the large windows. He whistled low and shook his head.

The wind was blowing stronger now, and he looked to the east as he tethered his horse and climbed onto the porch. The bad weather was approaching fast. Clay rapped the brass knocker, anxious to get back to town before the storm hit.

No one answered, so he knocked again and paced the porch, his gaze wandering. Paint was peeling under the windows. Looking closer, he saw cracks in several windowpanes. He turned. Weeds choked the flower beds. For all its beauty, the house could use some work. Odd, for one of the wealthiest men in Eldon.

When no one came to the door, Clay circled the house. In the rear lay a wide lawn, overgrown like the one out front. Barns, stables, a vegetable garden and orchards spread out in the distance. A small boy romped near the barn with a big dog, while a woman fought a valiant battle against the brisk wind that billowed the bed linens she tried to take down from the clothesline. Clay tensed. It was Kelsey. The wind blew wisps of hair across her face and tugged at her dark skirt as she stretched up to pull the pins off the line. He heard her mumble a filthy curse.

"Did your brother teach you to talk that way?"

She whirled to face him and covered her mouth. "I didn't mean for anyone to hear that."

He walked closer. "I'm not surprised."

"You shouldn't be sneaking up on people." Kelsey planted her hand on her hip. "What are you doing out here?"

His gaze raked her from head to toe. "Like I told you last night, I've got business to attend."

Beneath her skirt, Kelsey's knees trembled as the recollection of his kiss sent a warm flush through her. Then her heart slammed into her ribs. His business was tracking down outlaws. Did that now include the Schoolyard Boys?

"You're trailing the Dade gang? At my house?" She stretched up for a clothespin. "Too bad. You just missed them. Scully and all his men came by and had afternoon tea with me on the veranda."

He frowned at her sarcasm. "Morgan's payroll was stolen yesterday, by the Schoolyard Boys."

"Then shouldn't you be out tracking them down?"

He edged closer, watching her intently. "One of those boys was wearing widow's weeds."

"Oh? Had he just come from a funeral?"

"It was a disguise."

Kelsey tapped her finger against her chin. "Wearing black on a lovely day like yesterday? I would say a pink or yellow would have been more appropriate. Oh, yes, Marshall, a fashion crime has definitely been committed."

"You think this is pretty damn funny, huh?"

She rolled her eyes. "Why are you telling me all this?"

"Because I'd like to know why you've got a mourning dress stuffed in the bottom drawer of your bureau."

Kelsey gasped, too stunned at first to speak. Then anger coiled in her stomach. "You went through my belongings? My personal things? How dare you!"

He leaned closer. "Because it's my job."

Kelsey yanked a sheet from the line. "Since you've apparently been living in a cave for the last few decades, Marshal Chandler, let me inform you that every woman on the continent owns a mourning dress—including me! And for your further information, handling someone else's personal clothing is the height of ill manners and poor breeding. What were you doing in my room in the first place?"

"Getting my trousers back from you."

Kelsey's drew in a quick breath. "Well, that's different."

"Yeah? What's so different about it?" he asked her challengingly.

She whipped around, presenting her back. "It just is, that's all. I hardly expect you to understand."

"Can you tell me where those boys might have come by a mourning dress like that?"

She pulled another linen sheet from the line and turned to face him again. "How could I possibly know that? I'm just a hotelkeeper. No secrets. No surprises."

Screams and running feet sounded on the lawn behind them. The small boy Clay had seen near the barn hurried toward them, tears streaming down his face.

Kelsey knelt. "What is it, Toby? What's wrong?"

"Come quick, Mama! Please—you gotta!"

Stunned, Clay grasped Kelsey's arm and pulled her to her feet. "Mama?"

Chapter Seven

Toby grabbed Kelsey's hand and pulled hard. "Come quick! Buster's in the chicken coop! Tula gotted the gun!"

Clay held her arm. His gaze bored into her. "Mama?"

She looked up at him, then pulled free of his grip. "You stay here, Toby."

Kelsey gathered her skirt and ran across the lawn. Clay glared down at the boy, then hurried after her.

Hens squawked and feathers flew as the big black-and-white dog chased the chickens around the coop, darting playfully, barking and snapping at their tail-feathers.

"Buster, stop that!" Kelsey pulled the gate open. The dog loped across the coop, scattering the hens. She lunged for him, but he shifted direction and ran the other way.

"Ya'll better get back from that dawg, Miss Kelsey! I'm going to blow him to kingdom come!"

Kelsey threw up both hands. "No, Tula! Don't shoot!"

The short, round, gray-haired woman lumbered

down the lawn from the house, a shotgun tucked under her arm. "I done gone and had enough of that mangy animal! I'm a-gonna drop him on the spot!"

Clay ran up to the coop. He stepped in front of Tula. "Calm down. You're not going to shoot anything."

She looked him up and down and her back stiffened. "And who says so?"

"I do." Clay pushed the gun barrel upward, then pulled it from her hand.

Tula planted both hands on her ample hips. "Now just a minute—"

Clay darted inside the coop and propped the shotgun by the gate. Dodging chickens, he and Kelsey chased the dog until they finally cornered it by the henhouse. Clay grabbed the nape of its neck and pulled it out of the coop.

Kelsey bent down and pointed a finger at him. "Bad dog, Buster. Bad, bad dog."

The dog whimpered, then licked Kelsey's face and loped across the yard.

"That no-good dog." Tula shook her head and watched as Buster ran up to Toby and licked him furiously. "Them hens won't be laying now for a month of Sundays."

Kelsey grimaced and wiped off Buster's kiss with the back of her hand. "Tula, you can't shoot him. You know how much he means to Toby."

She mumbled under her breath, then sighed heavily. "That coop better get fixed good enough this time so that dog can't get in to them hens."

"I'll take care of it." Kelsey pushed a lock of hair behind her ear and sighed wearily. She gestured to Clay. "Tula, this is Clay Chandler."

The old woman squinted at him, then shook her

head. "And you're some kinda lawman. What a welcome we've given you to this house. I do declare, I don't know what-all has become of this family." Grumbling to herself, Tula went back up to the house.

Kelsey offered Clay an apologetic smile. "Tula is our housekeeper and cook. She's been with us for years."

He gestured toward the shotgun. "I don't want to know how she reacts if you don't clean your plate at suppertime."

Kelsey laughed, then stretched up and plucked a chicken feather from Clay's shoulder. Their gazes locked for an instant before Toby ran up and threw his arms around Kelsey.

"You saved Buster. I knowed you would."

"We can't let anything happen to Buster." Kelsey lifted him into her arms and hugged him tight. He wrapped his short legs around her and planted a wet kiss on her cheek. She smiled, then turned him to face Clay. "Toby, can you say hello to Marshal Clay Chandler?"

He held up his palm, fingers spread wide. "I'm this many."

A big boy for five, with green eyes and light brown hair. He looked like Kelsey.

"Me and Buster gotta go." Toby wiggled from Kelsey's arms and raced toward the dirt lane that led through the trees to the outbuildings.

"Toby! Wait!"

The wind whipped the words from Kelsey's lips and sent them sailing. Quickly she planted two fingers in her mouth and let out a piercing whistle. Toby stopped.

"Don't stay long! There's a storm coming! And watch out for snakes!"

He nodded and hurried to catch up with Buster.

Kelsey felt Clay's gaze upon her, and her cheeks pinkened at her own shameless, unladylike behavior. She smiled weakly at him. "My brother taught me."

"Yeah, I figured." Clay watched the boy and dog until they disappeared from sight. "Who, exactly, is Toby?"

"He's my brother."

Clay nodded. "So he's the one who taught you that hard drinking and sailor talk."

"No." Kelsey laughed gently. "I have an older brother, too. Toby calls me Mama sometimes. Our mother died a year ago. Her illness kept her bedridden for a long time, so I took over most of his care. He doesn't understand."

Thunder rumbled, and Kelsey glanced at the horizon. "I have to get the wash in."

To her surprise, Clay followed her back to the clothesline. He pulled the pins from the line and helped gather the bed linens, then carried the laundry basket to the back porch. Thunder rolled again, and the air was heavy with moisture.

Kelsey climbed the steps, bringing herself even with Clay. An odd feeling, being able to look him in the eye. "Storm is brewing."

Clay's chest tightened. A storm was brewing all right. He could feel it growing. God, she was a pretty woman. Tousled by the wind, her hair loose, her skirt whipping around her ankles, she looked inviting.

Clay lost himself in the depths of her green eyes for a moment. "Could be a hell of a storm."

Kelsey shifted uncomfortably, unsure it was the thunderstorm Clay was thinking of.

The back door burst open and slammed against the

house. A stoop-shouldered man stepped onto the porch, clutching a cane, his white hair bushy and unkempt.

"What's all the commotion out here? What's going on? Somebody's knocking on the door, then that dog is barking its head off. What's happening?"

"It's nothing, Papa. Everything is fine." Kelsey laid her hands on his flailing fists.

His wild, glassy eyes riveted Clay. "Who's that?"

"This is Clay Chandler. He's a federal marshal," Kelsey explained patiently.

"Stranger," he grunted. "I don't like strangers."

She patted his shoulder gently. "He's not a stranger, Papa. Clay is a friend of mine from town."

"I don't know about this...." He looked lost for a moment, then pointed a crooked finger at Kelsey. "I'm going to take this up with Miss Evelyn."

"All right, Papa."

"Where is she? I've not seen her all day."

"I don't know."

He glared at Clay, then made his way back into the house again.

Kelsey's shoulders sagged, and she touched her hand to her brow. Clay reached out and steadied her.

"What's wrong, Kelsey? Who is Miss Evelyn?"

She squeezed her eyes shut, gathering her strength, then looked at him. "Evelyn was my mother."

"But you said she died a year ago...."

Kelsey picked up the laundry basket and drew in a deep breath. There were reasons visitors seldom came to the house, and her father was only one of them.

"Well, I suppose you want to get back to town before the storm hits. I don't want to keep you," Kelsey said. She didn't want a federal marshal sleeping in her own home. Bad enough he was staying at her hotel.

Tula bustled through the door, her round face drawn in severe lines of disapproval. "What are you thinking, Miss Kelsey, sending a man out into this weather? And right here at suppertime? Have you lost all your upbringing? What would Miss Evelyn say, you acting like that?"

Kelsey felt her cheeks flush. "Marshal Chandler is a very busy man—"

The housekeeper pushed her wide girth between them and down the stairs. "I'm gonna get my shotgun and get that boy back up here to the house before the thunder scares him silly. I'll have Reuben take your hoss down to the barn. Now, get inside, both of you, before you catch your death of misery." Shaking her head, Tula trudged off through the yard.

Tula was right, of course. The weather looked terrible. And despite Kelsey's concern, Clay obviously didn't suspect her of anything, even though he'd questioned her about her mourning dress. If he had any facts, he'd have hauled her off to jail already. She was sure of it.

Kelsey managed a small smile. "Come inside. If you catch your death of misery, I'll never hear the end of it."

Clay hung his hat on a peg beside the back door as they walked into the kitchen. The addition connecting the old cookhouse to the main house had been completed years ago, replacing the earthen floor with tiles and increasing the cupboard and pantry space. A myriad of rich aromas mingled in the air—clean lemon soap, cherry pie and fresh bread.

Kelsey dropped the laundry basket on the worktable in the center of the room and rubbed her hands together. "Looks like Tula made fresh coffee."

Clay lingered in the doorway, watching as Kelsey tied an apron around her tiny waist and stretched up to open the cupboard. He crossed the room and reached over her head to take down two cups. The desire to ease himself closer, to touch her, nearly overcame him. Wild, sinful, delightful thoughts ran through his head. Clay stepped back and handed her the cups.

The kitchen door burst open, and Toby raced into the room, followed a moment later by Tula. She tucked her shotgun into the pantry and ambled to the stove. "Supper will be ready soon. Better get washed up."

Toby bounced on his toes and took Clay's hand. "Come on, Marshal Clay. Over here."

Clay allowed himself to be led to the sink, and stood by while Toby climbed up on a tiny footstool. He worked the pump as Toby awkwardly lathered his hands, dropping the soap over and over, and finally rinsed.

"Your turn." Toby wiped his hands on the front of his shirt and scrambled onto the counter to work the pump.

Clay rolled back his sleeves, washed and rinsed, then reached for the towel.

"Marshal Clay didn't wash good!" Toby made the announcement at the top of his voice.

Clay stood straighter. "Yes, I did."

Kelsey turned from the cupboard and pressed her lips together to keep from laughing. Clay looked absolutely indignant at the accusation, and totally flustered.

Kelsey sidled up next to Clay at the sink. "Let's have a look."

He sighed heavily and thrust his dripping hands out for inspection.

"He didn't wash the backs." Toby looked up at Clay. "You don't get no dessert if you don't wash the backs. And Tula makes the bestest dessert in the whole, whole world."

Kelsey grinned up at Clay. "You don't want to miss dessert, do you?"

Clay grumbled under his breath, glared at Toby and jerked up the soap again.

Toby pumped more water. "Tula said you're a lawman. She says you chaseded outlaws and putted them in jail."

"That's right."

Toby's eyes widened. "Gosh…"

"Kelsey! It's not fair!"

A long-suffering whine emanated from the hallway, and Clay turned to see a younger version of Kelsey come into the kitchen.

Kelsey winced. "Edwina, please. We have company."

Tula looked back over her shoulder from the stove, and rolled her eyes. She grumbled under her breath.

The young girl stopped and eyed Clay. "Oh."

"This is Marshal Clay Chandler. My sister, Edwina."

She gave him a cursory greeting, then turned on Kelsey again. "It's not fair. I want to go to the Morgans' party. Why can't I go? I'm fifteen. You went to parties when you were fifteen."

Kelsey crossed the room to the china hutch. "We've been over this a hundred times, Edwina. This isn't a party for young people."

She followed her doggedly. "But Jack Morgan is Papa's business partner. I should be there. Everybody will be there but me. It's not fair!"

Kelsey took down a stack of plates. "You're going to Sally Braden's birthday party in a few weeks. That will be more fun for you, anyway."

Edwina stamped her foot. "I don't want to go to some silly old birthday party. I'm old enough to go to adult parties."

"If you don't want to go to Sally's party, that's your choice. But I was going to have Miss Patterson make you a new dress for the occasion."

Toby leaned closer to Clay and whispered. "They talk about girl stuff all the time. Yuck! Girls are no fun."

Clay shook water from his hands and grinned. "I used to think that, too."

"Chasing outlaws is more fun. Huh."

For a moment, Clay took in the swish of skirts and the light feminine fragrance in the room. For months—years—all he'd thought about was his duty, bringing outlaws to justice, finding Scully Dade. But now...

Edwina's eyes had lit up. "Really? Oh, really, Kelsey? A new dress? Whatever I want?"

Kelsey considered it for a moment. "We'll decide on something together."

Edwina followed her across the room. "Can we go into town tomorrow and pick out the fabric? Can we?"

"Not tomorrow. The Morgans' party is tomorrow night, and Miss Patterson is rushing to get several gowns finished. I saw her this morning for a fitting, and she was in a panic because her measuring tape had disappeared." Kelsey passed the stack of plates to Edwina. "Set the table, will you? And think of which fabric you'd like to have. We'll go talk to Miss Patterson in a few days. I promise."

Edwina disappeared down the hallway to the dining room.

Toby slid from the counter and tugged at Kelsey's skirt. "Marshal Clay knowses outlaws—real outlaws. Can I go see the jail? Can I? Please, Kelsey?"

She smiled at Toby's admiration of Clay. "I don't think the jail is a proper place for a young boy to visit, Toby."

He ran to Clay and wrapped his arms around his long legs. "Make her let me, Marshal Clay. You're a lawman. She has to do whatever you say."

He didn't think for an instant that any man had a chance in hell of getting Kelsey Rodgers to do anything against her will. But he looked down at Toby and nodded seriously. "I'll talk to her."

Toby beamed with delight.

Clay edged closer to the sideboard, where Kelsey had gone to roll out the biscuit dough, and leaned over her shoulder until she elbowed him in the stomach. He went to the stove and watched as Tula stirred pots of vegetables. Edwina came through and asked him to move aside while she got the silverware. He wandered between the three women, generally being underfoot, until finally Kelsey took him by the arm and led him to the worktable.

She pulled out a tall stool. "Sit here. And stay put."

Grudgingly, Clay sat, and a second later, Toby scrambled onto the stool beside him. "Don't make her mad," he advised solemnly.

Clay shifted uncomfortably, though he didn't disagree with the advice.

Toby rested his elbows on the worktable and swung his feet, watching Clay intently. "I wanna be a marshal when I get growed up, just like you."

Stunned, Clay shook his head. "It's not always such a good job."

"How come?"

"You don't get to see your family much." The words slipped from Clay's mouth before he realized it.

"Oh." Toby bottom lip crept out. "Do you miss your mama?"

He did. And he hadn't even known it until this moment. Clay nodded slowly. "Yes."

Toby's little chin went up. "Kelsey's my mama now. You're lucky. You still gotted your mama."

Clay's chest tightened at the brave expression on the boy's face. "Kelsey seems like a good mama to me. I guess we're both pretty lucky."

He smiled and leaned his head against Clay's arm. Clay patted him gently on the back.

"Supper's ready." Tula looked at them seated together. "You two better get on in there."

"Come on, Marshal Clay, you can sit by me." Toby grabbed Clay's hand and pulled him from the room.

Tula sidled up next to Kelsey at the stove. "That man is big as a hoss. He's gonna eat every bite I got in the pantry. Then what we gonna do?"

"We'll manage. Just don't let on about how things are."

She frowned. "The man's got eyes, honey. He can see what's going on around here."

"You shouldn't have insisted he stay."

Tula's eyes bulged. "And have him think the Rodgers family don't know how to treat a guest? What would folks in town say when they heard that?"

"You're right." Kelsey took the platter of chicken from the sideboard. "Then pray the storm holds off so we can send him home tonight."

"Just so long as he don't go talking about Mr. Emmet when he gets back to town." Tula rolled her eyes. "Ain't nobody's business in town what's happened to him."

The marshal didn't seem inclined toward idle gossip. The town respected Emmet Rodgers, and Kelsey had done everything in her power to keep it that way.

They ate in the dining room under the massive crystal chandelier, with the delicate china her mother had brought with her when she married Emmet years ago. Rain fell steadily outside, but the fireplace warmed the room. Kelsey sat at the foot of the table, her father's spot at the head conspicuously empty. She couldn't remember the last time they'd had company, had the occasion to use the dining room or the fine tableware. Even Edwina refrained from her constant whining and used her best manners.

Clay sensed he'd grown to celebrity status in Toby's eyes, as the boy sat next to him, asking a hundred questions. But he didn't mind. It had been too long since he sat down with a family for a meal, instead of hunkered down around an open campfire, or isolated by strangers in nameless restaurants in nameless towns across the state.

He glanced at Kelsey as she ate and thought he could take every meal with her and never tire of seeing her at the table. A certain comfort came over him in her presence.

Afterward, in the parlor, Edwina played several selections on the piano, then retired to her room to think over dress fabrics and patterns. Tula brought in a tray of coffee and took Toby to ready him for bed.

Kelsey poured and passed the cup and saucer to Clay.

"Toby is quite taken with you. It's kind of you to be patient with him."

Clay sat back on the settee and sipped the coffee. "I don't mind. Besides, it must be hard, with your pa being bad-off, and all."

Kelsey froze, then her gaze collided with his over the top of her coffee cup. She shifted in the chair. "Yes."

"How long has he been like this?"

She'd held it in for so long, pretended to everyone in town that her father simply chose not to leave his home, that suddenly she couldn't do it any longer. She set her cup aside and rose from the chair.

"I don't know, really. Looking back, I see now it had been coming on for some time. We thought Papa was just becoming forgetful, misplacing things. Then, Mama died…"

Kelsey walked to the window and stared out into the dark rainfall. She heard the settee creak and felt Clay behind her. A warmth flowed from him, bathing her.

With extreme gentleness, Clay rested his hands on her shoulders, fighting the urge to wrap his arms around her and hold her tight against him until her worries vanished. He felt her grow tense at his touch, but she didn't move away.

"It must be hard on you." He whispered the words softly. "Taking care of this place, the hotel, looking after your pa, your sister, and that little fella. At times, you must have wanted to walk off and leave it to somebody else."

Kelsey turned and faced him, and in the dim light he saw hard determination burning in her eyes. "I'll keep my family together, Clay, no matter what I have to do."

Her words felt like spikes through his heart. She clung fiercely to her family; he'd walked away from his easily.

"Couldn't you use help sometimes?" he asked softly.

She relaxed marginally and nodded. "I'll have help as soon as Seth gets back."

"Your brother?"

"Yes." She managed a small smile. "The one who taught me to whistle through my teeth, drink brandy and talk like a sailor on holiday."

Clay chuckled. "You must have given your mother a fit."

"I certainly did."

"My sister and I were that way, too. We used to get into so much trouble together my pa threatened to send us to opposite sides of the country. He said it was the only way he could keep us apart." Clay smiled at the recollection.

"Sounds like Seth and me. Where is your sister now?"

Breath caught in Clay's chest. "She's dead."

Pain, raw and unchecked, was etched in the lines of Clay's face. It seeped through Kelsey. "How horrible for you. What happened?"

"I killed her...in a way."

Kelsey took both his hands and held them firmly. "I don't believe that, Clay."

He nodded, then lapsed into silence for a long moment. Finally, he drew in a deep breath and looked at Kelsey. "It happened a few years back. I caught a man I believed to be responsible for a string of a bank robberies. He convinced me I had the wrong man. I let him go."

Clay's grip on her hands tightened, and she nearly winced at the pain, but didn't say anything. The anguish he was going through was much worse. It showed in the tight, hard lines of his face, the rigid stance of his body.

"A week later, I saw him again." Clay's words were but a whisper. Slowly, he lifted his gaze to look at Kelsey. "He robbed a bank. I caught him escaping. There was a shoot-out on the street. Rebecca was hit."

Kelsey threw her arms around him. He held himself rigid, refusing to accept her comfort.

"She was in town to do some shopping. Just like she'd done a hundred times before. I tried to get to her. Bullets were flying everywhere. I shouted at her. I told her to get down, to take cover. But she froze. She just stood there. I tried, but—" Clay stopped. "She bled to death in my arms."

"Oh, Clay…" Kelsey tightened her hold on him, and finally he closed his arms around her. They clung to each other for a long moment.

"It wasn't your fault," Kelsey whispered.

Clay shook his head and pushed himself away. His features hardened again. "I shouldn't have believed him, shouldn't have let him go."

Her arms felt empty without him. "You made a judgment call, Clay."

"And my sister died because of it." Harsh, bitter words, held inside for too long. "I swore that day I'd never make that kind of mistake again."

Kelsey stepped closer. "That's why you left your family, isn't it."

He nodded. "My ma and pa said they didn't blame me for what happened. It didn't matter. I blamed myself. I couldn't face them, knowing what I'd caused."

Kelsey crossed her arms over her middle. "So they lost both their children."

Clay brought his gaze up quickly, stunned. Then he waved the thought away. "It'll be over, one day, when I bring that bastard to justice."

"Read me! Read me!"

Toby raced into the parlor in his nightshirt, waving a picture book. "I want Marshal Clay to read to me."

Kelsey took the child's hand. "Toby, I'll read to you."

"No!" He backed away, disappointment curling his bottom lip outward.

"It's okay. I'll read to him." Clay drew in a deep breath, his pain and anguish of moments ago gone.

"Are you sure?" she asked softly.

He nodded. "Yeah."

Toby scrambled onto his lap on the settee and made himself at home while Clay thumbed through the book. He read only a few pages before Toby fell asleep.

Kelsey rose from the chair across from them. "I'll take him up to bed."

Clay shifted the sleeping child onto his shoulder and stood. "I'll take him."

"I suppose this isn't the sort of evening you're used to." Kelsey gave him an apologetic smile.

"Nope." He shook his head. "But I'm not complaining."

"I wish I could say the same for my sister." Kelsey took the lamp from the table and led the way across the room. "I'm sending Edwina away to school in New Hampshire in a few months. I think the change will do her good."

Clay followed her across the foyer and up the wide,

curving staircase. "New Hampshire is a long way from home."

The lamplight cast shadows on the walls as they walked down the wide hallway. The big house was silent, except for the rain pattering against the windowpanes and the distant rumble of thunder.

"The school comes highly recommended. A good friend of mine attended."

"Mallory Morgan?"

She looked up at him in the dim light, surprised. "Yes. How did you know?"

"Just a hunch. Morgan's got the money to send his daughter to a fancy eastern school, so I hear."

Kelsey pushed open the door to Toby's bedroom and walked inside. "Jack Morgan can buy whatever he wants—or at least he thinks he can."

"From the looks of this place, I'd say your pa wasn't doing too badly himself. Why didn't you go away to school with your friend?"

"I had a mother to teach me all I needed to know." Kelsey turned back the coverlet on the bed. "She came from a very old family in Savannah. I didn't need to go to school to learn to be a lady."

"What about Mallory's mother?"

"She was very reclusive, because of an illness, or so Jack always claimed. He sent her away to a sanitarium outside of New Orleans the day after Mallory left for school."

Clay eased Toby into bed. "Did she get well?"

"She died there."

Toby moaned softly and buried his face against the pillows. Kelsey pulled the covers over him.

"He didn't even bring her home. Just had her buried

there.'' She looked up at Clay. "He didn't tell Mallory until months later, when she came home from school.''

Clay pushed his fingers through the hair at his temple. "What a bastard..."

Mallory had never forgiven her father for what he'd done, and Kelsey couldn't blame her. After that, Mallory had done everything in her power to irritate and annoy Jack Morgan, punishing him in whatever ways she could, her hostility finally escalating to armed robbery. Never, Mallory had sworn, would she be at the mercy of her father's whims, as her mother had been. And only money would ensure that.

Kelsey lit the lantern on the bedside table and turned the flame low, then placed a kiss on Toby's forehead. "Tula made up a room for you.''

His brows went up in mock surprise. "You're not sending me packing tonight?''

She looked solemnly up at him. "I'm expecting the Dade gang by for coffee and cake in the morning, and thought you'd like to be here when they arrive.''

He glared at her, then, in spite of himself, chuckled.

She grinned. "Besides, what kind of citizen would I be, turning a lawman out on a cold, rainy night like this?''

He gave her a playful grin. "So you consider this your civic duty?''

His gaze warmed her insides like the shot of brandy they'd shared the night before. "No, not entirely.''

He eased closer. "Then what?''

She wished she knew. But at the moment, logical thought escaped her, and some strange craving took over.

Slowly Clay traced a finger down her jaw and tilted her chin up. His arms encircled her and drew her tight against him. He kissed her gently, slowly acquainting himself with her, then deepened the kiss. Kelsey rose on her toes to meet his demands and circled his neck with her arms. He moaned softly and pressed himself closer against her.

He broke off the kiss, but didn't release her. Thunder rumbled in the distance as their hearts did the same. Gently he pressed his lips to her forehead, then stepped back.

He drew in a deep breath. "Maybe you should show me that room."

Fingers of fire tingled where he'd touched her, and at the same time she felt cold, abandoned, without his arms around her. Kelsey cleared her throat. "Maybe I should."

She took the lantern and led the way to the room at the end of the hall. She pushed open the door. Inside, golden lamplight shone from the bedside table and the coverlet had been turned back.

"It's Seth's room."

Clay gazed inside, then back at Kelsey. She looked so pretty in the soft light that he wanted to kiss her again. Improper though it was, he wasn't a bit sorry he'd already done it once tonight. Before he let his thoughts go any further, he stepped into the room. "Good night."

"Sleep well." Kelsey smiled faintly and disappeared down the hall.

Clay closed his door and banged his head softly against the casing. He doubted he'd sleep a wink tonight.

"Miss Kelsey, wake up."

She came awake with a start and pushed the heavy

coverlet back from her face. "What is it, Tula?"

"Somebody downstairs to see you."

"At this hour?" Kelsey sat up and squinted at the light of the lantern Tula held. "Who is it?"

Tula stepped back from the bed. "You'd best come see."

Breath caught in her throat. "It's not—? Oh, no." Kelsey scrambled from the bed and threw a glance into the hallway. "Hurry, Tula. And please, don't make a sound."

Chapter Eight

Kelsey threw her wrapper around her and tied it quickly. The cold floor tingled her bare feet as she followed Tula down to the kitchen. Against the glow of the fireplace, Holly paced back and forth, water dripping from her slicker, her wet braids wound tight against her head. She held a red bandanna against her lips, but it did little to muffle her tears.

Kelsey took the lantern from Tula. "Go back to bed."

Tula eyed Holly sharply, then turned her gaze on Kelsey. "You best be careful, Miss Kelsey." She bobbed her brows toward the second floor above them, and left the room.

Holly looked up, and collapsed into sobs. Kelsey hurried to her side and took both her hands.

"What is it? What happened?" Kelsey searched her face in the glowing light of the fireplace. Her eyes were red and swollen; she'd been crying for a while.

"Oh, Kelsey, they're not taking care of her. I saw her in the store, and she was crying." She pressed her bandanna to her mouth. "She was crying and crying and that woman was so busy with her shopping she didn't even pick her up. She had one of those other children tend to her.''

Despite her wet slicker, Kelsey put her arms around Holly and hugged her close. ''You rode all the way to Flint Valley in this rain?''

''I had to. I had to see her, Kelsey.'' She pushed herself back. ''I've got to get her back. Now! I can't wait any more!''

Kelsey glanced nervously over her shoulder, fearful their voices would carry upstairs. ''We're going to get her back, Holly. You and your daughter will be together. But not until you can afford to take care of her yourself. You know you can't take her to your parents' place to live.''

Fresh tears rolled down her cheeks. ''I hate them. I hate them both for what they did.''

''They had help,'' Kelsey reminded her. ''They couldn't have done it without Jack Morgan.''

Her bottom lip quivered. ''I hate him, too.''

Kelsey took her hands. ''We only need a little more time, then we'll have enough money to get your baby back.''

''What if they won't give her up? What if they really want to keep her?''

Kelsey pressed her lips together. ''If there's one thing I've learned, Holly, it's that cash speaks very loudly. You offer them enough money, and they'll give her back to you. They have other children. They only took her because they thought it was their Christian duty.''

She sniffed and nodded.

''And then you can leave this town for good. It won't be much longer, Holly, I promise.''

She wiped her eyes. "I know you're right. But it's just so hard waiting. She's growing so fast, Kelsey."

"You have to be strong, Holly. You can do it."

Holly swallowed hard and nodded. "All right. If you say so."

Kelsey opened the back door to a gust of cold wind and a spray of rain. "Be careful tonight."

Holly crammed the oversize hat over her head and hurried out into the rain.

Clay stepped back into the shadows of the dining room as Kelsey hurried down the hall and up the staircase. He'd heard voices from his room and thought Toby had been awakened by the storm. He'd been surprised when he looked out his door to see Kelsey hurrying down the staircase.

He'd been even more surprised by the late-night visitor. Clay rubbed his chin as he searched his memory in the darkened dining room. He'd gotten only a glimpse of the visitor from the doorway, but it had been enough for him to recognize the girl Deuce had told him about at the general store in town.

Holly Duncan, the girl who'd gotten in the family way, as Deuce had put it. He'd said Holly and Kelsey never spoke, because of a family feud. He hadn't been able to overhear exactly what the girls said, but he'd heard enough to know that Holly had come here to be consoled—and Kelsey had done just that. As a close friend would.

Clay walked to the window and stared out into the darkness. If Deuce had lied to him about Holly and Kelsey, maybe he'd lied to him about other things, such as his knowledge of Scully Dade's hideout.

Suspicion clawed at Clay's belly. Another talk with Deuce would be his first priority tomorrow.

Clay left the dining room, feeling his way toward the staircase. Still, something about that Holly girl bothered him. He was sure he knew her from somewhere. But where?

Bright morning sunlight brought Kelsey awake with a start. She pushed her hair off her shoulder and sprang from the bed, annoyed that she'd overslept. She washed and dressed quickly, in a dark green skirt and a white blouse, and twisted her hair into a chignon as she hurried out the door.

Across the hall, she caught sight of Clay's bedroom. The door stood slightly ajar. Her heart quickened as she glanced up and down the corridor, then peeped inside.

He was gone. Bed covers drawn up, curtains open, and not a sign of Clay Chandler. As if he'd never been there.

For an instant, Kelsey questioned her sanity. Had he been here last night? Had he kissed her? She touched her finger to her lips, and a tingle went through her. Yes, and he'd done more than kiss her—he'd made her toes curl.

A hot flush swept her and Kelsey hurried from the room, chastising herself for thinking such things, and silently cursing Clay Chandler for causing her to slip into a man's bedroom and have such thoughts.

The aroma of baking biscuits drew her down the stairs and into the kitchen. Disappointment registered when she stepped into the room and saw that Clay wasn't here either.

Tula looked up from the fireplace that covered the far end of the room. "Good morning, sleepyhead."

She brushed back a stray lock of hair. "Where is everyone?"

"Miss Edwina is still sleeping, and your pa is in his study, doing the Lord only knows what."

"And Toby?"

She inclined her head toward the back door. "Outside. He got up with Marshal Clay, long time ago."

"Oh."

Tula lifted a skillet onto the cookstove. "You needn't look so disappointed, Miss Kelsey. That man ain't gone and left yet."

Kelsey straightened. "I'm not disappointed. I was just—just concerned about Toby, that's all."

"Yeah, sure, honey." She turned back to the stove. "They both outside. You'd better fetch 'em. It's time to eat, soon."

Draping herself in what she hoped was an air of indifference, Kelsey marched out the door.

Golden rays of morning sun shone in the bright blue sky. Raindrops clung to the grass, trees and shrubs, sparkling in the light. Kelsey shaded her eyes as she crossed the lawn.

Clay stood backed against the chicken-coop gate, bending down to drive another nail into the wire that Buster had torn loose yesterday. His gun belt hung from a fence post. It was the first time she'd seen him without his gun strapped to his thigh. Hunkered down at his feet, watching his every action, was Toby. Buster lay in the grass beside them.

Toby looked up at Kelsey, his eyes bright. "Look, Mama, me and Marshal Clay are fixing the coop. I'm helping. See?" He shoved a fistful of nails toward her.

Clay looked up then, and Kelsey felt her stomach twist into a knot. He looked devilishly handsome this morning, and totally comfortable with the hammer in his hand. Apparently law enforcement and toe-curling weren't his only skills.

She eased closer to the fence and threaded her fingers in the wire. Clay's holster hung beside her and the scent of leather tickled her nose. "You two are mighty busy for so early in the day."

Toby sprang to his feet. "Me and Marshal Clay fixed everything. Didn't we?"

Clay pounded in a nail and straightened. "I noticed a few things that looked like they needed a little fixing-up."

"You didn't have to do that."

Toby lost interest in their conversation and hopped like a bunny alongside the coop, toward the henhouse. Buster got up and trotted after him.

Clay shrugged. "It's my way of thanking you for the supper and bed, and…everything."

Kelsey felt her cheeks flush. Was he remembering their kiss? "I never expected you to work for your meal, or bed, or…anything."

A little grin tugged at his lips. "I don't mind."

She cleared her throat and twisted her fingers together in an attempt to appear composed, though she hardly felt that way. "Well, thank you."

Clay's gaze swept the barn and the other outbuildings. "I know it's hard for you, running things by yourself, with your pa being like he is and your brother away, but your foreman seems to have let things go around here. If you'd like, I'll have a word with him."

"No, thank you. I'll handle it." Kelsey's chin went up a notch. She couldn't—and wouldn't—admit to

Clay, or anyone, that the Rodgers family simply had no funds for the upkeep of the big house and grounds. It was all she could do to put food on the table and keep the hotel running. And, of course, make the mortgage payments.

Clay shrugged. "I think—"

Toby let out a bloodcurdling scream and raced down the side of the coop, Buster barking at his heels. He darted behind Kelsey. "Mama! Mama! A snake! I sawed it! Hurry! Before it gets away!"

In a swift, easy motion, Kelsey pulled Clay's Colt from the holster, wheeled around, arms extended, and squeezed off two shots, striking the snake. She holstered the gun quickly and lifted Toby into her arms.

"There, it's all right now." She patted his back.

He buried his face against her neck. "I was scared-ed."

"I know." She rocked him gently. "But everything is fine. The snake can't hurt you."

Toby clung to her a moment longer, then sat up. "Can me and Buster go down to the creek today?"

Kelsey smiled and lowered him to the ground. Buster pushed his head under her hand; she petted his soft head. "No. The creek is too high after the storm. We'll go another day."

"Okay." Toby dropped to his knees and leaped like a frog toward the barn as Buster raced ahead.

Kelsey watched them and grinned, but then she caught sight of Clay and her smile dissolved. His gaze bored into her, asking—demanding—an explanation. Her stomach fell.

"I—I have to go to the house."

He grabbed her arm and pulled her against him. "Where did you learn to handle a gun like that?"

She pressed her lips together. "I told you, my brother."

His brows drew together, and he shook his head. "I never saw any woman shoot that well."

Kelsey jerked her arm away. "Well, maybe that's because you never knew a woman who could take care of herself, lawman. I don't need a man to protect me, and quite frankly, after the men who've been in my life, I'm not sure I want one."

She turned, stuck her fingers in her mouth and let out a piercing whistle. "Toby! It's time for breakfast!"

She threw Clay a defiant look and headed toward the house.

Clay watched her go, her nose in the air, her bustle swaying with each long, determined step. So Kelsey Rodgers didn't want a man to protect her? He shook his head slowly. Maybe she didn't need protection, but whether or not she needed a man was another question.

Clay waited until Toby came up from the barn, then walked into the house with him. Tension hung heavy in the kitchen as they washed up at the sink. Tula moved efficiently at the cookstove, and Edwina made quick work of gathering dishes from the cupboard. They both gave Kelsey a wide berth as she banged the spoon in the bowl of pancake batter at the worktable in the center of the room.

"We gotta go." Toby slid his damp hand into Clay's and pulled him toward the dining room.

Arms loaded with dishes, Edwina shot past him without a word.

Clay eyed Kelsey over his shoulder and stopped. "You go ahead."

"No." Toby gave him a worried look. "She's real mad. You gotta come."

"I'll be there in a minute." He patted Toby's shoulder and sent him into the dining room.

Kelsey beat the batter harder. Clay watched her, Toby's words echoing in his head. Maybe she was mad, maybe not. But he was certain of one thing. There was a lot of emotion bottled up inside her that needed to go somewhere.

He eased up to the opposite side of the worktable as Kelsey clanged the spoon against the bowl. "We have to eat that, you know."

Green eyes blazing, she pointed the spoon at him, batter dripping on the table. "Maybe you'd rather wear it?"

Tula bolted for the door. "I got things to check on."

Clay braced his arms against the edge of the table and leaned closer. "I'm not wearing it. But maybe you are."

In a quick motion, Clay plucked the wooden spoon from her hand and dragged it down her face, spreading pancake batter across her cheek.

Stunned, she gasped. He gave her a smug grin and waved the spoon, taunting her. Kelsey dipped her fingers into the bowl and flung batter up his shirt and across his face. Clay looked down at her uplifted chin, issuing a silent challenge. He grabbed for the bowl.

Kelsey squealed and yanked it away, locking it protectively in her arms. Clay dashed around the table and lunged for it, but she turned away, dipped her hand in the batter again and swiped it across his face. He grabbed her from behind and lifted her off her feet, but she held tight to the bowl. He ran his hand through the bowl and over her cheeks.

She collapsed into gales of laughter as they wrestled, smearing each other with batter, until Clay lost his footing and sat down hard on the floor, bringing her down with him. She landed with a thud in his lap, still holding the bowl.

Laughter rumbled deep in his chest as he circled her with his arms and grasped both wrists in one hand. He ran his finger through the bowl and touched it to her nose. She struggled to reach the bowl, but gave up in a fit of giggles.

"Now who's wearing it?" he asked, taunting her.

She wiggled sideways on his lap. Batter covered his cheek and forehead, dotted his shirt and plastered his hair down. She giggled wildly. "Looks like you are."

"Mercy be to goodness!" Tula stood in the doorway, arms akimbo, glaring down at them. "Look at what you-all have gone and done to my kitchen. Get yourselves out of here, before I take a switch to the both of you."

Trying to look contrite, but lapsing into giggles instead, they clambered to their feet and left the kitchen.

Clay dipped a wooden bucket into the rain barrel at the corner of the house and set it on the porch. He smiled down at Kelsey. "You're a mess."

And she was beautiful. Even the yellow batter splattered across her blouse and skirt, dripping from her fingers, sticking to her hair, gobbed on her nose, dabbed on her cheeks, made her more desirable than he could stand.

She dipped her hands into the bucket and grinned. "So, do you like my recipe for pancakes?"

He leaned down and touched his tongue to the batter coating her forehead. "Not bad. I'd like to taste it cooked, though."

She felt herself flush at his nearness, his strength, his warmth.

Clay scooped water from the bucket and rubbed it over his face. "I don't think I've heard you laugh this much before."

She looked up, surprised, and realized he was right. "I don't think I had reason to before."

And neither had he. Clay shook water from his hands.

They stared at each other for a long moment, and then Clay dragged his shirtsleeve over his face. "I'm hungry."

Kelsey grinned. "Me too."

They went inside and cleaned the kitchen, with Tula mumbling and grumbling the entire time. Finally they got breakfast on the table and all of them ate together in the dining room. And when it was time to leave, Clay didn't want to go.

Reuben brought his horse up from the barn, and Clay gave Toby a big hug.

"Can you come back for supper, Marshal Clay?"

He glanced at Kelsey, standing beside the porch. "I'll come back for another visit real soon."

"Promise?"

He nodded. "I promise."

He gave Buster a pat on the head, and the dog whined. Clay climbed into the saddle. "Well, thanks…"

Kelsey joined them and took Toby's hand. "You're welcome."

"I guess I'll see you in town."

She nodded.

He fought the desire to get down off his horse and give her the goodbye his gut urged him to deliver. Being with Kelsey's family left a heaviness in his chest and made his belly ache.

Clay touched the brim of his hat and rode away.

"Yoo-hoo! Marshal!"

Clay stopped his horse and pushed his Stetson back on his head. "Good morning, Miss Wilder."

She waved her flowered handkerchief at him and walked to the edge of her porch. "So good to see you. I hope you weren't caught out in that storm last night."

"No, ma'am."

Matilda Wilder's house sat on the edge of town, surrounded by a neat yard and a whitewashed picket fence. Just like a sweet little old lady's house should look, Clay thought, as he made the decision not to divulge that he'd spent last night at Kelsey's place.

But he hadn't exactly left Kelsey behind. The mental image of her, anyway. Soft and vulnerable in his arms the night before, a spitfire and a dead shot this morning. He shifted in the saddle. The woman was a well of contradictions.

"Come inside for a cup of tea. It's a bit chilly."

The afternoon sun shone bright overhead, quickly drying the puddles left by the storm, and Clay felt neither chilly nor in need of a cup of tea.

"No, thank you, Miss Wilder. I've got some business to take care of."

She nodded proudly. "Well, of course you do, dear. You just keep going with your marshaling work."

Clay noticed the stack of wooden packing crates piled beside her front door. "You're not leaving town, are you?"

She tittered and waved her handkerchief at him. "You know my nephew has been after me for some time now to move with him to Memphis. He's got a lovely new home there, you know. I'm sending him my books for his library."

Clay stroked his chin. "You're not going to try to move those crates yourself, are you?"

Miss Wilder drew in a deep sigh. "I asked those nice young men from the express office to bring them inside for me, but, well, you know how busy some people are. They just didn't have the time. I'll manage."

Clay pulled his hat low on his forehead, looked at the crates, then at the frail Miss Wilder. He swung down from his horse.

"Oh, no, Marshal, you're much too busy," she protested as Clay tethered his horse to the picket fence. "You have such a heavy responsibility on your shoulders already."

"It's no bother."

She smiled sweetly up at him. "You're such a nice young man."

Clay lifted one of the wooden crates and followed her inside.

While the house looked as he'd imagined, with white doilies on the furniture, lace curtains and delicate figurines, it was also packed and piled with an assortment of oddities—scissors, buttons, tiny vases, pincushions, shell casings, copper pots, blue-speckled cups, pencils, inkwells, small writing tablets, measuring scoops. The mantel, every table and shelf, every cabinet, was nearly buried, as if everything the woman had ever purchased had been brought home and simply laid down somewhere. Very odd.

Clay followed her to a small room in the back of the house and set the crate where she indicated. Shelves lined all four walls to the ceiling, filled with hand-

tooled, leather-bound books. In the center sat an upholstered chair, a small table and a lantern.

Miss Wilder pressed her handkerchief to her throat
and sighed heavily. "I spent my life teaching school,
molding and shaping young minds, sharing the joy of
books. Oh, how I wish I could read these volumes one
more time. My eyes, they aren't what they used to be.
Sanford will have to enjoy them for me."

A pang of sadness tugged at Clay at the thought of
Miss Wilder devoting her life to her job, sitting alone,
reading, never marrying, never having a family. And
now, with advancing age and failing eyesight, sending
her books away.

"I didn't know you were the schoolteacher here."

"Oh, yes. But I haven't taught in years. Miss Chalmers has the class now. She lives right across the road.
We get together occasionally and talk." She laughed
softly. "Few people like books, you know. My nephew
Sanford, the dear boy, provided me with sufficient fi-
nances to pay someone to catalog the books and pack
them properly. But, well, young people today just
aren't interested in such things. Some of these volumes
are very rare, you know."

"Yes, ma'am." Clay left her standing alone with her
books and made quick work of bringing the remaining
crates inside.

She thanked him profusely from the porch and insisted he have a cup of tea, but Clay climbed onto his
stallion and left, uncomfortable in the house and in
Miss Wilder's presence. It seemed more empty than he
could bear, especially after the time he'd spent with
Kelsey's family.

He rode into town and pulled his horse to a stop at
the sight of Deuce coming out of Morgan's Grain Com-

pany, stooped beneath a fifty-pound sack of feed. The boy struggled across the boardwalk, the sack precariously balanced on his shoulder, and heaved it into the back of the livery-stable wagon, its weight pulling him into the wagon, as well. He pushed himself upright, and swiped his bangs out of his eyes.

"You and me need to have a talk, Deuce." Clay swung down from his horse and tied it off to the hitching post.

Deuce spun around, his shoulders rising and falling with each heavy breath. A dozen sacks filled the wagon, and he looked as though he'd carried them all himself.

"Hello, Marshal." He saw the frown on Clay's face. "What's wrong?"

Clay stopped in front of him, his feet braced wide apart. "I don't like being lied to."

"I didn't tell you a lie, Marshal. I swear."

"Looks to me like you did. And I figure if you're lying about one thing, you're probably lying about other things—like the location of Dade's hideout."

Deuce glanced over his shoulder at the entrance to the grain store. "My pa's inside. He'd be powerful mad if he thought I was in trouble again."

Clay relaxed his stance. He didn't want Deuce to endure any more of his father's punishment on his account. "Then explain something to me. You told me Holly Duncan and Kelsey never spoke to each other. But I saw them together."

"No, sir. You must be mistaken. If Holly and Kelsey see each other on the street, they turn up their noses and walk the other way. I've seen them do it. So has everybody else in town. The Duncans don't go to the hotel and the Rodgerses never go to their dry goods store.''

''I'm telling you, I saw them talking. Talking like best friends.''

Deuce shook his head. ''There's bad blood between their families because of that business deal that went bad, and because of Holly getting…you know.''

Clay pulled at his neck. ''Because of Holly getting pregnant? What's that got to do with the Duncans and Rodgerses not speaking?''

''Didn't I tell you that part?'' Deuce scratched his head. ''It was Kelsey's brother that got her that way.''

Stunned, Clay leaned closer. ''Kelsey's brother, Seth, is the father of Holly's baby?''

''Yes, sir.''

''Then that would mean Kelsey's brother is in prison.'' Clay whispered the words, his mind whirling.

Deuce sat down on the tailgate of the wagon, his legs swinging. ''Remember, I told you he couldn't marry her because he got caught robbing Morgan's Hardware Store. I guess it suited Holly's pa real good, because he was already mad at Emmet Rodgers over that business deal. If Seth hadn't robbed Mr. Morgan's store, he and Holly would be married today. That's what my ma says.''

Clay blew out a heavy breath. ''Seth sure fouled up his whole life.''

''A lot of people wondered why he robbed the store in the first place, what with the Rodgers family being pretty rich, and all. Seth claimed he was meeting Mr. Morgan there late that night, but Mr. Morgan didn't know anything about it.''

''Jack Morgan was personally involved?''

''Yeah. But he had no reason to lie, leastwise none

anybody could figure." Deuce shrugged. "Why would Mr. Morgan want Seth Rodgers to go to jail?"

Why, indeed? And why, when Kelsey mentioned her brother, had she not said he was in prison? She'd simply said he was away. Thoughts, possibilities, ran through Clay's mind, but none that made much sense, except that she was simply embarrassed.

"You believe me, don't you, Marshal?"

Jarred from his thoughts, Clay nodded. "I believe you."

"I wouldn't lie to you, I swear. I don't want anybody thinking bad of me, especially—"

Ben Tucker stepped onto the boardwalk from the grain store, talking with Jack Morgan.

Deuce jumped to his feet. "I loaded all the grain, Pa."

Ben broke off his conversation and shoved a sheaf of paper at Deuce. "Take this and get on back to the livery. That's my receipt, so put it in the desk, and don't lose it."

"Yes, sir." Deuce took the paper.

"Afternoon, Marshal," Ben said.

Jack Morgan hung his thumbs in his vest pockets. "Find out anything new on my stolen payroll, Chandler?"

"I'm working on some leads," Clay told him.

Deuce glanced over the paper his father had given him, then looked up. "Pa—"

Ben frowned. "Get on over to the livery, like I told you."

Deuce held out the paper. "But, Pa—"

"You're not sassing me, are you, boy?"

He drew back. "No, sir." He gave Clay a troubled

glance before hurrying into the wagon and driving away.

Annoyed by both Jack Morgan and Ben Tucker, Clay left the two men standing on the boardwalk and headed over to the jail. Sheriff Bottom sat behind his desk.

"So there you are, Chandler." The sheriff reared back in his chair. "I thought maybe you'd left town before I had a chance to give you the news."

Clay sank into the chair across from him. "What news?"

"We had a break in the payroll robberies. Seems your lady outlaw is none other than Miss Kelsey Rodgers."

"What?" Clay surged to his feet.

Sheriff Bottom smiled broadly. "Yep. It's true. My deputy broke the case."

"Christ..." Clay pulled off his hat. "That Elder kid is crazy as a three-legged toad. It's not Kelsey."

"We've got some pretty strong evidence."

"Like what?"

"Well, for one thing, you yourself said one of them Schoolyard Boys is a girl. And as it turns out, Kelsey owns the horse that was used in one of the robberies. That looks pretty convincing to me."

"That doesn't prove anything."

Sheriff Bottom eyed him sharply. "You're trying mighty hard to say it wasn't her. Any reason for that?"

"No." His quick answer didn't sound convincing, even to him. Clay sat down in the chair again. "Who told you Kelsey owned the horse?"

"Luther. He said Deuce was bringing the mare back from the livery and told him it belonged to Kelsey."

"Luther is no more reliable than that kid deputy of

yours." Clay leaned forward. "Look, Sheriff, I got a pretty good look at the girl when she fell off her horse, and I can tell you for sure it isn't Kelsey Rodgers."

"Then who was it?"

He sat back. "I don't know."

"Well, you'd better find out."

"Did you tell Morgan about this?"

The sheriff shook his head. "No, not yet."

"You'll look like a fool," Clay told him. "Especially when it proves not to be true, and Morgan finds out you've done nothing to track down the real robbers."

"I'll tell Morgan when I'm ready."

Clay's brows drew together. "You can't go throwing out accusations with no more evidence than this."

Sheriff Bottom rose from his chair. "Look, Chandler, Jack Morgan is an important man in this town. He carries a lot of weight around here. I'm looking to retire from this job come fall, and I don't intend to lose my pension. As far as I'm concerned, Kelsey Rodgers is a suspect. If she commits one suspicious act—I don't care how small—I'm arresting her on the spot. No questions asked."

Clay mumbled a curse. "You're making a mistake, I tell you. I saw the girl. It wasn't Kelsey."

"Then you'd better round up that gang of boys and their lady friend, or Kelsey Rodgers might find herself behind bars." The sheriff gave him a quick nod. "I'm not losing everything I've worked for in this town over a gang of kids."

Clay pulled his hat on and stalked out of the jail. Damn stupid deputy. And the sheriff was no better. It galled him, but he'd have to step up his efforts to find those Schoolyard Boys. Scully Dade would have to wait.

A freight wagon thundered down the street, the horses kicking up mud and water. Clay waited on the boardwalk until it passed, then heard shouts from down the street. His heart rose in his chest as he saw Deuce run blindly out in front of the wagon, barely missing the lead horses as he rushed across the street and down the alley.

Clay stepped off the boardwalk. He'd only caught a quick glimpse of the boy, but it had been enough for him to see that his face was covered with blood.

Chapter Nine

Clay rounded the corner of Braden's Dry Goods Store and found Deuce on a bench at the back of the shop, nearly hidden amid stacks of barrels and wooden crates. His forehead rested on his drawn-up knees, and his shoulders shook as he sobbed softly.

Clay wound his way through the maze and sat down beside him. He laid his hand on Deuce's shoulder. "What happened?"

He raised his head quickly, startled to find Clay next to him, and sprang from the bench. "Nothing—"

Clay caught a handful of suspenders and pulled him onto the bench again. "Slow down, Deuce. You're bleeding."

He looked down, horrified at the blood dripping from his nose onto his shirt. His shoulders slumped, and another tear rolled down his cheek. "My ma's going to kill me for messing up this shirt. Now I won't get supper tonight."

"Come here, son." Clay pulled his handkerchief from his hip pocket, leaned Deuce's head back and pressed it against his nose. "Calm down. Everything will be all right."

He tried to sit up. "But my ma..."

Patched elbows, mismatched buttons, frayed cuffs and collar—the hand-me-down shirt wasn't fit to be worn, but Clay knew Deuce would catch hell for it anyway. He looped his arm around Deuce's shoulder, pulled him back and held the handkerchief gently in place. "Sit still until it quits bleeding."

He quieted, and after a few minutes Clay lifted the handkerchief. "There, it's stopped. Go wash your face."

Slowly, he rose and rinsed his hands and face in the rain barrel at the corner of the building, then plopped down on the bench again.

Clay drew in a deep breath. "Who busted your nose?"

Deuce hung his head. "I fell down."

Suspicion tightened Clay's chest. "You just fell? All by yourself?"

"Pa hit me." He turned his face, and Clay saw swelling around his left eye. "He hit me and I fell. I guess I banged my nose on the floor."

Anger coiled deep inside Clay. He had no tolerance for any kid getting hurt, and though Ben Tucker called it discipline, in Clay's mind he'd gone too far. But for Deuce's sake, he remained calm. "Why did he hit you?"

"He said I shamed him. Because of this." Deuce dug into the pocket of his baggy trousers and handed Clay a stack of crumpled papers. "It's feed bills from Mr. Morgan's grain store. He's been cheating my pa."

Clay shuffled through the bills, which dated back over a year. "How did you find out about this?"

"I noticed it this morning when Pa handed me the

bill. It was totaled up wrong, charging Pa too much. I tried to tell him, but he wouldn't listen.''

Clay pushed his hat back on his head. ''A man as rich as Morgan actually works in the grain store?''

''He works in all his stores, from time to time. My ma says it's so he can keep an eye on his clerks, so he doesn't get cheated. But Mr. Morgan is the one doing the cheating.''

''Maybe it was just an honest mistake.''

Deuce sat up. ''No, sir. When I got back to the livery, I looked at the other bills Pa had in his desk, and all of them were wrong. Every time Mr. Morgan made out the bill, the numbers didn't add up and Pa got charged too much. But when anybody else in the store made it out, all the numbers were right. Mr. Morgan cheated him on purpose.''

''Bastard...'' Clay shook his head. The more he learned about Jack Morgan, the more he disliked the man. He passed the bills back to Deuce. ''So why did your pa hit you? Looks like he'd be mad at Morgan, not you.''

''Pa never had real schooling. He can't read and cipher much. He said I shamed him and made him look like a fool because he didn't figure out what Mr. Morgan was doing.'' Deuce hung his head. ''I thought he'd be proud of me.''

Clay's gut ached. He patted Deuce on the knee. ''Well, I think you did a good thing. You're pretty smart to figure it out, and you did right telling your pa. He had no call to slap you.''

''You really think so?'' Tears welled up in Deuce's eyes.

''Yes, son, I do.'' Clay rose. ''Come on, let's go get a beefsteak for that eye.''

He wiped his face with his shirtsleeve and followed Clay into the alley. "Where are we going?"

Without realizing it, Clay was heading for the place that felt most comfortable to him. The one place that felt closest to a home. The Eldon Hotel. Where Kelsey would be.

The kitchen should have been alive with the scurrying of feet and the smell of supper, but the room was quiet when they walked through the back door. A single pot simmered on the stove, with no sign of Etta Mae to tend it. Kelsey sat at the table, writing. She looked up when Clay stepped into the room, then rose when Deuce followed.

"My goodness, what happened to you?"

Embarrassed, Deuce glanced up at Clay. "I—"

"Got into a fight." Clay grinned and slapped him on the back. "You should see the other fella."

"Honestly, you men. Deuce, I'd think you'd know better than to settle an argument that way." She threw a scathing look at Clay. "And you—a lawman—condoning it. Sit down, Deuce. I'll get something for your eye."

Deuce gave Clay a grateful look and eased into a chair at the table.

"No supper cooking?" Clay asked.

"With the Morgan party tonight, I figured we wouldn't have much of a turnout, so I gave Etta Mae the night off." Kelsey stepped from the pantry unwrapping a beefsteak. She leaned Deuce's head back and placed it over his eye. "Hold it there. Maybe you won't have much of a shiner."

"Well, what are the hotel guests supposed to eat?"

"I recommend the Blue Bonnet Café."

Clay disregarded her suggestion with a wave of his

big hand. "I'm not eating at some café. What's in the pot?" He ambled to the stove and lifted the lid. "Smells good. I'll eat this. Got any bread?"

Kelsey rolled her eyes. "It's just a simple stew I threw together for myself."

"There's plenty for all of us." He made himself at home, going through the cupboards finding bowls and spoons.

"Well, by all means, join me."

He ignored her sarcasm. "Don't mind if I do."

"Wash your hands." She went to the pastry safe and took out a loaf of fresh bread. "I'll be leaving for the party in a while, so don't get too comfortable."

Clay pumped water into the bowl at the sink. "You're going to Morgan's soiree?"

"Yes. Mallory insisted."

He eyed her critically. "In that?"

She looked down at her simple green skirt and blouse. "No. I'm taking my things with me, and I'll change there. Mallory saved me a room to use, though heaven knows how she managed, with all those guests from back east. I told her I'd dress here, but she wouldn't hear of it."

"Maybe she wanted to make sure you wore that gown she picked out for you." He rolled back his sleeves.

"How do you know about my gown?"

Clay turned his back and plunged his hands into the basin. He couldn't tell her he'd eavesdropped on her conversation with Mallory in the dress shop and overheard her concern that her breasts might tumble from the gown. Desire coiled in him at the memory. "You and your sister talked about it. Remember?"

"No, I don't—"

Clay shook water from his hands. "How about some coffee with supper?"

Kelsey tossed him a linen towel. "Stop dripping on my floor."

The towel struck him in the face and fell into his hands. "Got any of that apple pie left? Deuce, you like apple pie, don't you?"

"Yes, sir." He pulled the beefsteak from his eye. "You two act like married people."

Clay and Kelsey glared at each other, stunned. A long moment dragged by. Then both turned and busied themselves getting supper ready.

They settled around the table over bowls of hot stew, warm bread and steaming coffee. Both Clay and Kelsey made certain Deuce sat between them. They talked easily in the quiet, warm kitchen.

Deuce scraped the last of his second piece of pie from the plate and looked out the window. Dusk was settling over the town. "I better get home. Thanks for supper, Miss Kelsey."

"You're very welcome. And take care of that eye." She wagged a finger at him. The dark circle under his eye worsened by the minute.

Clay walked with him to the door. "I'll go home with you, if you'd like."

He shook his head. "No thanks. Pa will most likely be in bed by the time I get there."

"I know things are tough right now, Deuce, but you've got a long road ahead of you. It will get better."

He shrugged, as if he doubted it, and left.

Clay plowed his fingers through his hair and closed the door. "Thanks for feeding the boy supper. He wouldn't have gotten any at home."

Kelsey gathered dishes from the table. "I thought

more was going on here than you were telling. What's wrong?''

"His pa gave him that shiner.''

"Ben hit him that hard? Why?''

Clay crossed to the sink and pumped water into the kettle. He sat it on the stove. "He found out Jack Morgan was cheating his pa on the feed bill. Ben didn't appreciate his son telling him Morgan had been making a fool of him for years.''

"Poor Deuce.'' Kelsey carried dishes to the sink. "It's always been so hard for him, with his twin brother being so close to their pa. He never quite fit in.''

"The boy wasn't meant to work in the livery. He's too small.'' Clay poured warm water from the kettle into the basin. "He needs something else to occupy his time and keep him out of trouble.''

"He used to go to school. I saw him there sometimes when I went to check on Edwina's progress with Miss Chalmers.'' She eased the dishes into the basin and began to wash.

Clay took up a towel. "Ben says she won't let him come back to school anymore.''

"Too bad. I always thought Deuce was a nice boy.''

"There must be something else he can do.''

Kelsey grinned. "You seem like a very resourceful man, Marshal. I'm sure you'll come up with something.''

They washed and dried the dishes together, and then Clay took his hat and opened the back door. "Thanks again for supper. Put Deuce's meal on my bill.''

Kelsey rested her hand on the doorknob. "Both are on the house. I enjoyed the company.''

He gazed into her eyes, lost in those depths of deep

green. "Yeah, me too." A moment passed before he found himself again. "I reckon I'll see you later tonight at Morgan's."

"You're going to the party?"

"Not so much as a guest, but as an extra pair of eyes. Some of those businessmen from back east have their wives with them, showing off the trinkets their husbands bought them. Morgan doesn't want any trou ble. I've got nothing better to do, so I said I'd come over. Maybe I'll see you there."

"Maybe."

He wasn't sure it was safe for him to see her in that gown she planned to wear. But then, he didn't like the idea of all those other men looking at her and him not.

Clay touched the brim of his Stetson and left. At the corner he saw Deuce sitting on the boardwalk, staring at his feet. He started to go talk to him, but didn't, deciding the boy needed some time alone to think things through.

But Clay had done all the thinking he needed to on the situation, and he walked to the edge of town to the schoolmarm's house. Across the street he saw a single lamp burning in the window of Miss Wilder's tiny house. Was she sitting in there, trying to read her books with her failing eyesight? Or had she given up on reading and was simply sitting alone? Disturbed by the thought, Clay knocked on Miss Chalmers's door.

After a moment the door opened slightly. "Yes?"

He tipped his hat to the crack. "Evening, Miss Chalmers. I'm Marshal Clay Chandler. I wonder if I might have a word with you?"

"It's late to come calling, Marshal."

Her voice was stern and disapproving. Clay shivered. It reminded him of his school days. Did all teachers talk that way? Was it a requirement for getting teaching credentials?

"I'm sorry, ma'am. It can't wait." He sounded contrite, and couldn't help himself.

"Well, all right."

Miss Chalmers stepped onto the porch. She looked the way she sounded, tall, thin, hair drawn back in a severe bun, dressed in somber black. He couldn't guess her age, beyond older than Eve.

"Well?"

Clay spoke quickly, afraid she might rap his knuckles with a ruler. "I wanted to talk with you about Deuce Tucker."

Her lips drew together in a tight pinch. "You mean Dennis Tucker."

"Yes, ma'am. Dennis. I understand you won't let him back in school anymore, and I—"

"That is incorrect."

He wondered if she planned to give him a grade on presentation. "His pa said—"

"What I said was that there was no reason for Dennis to return to school. He'd gone as far as he could. I could no longer justify taking time away from the other students to keep him occupied."

"So he was a behavior problem?"

She looked down her long nose at him. "Is that what I said?"

"No— Yes— I—"

Miss Chalmers folded her hands in front of her. "What I said was, that Dennis had advanced beyond the academic structure of the class."

"You mean he's smart?"

She pursed her lips. "Yes, Marshal."

"Did he like school?"

"Dennis was an exceptional student, always eager to learn. Excellent at math, reading, writing. I wish I had a whole classroom of Dennis Tuckers. I recommended to his parents that he be sent to college, but frankly, I hardly expected Ben Tucker to send him. And I was right, as you can see."

"Dennis is having a tough time right now. Any chance you could take him back in your class?"

"None. He's read every book I have, worked through all the arithmetic in my curriculum. I have no more materials with which to teach."

"Maybe he could help teach the other students?"

Miss Chalmers's back stiffened. "I assure you, Marshal, my students already receive more than adequate instruction. But if you would like to address the town council on appropriating additional funds to pay his salary, you may do that. However, I must tell you I feel strongly that any additional money set aside for the school should go to books and materials, not an additional, uncredentialed teacher."

"Thank you, ma'am. Good night." Clay left, sure he'd earned no gold star from Miss Chalmers. He headed back to town.

"Pssst! Hey, boy. Get yourself over here."

Deuce cringed, sorry he'd cut through the alley behind the jailhouse. He stepped into the light that shone from the window. "How you doing, Luther?"

"How am I doing? How do you think I'm doing in this gol-darn jail cell? Locked up in here with no decent food, a bed full of bugs and not a drop of liquor." He pressed his face against the bars. "They took that bottle you bought me, boy. How come you didn't come back like I told you?"

Deuce shoved his hands deep into his pockets. "My pa is powerful mad, Luther. If he found out—"

"Your pa! Is that all you got to worry about?" Luther glanced back inside his cell. "That sheriff threw them two old drunks in here next to me last night. You know, them two that's always hanging all over each other over at the Lucky Lady, drinking 'till they puke."

Deuce nodded. "You mean Herb and Wayne?"

"Herb and Wayne. That's them." He gripped the bars. "They're over here in this cell together, and I don't want nobody thinking I've got anything to do with them two. I got to get out of this place. You got to bust me out of here."

Deuce backed up a step. "I can't do that."

"You got to. Come on, Deuce. It will be just like it used to be, you and me, riding free. We'll hook up again with Scully and the gang."

"I don't know, Luther."

His eyes bulged. "You like living under your papa's thumb? Shoveling up after horses, getting hay down your back, sweating 'till you stink?"

"Well, no, but—"

Luther pressed his face against the bars. "Who give you that shiner? It was your pa, wasn't it?"

"Yeah," he admitted.

"You bust me out of here, boy, and you'll never have to see your pa again. That'll show him. Scully will teach you everything about outlawing, so's that you have all the money you need. And people will be afraid of you, boy. You'll be the one giving out the shiners."

"You think so?"

"I know so." Luther licked his lips. "The sheriff and deputy are going over to that big shindig at Morgan's place tonight. Some yahoo is watching the jail, but he don't know nothing. It'll be easy."

Deuce glanced up and down the alley. "We could go far away? And never come back? Ever?"

"That's right. Show your pa he can't push you around and expect you to just stand there and take it." Luther tightened his grip on the bars. "Now here's what you do. Wait 'till it's late, real late, and that yahoo watching the jail has dozed off. You can get the drop on him then. Bring a couple of horses with you, and some grub. Got it? Now, don't let me down."

Stomach gnawing at him, Deuce left the alley. At the corner, he ran square into Clay. He gasped and jumped back, lost his footing on the boardwalk and fell into the street.

"What's the matter with you, Deuce?" Clay grabbed his arms and pulled him to his feet.

"Nothing. I swear." He swallowed hard and glanced down the alley. "I wasn't doing nothing. Really..."

The denial naturally aroused Clay's suspicious nature. He looked down the alley behind the jail, but saw no one. "I think I found you a new job, Deuce. One you'll like a whole lot better than working for your pa."

"Huh?"

"I stopped by Miss Wilder's place this morning, and she's willing to pay somebody to catalog her books and ship them out to her nephew. I figure you're the man for the job."

His eyes rounded. "Miss Wilder's got books?"

"A whole roomful. And I think she'd like it if you read a few of them to her before they got shipped off. So, what do you think?"

"I—I don't know."

"I want you to go over there in the morning and talk to her." Clay fished a half eagle from his pocket and pressed it into Deuce's hand. "First thing tomorrow, you need to get a haircut. Then buy yourself a new shirt, and some trousers that fit."

Deuce looked down at the money, then up at Clay. "I can't take money from you, Marshal."

"Your pa's not paying you, is he?"

Deuce shook his head.

"I didn't think so. Listen, son, you're going to ask for a job, and you've got to look proper. Meet me in the hotel lobby tomorrow morning and I'll walk over to Miss Wilder's with you. And don't worry about your pa. If you get the job, I'll talk to Ben and make him see this is best." Clay patted his shoulder. "Get a good night's sleep. I'll see you tomorrow morning."

Deuce watched Clay disappear down the boardwalk, then gazed off down the alley. Luther pressed his face against the bars, straining to see. Deuce looked at Clay again, then back at Luther.

He touched his finger to his swollen eye and walked away.

Chapter Ten

"You look perfect. Quit fussing and come on. I've got guests arriving."

Kelsey turned away from the mirror and shot Mallory a scathing look. She hitched up her bodice. "I can't believe I let you talk me into wearing this gown."

Mallory beamed. "The men won't be able to take their eyes off you." She turned in a quick circle. "How do you like my dress?"

"Gorgeous, of course." Mallory had selected a lavender gown for the party that turned her eyes violet. "Not one single man will know I'm in the room once you walk in."

"I doubt that, Miss Buxom." Mallory giggled. "Come on."

Kelsey moaned and followed her out of the bedroom. Tiny, tucked away at the end of the hallway on the second floor, the room held little appeal, furnished sparsely with a poster bed, dresser, mirror and washstand. But at least, as Mallory had promised, she'd had a private place to dress for the party and draw up the courage to face the guests in the daring gown.

In the hallway, they greeted two ladies leaving their

bedrooms, wives of the eastern investors Jack Morgan was wooing. The women had been ensconced in their room since Kelsey arrived.

"Good evening, ladies." Mallory smiled a well-practiced hostess's smile. "I'd like you to meet a dear friend of mine. Mrs. Constance Higgins-Smythe, Mrs. Abigail Henry, this is Miss Kelsey Rodgers."

"How do you do?" Mrs. Higgins-Smythe shifted her wide girth and eyed Kelsey up and down.

"Very nice to meet you ladies. I hope you're enjoying your stay in Eldon," Kelsey said.

Though both looked fiftyish, they appeared a mismatched couple, with Mrs. Henry towering over her companion. Both wore expensive gowns and lots of jewelry. Trinkets being shown off, Clay had said. That certainly seemed true.

"Well, to tell you the truth, it's been quite an adventure," Mrs. Henry said. She had a long face, large, protruding teeth and equine features. She laughed suddenly, and it sounded like a whinny.

"Humph! Adventure..." Mrs. Higgins-Smythe jerked her chin.

Mrs. Henry squinted over her long nose. "Miss Rodgers, that is a beautiful necklace."

Kelsey touched the diamond-and-sapphire piece. "Thank you. It belonged to my mother."

"Exquisite." She whinnied again. "Come, you must see the brooch my husband gave me for our anniversary. It's very similar to your necklace."

The ladies followed Mrs. Henry into her bedroom.

"Really, Abigail, I can't believe you're so careless with your jewelry," Mrs. Higgins-Smythe droned. "You should lock your pieces away, as I do."

"This is the beauty of it, don't you see?" Mrs.

Henry picked up a small satin bag from the clutter of combs, brushes and pins on the bureau. She dumped the contents into her hand, a tangle of diamond, sapphire, ruby and pearl. "No one would suspect all this jewelry to be lying about in this simple bag, now would they? It's so innocent-looking, why would anyone think to steal it?"

"You're not in New York, Abigail. This place is barely civilized." Mrs. Higgins-Smythe put her nose in the air.

Mrs. Henry whinnied again. "Constance, you're such a worrier!"

Kelsey admired the jewelry cupped in Mrs. Henry's hand. "You have some beautiful pieces."

"Your husband is very generous," Mallory said.

"Oh, yes. My Wilford is such a dear. He surprises me with a bauble or two, sometimes, for no reason at all."

Mrs. Higgins-Smythe arched her brows. "There is always a reason."

Mallory glanced at the door. "I really must see to my guests."

"Oh, yes, yes, we must go." Mrs. Henry dumped the jewelry into the bag and tossed it onto the bureau. She stole a quick glance in the mirror, touched her carefully sculptured hair and whinnied. "I love parties!"

Kelsey followed the ladies down the sweeping staircase. Light from the massive crystal chandelier above the foyer sparkled off the marble floor. Vases of fresh flowers scented the air. Mallory's preparations for the party had been learned at finishing school and displayed to perfection tonight. Kelsey only hoped Edwina would do as well at the school, for surely one day the Rodgers family would entertain again.

Bitter anger rose in Kelsey as she walked down the hallway into the huge ballroom at the rear of the house and saw Jack Morgan greeting his guests. Elegantly attired, he appeared confident, flaunting his money and his position in Eldon, both gained by stepping on so many people. Including her own family.

Kelsey slipped away from the receiving line and melted into the crowd at the edge of the dance floor. Seeing Jack Morgan like this, being in his house, was harder than she'd imagined.

Across the room, a small orchestra played, and several couples whirled to the music. Others stood together, chatting, occasionally slipping through the French doors onto the terrace. Behind her in the dining room, a lavish buffet was laid out under twin chandeliers. Kelsey had no appetite. She wound her way through the crowd to the far corner, where the spinsters and grandmothers had sequestered themselves. As she'd expected, she found Holly seated there.

Her mother sat beside her, head bobbing as she whispered and discreetly pointed. Kelsey's anger simmered. Estelle Duncan tried to push Holly toward every bachelor in town, and now, with fresh prospects available— wealthy prospects—her efforts had apparently doubled. She saw Holly fold her arms and stare off at nothing in silent refusal. It brought Kelsey a modicum of comfort to know Holly remained faithful to her brother, Seth, locked away in his prison cell.

She'd hoped to find a discreet moment to get a word with Holly, but that seemed unlikely now. Clay Chandler could arrive any minute, or might even be here already, and Holly should be warned to steer clear of him. She'd told Mallory to alert Holly to his presence, but with all her hostess duties, Kelsey feared it would slip her mind; Holly's predicament had never been a concern for Mallory, anyway.

At that moment, Clay walked into the ballroom. He bore no resemblance to a federal marshal tonight, wearing a crisp white shirt, string tie and dark coat. No badge rode on his chest. Kelsey flushed at the sight of him. Jack Morgan approached, and they fell into conversation with several men Kelsey didn't recognize.

"Forgive my bold interruption, but there seems to be no one near for a proper introduction."

Kelsey felt a hand brush against her elbow and turned to find a man at her side. Short, portly, with graying whiskers and an expensive suit, he offered a shallow bow.

"Wilford Henry, at your service."

Abigail's husband, she realized, the bestower of a bauble or two for no reason. Kelsey fought the urge to shudder as she felt his gaze cover her. "Good evening, Mr. Henry. I'm Kelsey Rodgers."

He eased closer. "Charmed, my dear."

Kelsey backed up a step. Having just seen Clay, she found the man decidedly unappealing. "I met your wife earlier, Mr. Henry."

His expression soured. "Ah, yes, Abigail." His gaze raked her again. "May I say, Miss Rodgers, you look stunning tonight?"

Kelsey's stomach rolled, and she silently cursed herself for being talked into wearing the low-cut gown. "Thank you, Mr. Henry."

He touched the thin mustache over his lip. "Perhaps we can find a moment to get to know each other better."

"I'm afraid my evening is quite full already, Mr. Henry. But thank you just the same. If you'll excuse me, please."

She left quickly, darting between the other guests, and ended up in the dining room, amid the crowd surrounding the buffet table. She'd been on the receiving end of distasteful leers from the Wilford Henrys of the world before, but had never grown to tolerate them.

Clay walked through the doors and eased up to the buffet table, and Kelsey was relieved to see a friendly face in the crowd. He turned her way, and she smiled. But he didn't return the cordial greeting. Instead, his expression darkened and he pushed his way over to her. She stepped back as he towered over her. Suddenly he grasped her elbow and guided her to the far side of the room. He planted her in the corner and stood in front of her, blocking out the room.

Clay looked her up and down, still too stunned to speak. Accented with jeweled combs, her hair was done up in a intricate coif. Tiny gems dangled from her ears. The soft light from the wall sconces made her porcelain features as delicate and refined as always, and her lashes were thick and dark against her milky-white skin. Her eyes looked greener than emeralds tonight. His gut ached just from looking at her.

But the dress—he couldn't let any other man lay eyes on her in that thing. It fell over her hips in layers of rich blue fabric and hugged her waist, then rose to capture the swell of her breasts. *Barely* capture them. If she drew a deep breath, he feared, they might tumble completely out. And if that wasn't bad enough, she wore a necklace that dangled between them, guaranteed to draw the eye of every man in the room to that spot.

Clay frowned down at her. "Haven't you got a coat or something you can put on?"

"What?"

He looked her up and down, trying to ignore the urges pulsing through him. "A coat. Put a coat on."

She thought he'd taken leave of his senses. "Why on earth would I put a coat on?"

"Because...it's chilly in here."

He appeared to be melting, right before her eyes. "It's not chilly."

"Well, put a coat on anyway. I don't want all these men here looking at you in that dress."

She'd thought all along that the dress was too daring, but she certainly wasn't going to have Clay Chandler dictate what she should and shouldn't wear. She drew in a quick breath. "And what is wrong with my dress?"

Her breasts swelled higher over the top of the gown, and Clay's knees weakened. "It's not proper."

She pursed her lips. "Yes, it is. Every woman in the room is wearing a similar bodice."

But not every woman in the room filled hers the way Kelsey did. Desire pounded through him. "I won't have you wearing it."

Her back stiffened, and her nose flared slightly. Clay knew he'd made a fatal mistake.

"For your information, Marshal Chandler, what I choose to wear is my business, and my business alone. And I will thank you to keep your opinions to yourself." She glared up at him, willing him to step aside and let her out of the corner. He didn't. "Move!"

Clay made one final attempt. "Do you think your brother would want you parading around in a dress like that?"

Anger and hard determination narrowed her eyes. "The next time I go to see him, I'll be sure to wear it and ask his opinion."

Oh, God, no, she wouldn't really wear that thing to the prison! He pointed a finger at her. "You listen to me—"

Kelsey shoved him with both hands. He didn't budge, his chest as solid as a stone wall. "Get out of my way."

Fingers of fire crawled down his chest. Instinct urged him to lean closer, but he stepped aside.

She tossed her head. "Thank you."

In a flurry of skirts and petticoats, he watched her cross the room and slide her arm through that of young Ernie from the express office. He stuttered and stammered and his face turned red as Kelsey hauled him off to the dance floor.

"Damn." Clay cursed himself and his uncomfortable condition as he craned his neck to see Ernie ogling Kelsey's bustline as they swept around the dance floor together.

"Why, good evening, Marshal."

At the familiar twitter, Clay found Miss Matilda Wilder at his elbow. She wore a dark brown gown, with about two hundred buttons up the front and a collar that tickled her chin. Now *that* was how a woman ought to dress.

"Evening, Miss Wilder." He smiled politely.

She shifted her straw satchel to the other arm. "Isn't this a lovely home? Are you enjoying the party?"

Clay glanced at the dance floor again. "Oh, yeah."

"It looks as though everyone in town is here tonight."

He glared at Ernie. Maybe one person too many was here tonight.

"Enjoy your evening." Miss Wilder smiled sweetly and drifted away.

The urges twisting Clay's belly into a knot turned from longing to anger as he watched Ernie hold Kelsey in his arms as they spun around the dance floor. One hand dipped a little too low on Kelsey's back, and he hadn't lifted his gaze from her breasts once during the whole dance, none of which suited Clay in the least. He headed across the room to tell Ernie just that, only to have Sheriff Bottom walk up.

"Looks like Morgan took your advice."

Annoyed, Clay stopped. "What are you talking about?"

"Taking precautions with his next payroll, like you said. Sending it out on one of his own wagons instead of the stage. Guarding it, too."

Clay pushed past the sheriff. "Good for him."

"With your help, of course."

He spun around. "My help?"

"Yep. You and some of the hired hands will be guarding it." Sheriff Bottom leaned closer and lowered his voice. "Lot of money. He's sending three months' payroll at once."

"Three months? With hired hands to guard it?" Now Clay was annoyed at Morgan as much as at Ernie.

Sheriff Bottom nodded. "Morgan says if he's taking his men off their regular jobs for guard duty, he's sending three months' worth of payroll so they don't lose time again so soon. Says he's got a safe out at the mine. Payroll will be secure there."

Clay raked his fingers through the hair at his temple. "He's having hired hands guard it?"

"Yeah. Along with you." Sheriff Bottom hitched up his trousers. "Billy's coming along, too."

"Jesus…"

"Well, you ought to be happy, Chandler. Morgan's just doing what you suggested."

Happy? Clay glared at the back of Sheriff Bottom's head as he burrowed through the crowd at the buffet table. He wouldn't be happy until he saw the last of this town, once and for all.

Clay turned and spied Kelsey, still on the dance floor with Ernie. His gut churned again, and at that moment he wasn't the least bit sure anything could make him happy—except maybe punching Ernie square in the mouth. He headed for the dance floor.

Kelsey caught sight of Clay moving through the crowd as Ernie turned her around the floor, and felt her anger grow. That arrogant man. What nerve! Because he'd kissed her twice, did he think he owned her? Well, it would be a cold day before she allowed him to touch her again.

She danced another number with Ernie, then smiled sweetly as they stepped into the crowd at the edge of the dance floor. "Would you mind terribly getting me a glass of punch, Ernie?"

His gaze clung to her breasts. "I'd be proud to, Miss Kelsey. Now, don't you go anywhere. I'll be right back."

Kelsey watched him push his way toward the dining room. Ernie had fallen all over himself trying to please her, and Clay had wanted to swathe her in wool to hide her—and all because of her bosoms. She'd not known the sight of her breasts was so powerful.

"Ah, so we meet again." Wilford Henry stepped in

front of her. "You look as though you could use a breath of air. Shall we step out onto the terrace?"

She easily read the motive lying beneath Wilford Henry's suggestion, and it made her skin crawl. She had to get away from this man. At that moment, she caught sight of Clay, heading her way. She forced a smile. "Thank you, Mr. Henry, but I've promised this dance to someone."

Without giving him a chance to respond, Kelsey slipped around him and blocked Clay's path. "Dance with me. Now."

The last thing he'd expected from Kelsey after their exchange in the dining room was an invitation to dance, and though it sounded more like an order than a request, he wouldn't let the opportunity pass. So he went willingly when Kelsey ran her arm through his and threaded them through the gathering to the dance floor.

Clay took her in his arms, and they fell into step with the other couples sweeping around the room. And what a delight she was in his arms. Her skin felt soft, her hand tiny and fragile. A delicate scent wafted over him. Clay nearly groaned aloud at the view of her breasts displayed for him alone.

He dragged his gaze to her face. "I have to tell you, Kelsey, I didn't expect to be dancing with you tonight."

She cast a glance over her shoulder, hoping to find Mr. Henry gone; he wasn't. "I'm not dancing. I'm escaping."

He followed her line of vision to the men crowded near the spinsters and grandmothers. "So, you're just using me?"

"Yes." Kelsey realized what she'd said and looked up at him. "Well, maybe *using* isn't the right word."

"How about *rescue?*" he suggested.

It pricked her pride, but she nodded. "You don't mind, do you?"

He felt his innards melting from the raging fire of desire. "No. Not at all. Does this mean you're not mad at me anymore?"

She considered it a moment. "It's difficult to dance and be mad, isn't it?"

It was difficult to dance and be in his present condition, also. He nodded toward the crowd. "Who am I rescuing you from?"

Kelsey shuddered. "Mr. Henry."

Clay scanned the crowd. "Looks like he's interested in your friend at the moment."

She glanced over her shoulder and saw Wilford Henry seated beside Holly. Was no one safe from that lecher? "Holly Duncan is not my friend."

"That's right, your families aren't speaking."

"How did you know that?"

"I hear rumors from time to time."

"I hope you don't repeat any rumors you hear about me, Marshal. But I couldn't care less what you say about Holly." The words tasted bitter on her tongue, but Kelsey got them out; publicly continuing the feud with the Duncan family was easy, except when Holly was involved.

Clay gazed across the room, then looked at Kelsey again. "I swear I've seen her before, but I can't think where."

Kelsey's blood ran cold. The day in the meadow, when they rescued him from hanging, he'd seen Holly when she fell from her horse. If he ever made that connection, Holly would be in jeopardy.

The song ended, and Kelsey stepped from his arms. "Well, thank you."

"Let me know if you need rescuing again."

"No, we're even now."

Clay frowned. "Even?"

Kelsey bit down on her lip; Clay, of course, didn't know it was she who had rescued him from hanging. "You stayed at my house instead of riding home in the rain. That was a rescue...sort of."

Kelsey smiled and eased away, anxious to be gone before she said anything else foolish. She found Mallory standing at the hallway leading to the foyer.

"What are you doing dancing with my beau?" Mallory asked teasingly. "How am I going to get the stage schedules from him if you turn his head?"

She'd had her fill of men tonight. "Ernie is all yours. You can have him."

"There is a certain recklessness in his passion," she mused. "Comes from being so young, you know."

Startled, Kelsey said, "Mallory, you and Ernie didn't—"

"Now, take Mr. Wilford Henry, for example." A knowing grin parted her lips. "An older gentleman, of course, but—"

"A lecher. He makes my skin crawl."

Mallory lifted one shoulder noncommittally. "But a very generous man. In many ways."

"Mallory, what are you saying?"

She giggled. "I think I know why Mrs. Henry is so often surprised with a bauble or two."

Mallory's recklessness often alarmed Kelsey. She'd always been this way as a child, albeit to a lesser degree. But since she returned from school back east and learned of her mother's death and how her father had kept it from her, she'd gotten worse. Kelsey worried what Mallory was actually capable of doing.

"Mrs. Henry invited me to return to New York with them." Mallory giggled low in her throat. "She wants to introduce me to eastern society."

"Are you going?"

"I'll think on it, then do whichever will annoy Papa the most. An engagement or two to a roguish scalawag has all sorts of possibilities." Mallory dismissed the subject with a toss of her head, then turned her attention to the dance floor. "I see your marshal is here tonight."

Kelsey spied Clay winding his way through the crowd, nearly impossible to miss, standing a head taller than most. "Why did you invite him?"

"Papa's idea." She heaved a bored sigh. "He's so worried about these investors, he's been a bear all week. He really needs their cash."

Kelsey tugged at her bodice. "Well, I wish he hadn't shown up."

"I think Holly might wish the same. Looks like he's heading her way."

Kelsey gasped and grabbed Mallory's arm. "He got a look at Holly's face when she fell from her horse. What if he's recognized her?"

Mallory giggled. "An arrest at Papa's party? Wouldn't he just have a fit?"

"Mallory!"

She shrugged and rolled her eyes. "I'm kidding."

Kelsey wasn't so sure. "You go head off the marshal. I'll get Holly out of here."

She squealed and shivered. "This is going to be fun."

Kelsey ignored her and hurried through the gathering, formulating a plan and keeping an eye on Clay as he made his way in Holly's direction.

Ernie popped up in front of her. "Here's your punch, Miss Kelsey." He held up the crystal cup, his gaze glued to her bosoms. "Can we dance again?"

Good grief, where did he come from? And why now? Kelsey sampled the punch and smiled sweetly. "Delicious. Would you mind getting me a bite of cake?"

"Sure thing. What kind?"

Kelsey batted her lashes coyly, when what she really wanted to do was scream. "You decide."

"I'll be right back. Don't go away, now."

Quickly, Kelsey located Clay, halfway across the dance floor, with Mallory in front of him, talking nonstop. She only had a few minutes; Clay wouldn't be deterred for long, even by Mallory. She walked deliberately past Holly and dropped her glass of punch onto her lap.

Holly gasped as the deep red liquid ran in rivulets down her skirt. Kelsey leaned down to pick up her cup and whispered, "Meet me outside the kitchen door. Now. Hurry!"

Kelsey straightened and looked down at Holly indifferently. "Oops. Sorry." She strolled away without a backward look.

She lingered near the French doors for a moment, pretending to watch the dancers. Then, assured that Clay was still busy with Mallory, she slipped out onto the terrace.

The evening air tingled against Kelsey's bare shoulders as she hurried silently down the stone steps onto the lawn. After years of visiting the Morgan home, she knew the house and grounds as well as she knew her own. Kelsey lifted her skirt and dashed through the rose garden, around the corner to the kitchen. Holly stood by the door.

"What's going on?"

"Shh!" Kelsey grasped her arm and pulled her to the side of the house. They slipped between the bushes.

"Kelsey, my dress—"

"Sorry. But I had to get you out of there." She glanced around quickly, but saw no one.

Holly's shoulders sagged. "Do we have to keep pretending we're enemies?"

"We agreed this is best. It will keep suspicion off either of us if one of us should be connected with the stage robberies."

Her shoulders sagged further. "Yes, I know, but—"

"The whole town knows our families hate each other. It's a perfect cover."

"Still, I wish if could be different." Holly heaved a deep sigh, then straightened. "I guess it wouldn't be fair to you, after I get my baby back and leave. Mama and Papa would blame you, somehow, because of Seth. Who knows what they might do to you? Look what they did to Seth."

"No time to worry about that now. We've got a bigger problem. Marshal Chandler is here tonight. I think he's suspicious of you."

Holly gasped and swayed against the side of the house. "Oh, no…"

Kelsey grabbed her arms and pulled her to her feet. "This is no time to swoon. Go home and stay there. Don't come out. Don't show yourself in public."

"But, Kelsey—" Panic crept into her voice.

Kelsey forced herself to sound calm. "Don't worry. Everything will be fine. He doesn't know anything for certain. As long as he doesn't get a good look at you again, we'll probably be safe."

"Well, all right." Holly turned to leave, then whirled back. "I wish Seth were here."

A lump of emotion rose in Kelsey's throat. "Me too. But think of how marvelous it will be when he comes back. You'll have your baby and be safely away from Eldon, away from your parents and away from Jack Morgan. You three will be a family. And you'll have all the money you need to support yourselves until Seth gets on his feet again."

"It will really happen like that, won't it, Kelsey?"

It had to. "Yes. I promise. Now, go home. I'll get word to you if anything changes."

Kelsey stood in the darkness, listening to the faint sound of music, laughter and voices, and told herself for the thousandth time that she was doing the right thing. The only thing, in fact, that she could do. Circumstances gave her no alternative. Family came first, before anything. She'd keep them together. She didn't care what it took, as she'd proven each time she relieved Jack Morgan of the payroll money.

Kelsey turned back toward the house. Thoughts of Ernie and Wilford Henry loomed large in her mind, and she didn't relish the idea of being pursued by them any more tonight. She'd have to go back inside, sooner or later, but for now she felt content to enjoy the crisp night air and the solitude. She'd take the back stairs through the kitchen, in a while, and freshen up in her room. Maybe things would look better then.

* * *

She'd been gone a long time, and if that wasn't worrisome enough, he hadn't seen that little snot Ernie, or the lecherous Wilford Henry, either. Clay scanned the dance floor. He'd positioned himself in the hallway, where he could keep an eye on most everything, but so far he'd seen nothing more interesting than Estelle Duncan leaving in a huff and Miss Wilder teetering down the staircase.

"Damn..." Clay made his way across the ballroom and out onto the terrace. A few couples sat on benches, but no sign of Kelsey. He paused at the top of the steps, waiting for his eyes to adjust to the darkness. His gut tightened. Somehow, he knew Kelsey was in trouble.

He wandered through the gardens, making his way slowly in the darkness, but saw no one there. The moon offered precious little light as he circled the house. Finding nothing, he headed back toward the terrace, but voices—angry voices—drew him to an open window. Inside, he glimpsed Jack Morgan and Sheriff Bottom in the study.

"Damn it, I was afraid something like this would happen." Jack Morgan was pacing in front of a cherry desk. He turned to face the sheriff. "Wilford Henry, of all people. The man's got more money than everybody in this whole town put together. Where's that deputy of yours? Where's Chandler?"

"Billy is outside, Mr. Morgan, but we don't need the marshal." Sheriff Bottom hung his thumbs in his vest pockets. "I already know who stole Mrs. Henry's jewelry."

"What? Then why the hell are you standing here? They're getting away."

"They ain't going nowhere. And, by the way, this

will put an end to them payroll robberies of yours.'' The sheriff nodded confidently.

Morgan glared at him. ''What are you talking about?''

''They're one in the same, this robbery and your payroll robberies. You just let me make the arrest, Mr. Morgan. I'll get Mrs. Henry's things back before they've even left this house. And you won't have no more problems getting your payroll through, either.''

''Who is it? I want to know.''

Sheriff Bottom shook his head. ''Just let me do my job.''

His eyes narrowed. ''You bring him to me. I'll deal with this man myself.''

Sheriff Bottom chuckled. ''What makes you think it's a man?''

Clay stepped back into the shadows, holding in a vicious curse. The sheriff was more interested in his pension than in justice. As he'd promised, he was going after Kelsey.

Clay hurried across the back of the house, past the terrace. If Kelsey wasn't at the party and wasn't outside, she could be in only one other place. He found the kitchen and dashed inside. The servants across the hot, steamy room didn't notice as he bounded up the staircase. In the second-floor hallway, he walked swiftly, peering into open doors, listening for voices, hoping his hunch would pay off. He had to get to Kelsey before the sheriff did.

A door opened ahead of him, and Kelsey walked into the hallway. Clay was in front of her in three long strides.

He grabbed her arms. ''What do you know about Mrs. Henry's jewelry being stolen?''

"What?" Stunned, she looked up at him.

He tightened his grip on her arm. "Do you know anything about the jewelry being stolen tonight?"

Kelsey gasped. "Mrs. Henry's lost her jewelry? Someone stole it?"

Clay heard voices on the staircase. He pushed Kelsey inside her bedroom and eased the door shut. Lanterns burned in the wall sconces and by the bed.

She pulled her arm from his grasp. "What are you doing?"

Clay stepped closer. "Take off all your clothes and get in bed."

Chapter Eleven

"What?"

"Take off all your clothes and get in bed."

Her cheeks burned with indignation. "I'll do no such thing."

Clay glanced over his shoulder and pulled loose his string tie. "The sheriff's on his way up here. He thinks you stole Mrs. Henry's jewelry."

Panic sliced through Kelsey. "But why? I mean, how could he think that? I only saw her jewelry for a moment."

His eyes narrowed. "So you did see the jewelry."

"Yes, she showed it to Mallory and me. Mrs. Higgins-Smythe was there, too. She even told Mrs. Henry to be more careful with it."

"And you knew where she kept it hidden?"

"Well, yes, but—" Kelsey bit her bottom lip. The incident had seemed innocent at the time, but now it made her seem as if she were a party to robbery.

"Have you got an alibi?" Clay popped open the top button of his shirt.

"A what?" Fear tightened her chest.

"An alibi, Kelsey. You haven't been at the party or on the terrace. Where have you been?"

Holly. A lump of emotion rose in her throat. She'd been with Holly. But telling him would compromise the cover they'd spent months concocting. At the very least, he would question Holly, and he might link her with the stagecoach robberies.

Clay grasped her upper arms. "Where were you, Kelsey?"

She looked up at him and swallowed hard. "In the gardens. I was in the gardens."

He glanced over his shoulder again. "Who were you with?"

"No one."

"Damn it..." Clay shrugged out of his coat and flung it across the room. "The sheriff thinks you stole those jewels. He's on his way up here to arrest you."

"Me! Why would he think I did it?"

"I've got no time to explain." Clay yanked his shirt from his trousers. "Get out of those clothes. Now."

Her eyes bulged. "I will not—"

"Have you got a better alibi?" He caught her wrist and pulled her closer. "Have you?"

The breath went out of her. Her only alibi might implicate Holly, then Mallory, and eventually even lead to her own arrest.

"No." The word came out in a whispered rush. "I have no alibi."

Clay released her arm. "Hurry. The sheriff is on his way."

Panic seized her, and she struggled with the fasteners on her dress, stepped out of it and kicked off her slippers, her ears straining for the sound of footsteps in the hall, a knock at the door. Images of herself on the hangman's scaffold, Toby crying, the ruined name of the Rodgers family on everyone's lips, raced through her mind.

"Take down your hair."

His voice sent a shiver through her. In her rush, she'd forgotten about Clay. He stood before her now in his bare feet, shirt off, trousers unfastened. The fabric of his long johns stretched across his wide chest; dark hair curled at the opening. She shrank back.

"Take down your hair," he repeated.

She pulled her dress in front of her. "I..."

Clay froze and leaned toward the door. "I hear footsteps on the stairs. Hurry."

A little squeal slipped from her lips, and she tossed the dress aside. Frantically she removed her petticoats and flung them aside, following them with her stockings and bustle. Her fingers tangled in the strings of her corset.

"Turn around." Clay grasped her shoulder and spun her, then pulled loose the knotted strings.

Kelsey dropped the corset at her feet, jerked back the coverlet and sheet and leaped into bed wearing her chemise and pantalets. She glanced back at Clay as he dropped his long johns on the floor. A hot flush shot through her. He was naked. She'd seen her brother shirtless before, but he'd never—ever—looked like Clay Chandler.

Every nerve ending she owned stood on end as Clay stretched out beside her and pulled the covers over them. Heat radiated from him. The mattress shifted, leaning her in his direction. Their arms touched. Kelsey scooted away, toward the wall.

"I told you to take your hair down."

He rolled above her onto his elbow. His shoulders

were wide, his arms heavily muscled. Crisp black hair covered his wide chest.

Clay took a comb from her hair.

She pulled away as her hair tumbled down. "But—"

"Nobody does this with their hair up." He reached for another comb.

"And I'm supposed to know that?"

His hands stilled, and he looked down at her in the light from the bedside lantern. "Sheriff Bottom will know it."

She let out a tiny whimper and tore the rest of the combs and pins from her hair.

"Open your top."

She grasped it with both hands.

"Open it. And pull your arms out. We've got to convince the sheriff this is the real thing."

Kelsey loosened the laces in her chemise and slid her arms from the sleeves. She pulled the coverlet up to her chin.

"Come closer."

Clay looped his arm around her waist and pulled her against him. Her flesh burned where his leg touched hers. His hard chest pressed against the side of her breast. His arm rested casually across her belly. Kelsey held her breath, afraid to move.

Minutes dragged by as she strained for the sound of Sheriff Bottom's boots in the hall, his fist against the door. She heard nothing.

"Maybe—"

"Shh..." Clay nuzzled against her ear. "Don't talk."

Another long moment passed, then another and another. She felt Clay's arm relax across her belly and his fingers graze her flesh between her chemise and pantalets. He shifted slightly, and his leg crossed over hers.

"Clay, maybe—"

"Quiet." He brushed his lips against her hair and spoke softly into her ear.

Kelsey lay there for another moment, listening to the silent house and the sound of Clay's deep, even breaths. He shifted on the bed, drawing her closer. Suspicion coiled deep in her belly, then bloomed into anger.

"You sneaky, low-down polecat." She ground out the words in a low, menacing voice.

"Shh—"

"Of all the rotten, underhanded tricks I've ever heard of!" Kelsey drew back her elbow and jabbed him in the belly. "Get off of me!"

A little *whoof* slipped through his lips as he grabbed his stomach. "Quiet, Kelsey, the sheriff will be here—"

She pushed him away with both hands and sat up. "You must think I'm a fool, believing this trumped-up story of yours. Sheriff coming to arrest me. Stolen jewelry, my foot! Of all the men I've known, Clay Chandler, you are the lowest, filthiest, rottenest skunk I've ever met!"

He sat up and braced his arm against the pillow. "Look, Kelsey, you've got it all wrong. I—"

Kelsey scooted sideways in the bed and reared back against the wall. "Get out!" She kicked him with both feet.

Clay tumbled backward onto the floor. He sprang to his feet and planted his fists on his hips, glaring down at her.

Kelsey's cheeks flamed when she saw his body. He

was naked. She plastered her hands over her face. "Cover yourself!"

"Okay!" He caught a fistful of the coverlet and yanked it off her.

She squealed and grabbed for it. "No!"

They pulled it back and forth between them, and then Clay tugged it hard and Kelsey flew across the bed with it and landed crossways on her belly. She pushed herself up and arched her neck, to find herself staring at his crotch. She squealed again and jumped back.

"You're slimier than pond scum!" She drew back her fist.

Clay caught her wrist and pushed her back onto the bed. She swung the other hand at him, but he captured it, too, then straddled her hips, pinning her to the bed.

She thrashed wildly beneath him, but he held her easily. "Look, Kelsey—"

"Open up in there!"

The door burst open and Sheriff Bottom strode into the room, gun drawn. Kelsey screamed, and Clay whirled around.

He eyed them for a long moment, then shoved his pistol into its holster. "So the lady likes it rough, huh?"

Mortified, Kelsey wished the bed would swallow her whole.

Clay sat up, shielding her from the sheriff's view. Kelsey pressed herself close to him, thankful for having his big, wide back to hide behind. Her tangled hair fell over them both.

"What do you want, Sheriff? I'm kind of busy right now."

He peered around Clay. "Is that Kelsey Rodgers you've got back there?"

She shrank lower behind Clay.

He shifted to block the sheriff's nosy gaze. "Yeah. What do you want?"

Sheriff Bottom hung his thumbs in his gun belt. "Just checking on something. She been in here with you long?"

"Not quite long enough, if you've got to know."

He rocked back on his heels, straining to see around him. "Seems like somebody went and stole—"

"Get out."

Kelsey bit her lower lip, praying Clay wouldn't get up off the bed and throw the sheriff out. If that man saw her in her underwear, she'd die, right there on the spot.

The sheriff lingered for only a second longer, then sauntered to the door and chuckled. "I see why you were so anxious to defend her the other day. Not that I blame you."

"Get the hell out of here."

With a smug grin, the sheriff closed the door softly behind him.

Trembling, Kelsey scooted back against the wall and drew up her knees. She pulled a corner of the coverlet up around her chin, and held it with both hands.

Clay watched the door until the sheriff's footsteps faded away, then pulled the coverlet over his lap and turned to face Kelsey. "Are you all right?"

She drew in a deep breath. "I don't know."

They were quiet for a long moment. Finally, Kelsey looked across the bed at him. "Why did you do this?"

Why had he? He'd stuck his neck out a mile to protect Kelsey, when he had no actual proof of her innocence, only his gut instinct. Clay shrugged. "The sheriff is more interested in himself than justice. He'd have sent you off to prison without a second thought, just to keep his pension and save face with Morgan."

Kelsey nodded slowly as the full impact of what Clay had done dawned on her. Without his interference, she'd be on her way to the jail right now.

"And I didn't want to be one of the others."

She looked up, jarred from her thoughts. "Who?"

"The men you mentioned out at your place. The ones who couldn't take care of you, who let you down." He eased closer on the bed. "Who were they? Your pa?"

Kelsey's stomach coiled into a knot at the thought. Clay had figured right. Her father had mortgaged everything the family owned, then lost his mind. "Yes," she whispered.

Gently Clay pushed the mass of her brown hair back off her face. "What happened to your brother?"

The joy mixed with anger that she always felt at the mention of Seth's name swept over her. She blew out a heavy breath. "I told him not to go to Morgan's place that night by himself, but no, he didn't listen."

"You don't believe he robbed the hardware store?"

"I know he didn't. It was a trap." Kelsey forced down her anger. "My father had a business deal with Nate Duncan. It went bad. Mr. Duncan lost a lot of money. He thought my father had purposely cheated him. He was furious."

"Was it true? Did your pa cheat him?"

"Probably." Kelsey sighed and drew her fingers through her thick hair. "But not purposely. Papa's mind was cloudy, he got confused. I'm not sure he knew what he was doing. Seth took over most of Papa's business after that.''

''But that didn't appease Duncan?''

''No. During that same time, Seth was seeing Holly. When the Duncans found out Holly was— Well, Mr. Duncan decided to exact his revenge on Seth, with the help of Jack Morgan.''

''Why would Morgan get involved? What did he have to gain?''

Kelsey kept the truth of her suspicions about Jack Morgan to herself, lest she provide Clay with her motive for robbing the man's payroll. She lifted one shoulder. ''Jack Morgan has his reasons, not always clear to everyone. Anyway, Seth got a message to meet Mr. Morgan at his hardware store one night to discuss business. Seth had begun to handle all of Papa's affairs by then, since he could hardly do it himself. When he arrived, Seth found the place locked up tight, just before he got hit over the head from behind. He woke up inside the store, his pockets full of money and the sheriff standing over him.''

''What makes you think the Duncans were involved?''

''It was Nate Duncan who supposedly witnessed the break-in and sent for the sheriff.''

Clay stroked his chin. ''And you believe Jack Morgan was a party to this, too?''

''The trial was over almost before anyone knew about it. Seth was sentenced to five years in prison.''

''Five years? What judge would—'' His back stiffened. ''Kingsley. Judge Kingsley.''

Kelsey nodded. ''Morgan paid him off. I'm sure of it.''

''Morgan and dozens of other people. Kingsley was

the richest judge in the state when we finally got rid of him.'' Clay nodded slowly. ''So you think your brother was framed by Duncan and Morgan. Duncan, to get him out of his daughter's life. And Morgan?''

She looked away. ''I don't know why Morgan did it. But I'm certain of his involvement. Nate Duncan didn't know Kingsley well enough to arrange—and afford—a five-year prison sentence.''

''And you're sure Morgan did?''

Anger darkened her face. ''Kingsley stayed with the Morgans whenever he was in town.''

Clay pulled at his neck. The story sounded true, especially given that Seth had had no motive to rob the store in the first place.

Clay touched her chin and lifted her face. ''So, did I succeed?''

His gaze felt soft and gentle upon her, caressing her, yet burning with an intensity she'd never seen before. It washed over her, seeped deep inside her, and touched a spot at the very core of her being.

He lowered his head and touched his lips softly to hers, pressing them together with exquisite gentleness. He looped his arm around her waist and drew her nearer. Her breasts yielded to his hardness.

A groan rumbled deep in his chest and he thrust his hand into the thickness of her hair. Kelsey tipped her head back and he deepened the kiss, twining his tongue with hers.

Urgency claimed him as he eased her onto the bed and stretched out above her, his legs coiling intimately with hers. She felt like velvet as he drew his hand across her belly and slid his fingers past the laces of her chemise. He pressed deeper, cupping her breast, kneading her, and circled his fingers over the crest, bringing it to life.

She moaned and looped her hand around his neck as his fingers moved slowly over the mound of her breast. She pressed closer, aching with need. He pushed back the fabric and kissed a hot trail down her throat and chest, circling the tiny bud with his tongue, then laid claim to it.

Kelsey gasped and drew her hand across his chest, combing her fingers through his dark, curly hair until she touched the tiny copper disks buried there. He moaned and covered her mouth with a demanding kiss.

Urgency claimed them both as Clay slid his hand down the curve of her hip, pushing away her pantalets. She kicked them off and ran her leg the length of his, touching him intimately.

Instinct told him to rush, but he didn't. She was so sweet, so pure he could have done it easily. But that wasn't what he wanted from Kelsey, nor was it what he wanted to give her.

Clay kissed his way the length of her body, dragging his tongue in a hot trail, devouring her thighs, her hips, nipping her breasts as she writhed against him. He lifted his gaze and looked at her, head thrown back, tossing on the pillow. She was so vulnerable, so trusting, giving herself to him. Clay's heart swelled in his chest, pumping his body taut with need.

Desire, demanding and urgent, coiled deep within him. Clay rose above her and settled between her thighs. He wrapped his arms around her as he eased himself into her. She felt so tiny beneath him, around him, and he'd never been so swollen in his life. For a second, he nearly lost all control. He grasped a fistful of the pillow and gritted his teeth.

Slowly, gently, he moved within her, until she responded. Tentatively at first, then with the same desire that had claimed him.

Kelsey threw her arms around his neck and grabbed a fistful of his hair. His movements sent all thought from her mind, leaving instead primitive instinct. She moved with him, arching up to meet him over and over, until great waves of passion broke through her.

Clay twisted his fists in the pillow, holding back until he was certain, then wrapped her in his arms and thrust deep inside her, again and again, pouring out his feelings as he moaned her name.

Spent, he rolled beside her and pulled her near. She snuggled close, wrapping her arm over his chest. They lay, contented, in each other's arms.

Kelsey gazed up at him, listening to the even rhythm of his breathing. He hadn't said he loved her, hadn't even said he cared. Not with words, anyway. But she felt no remorse for what she'd done. His arms around her, his presence, all brought her a contentment and comfort she'd never felt before. And for now, that was enough.

A few moments later, Clay roused and planted a kiss on her forehead. She looked beautiful in the pale light, rumpled and disheveled, glowing with their lovemaking. He wished he could stay here with her forever.

"I think we'd better go." Kelsey sat up. "Someone else might come looking for one of us."

He didn't want to leave, but he didn't like the idea of someone else walking in on them. Clay rolled out of bed and reached for his long johns. Though they'd just shared the most intimate act possible between a man and a woman, Kelsey seemed embarrassed to look at him, so he gathered his clothes scattered everywhere in the room and dressed quickly.

"I'll wait outside," he offered. Still seated on the bed, her back to him, swathed in the coverlet, Kelsey nodded, and he left her alone.

A few moments later, she stepped into the hallway, dressed in the simple skirt and blouse she'd had on earlier in the day, her hair twisted in a neat chignon.

Kelsey shifted her carpetbag from one hand to the other. She had no idea of the proper etiquette for such an occasion. A kiss? A handshake? A thank-you hardly seemed appropriate. "Well, good night," she finally said.

"I'll walk you home."

"Oh."

He took her bag and led the way to the head of the staircase that descended to the kitchen.

She stopped on the first step. "You don't have to. I'll be fine."

"I want to." He gazed down at her and felt his insides melting all over again.

Still, she didn't move. "I don't think we should be seen leaving together. People talk."

Clay berated himself for being so thoughtless. Of course, she'd be concerned about gossip.

"I'll go down first and wait for you out back. The kitchen staff is pretty busy, I doubt they'll notice."

Kelsey touched her hand to her forehead. "I suppose the sheriff will spread this all over town by tomorrow morning."

"Only if he wants to admit he was a complete fool thinking you'd taken that jewelry. He won't open his mouth." And if he did, Clay would take great pleasure in closing it with his fist.

Kelsey nodded, a little relieved. "All right. I'll follow you down."

The kitchen of the Eldon Hotel felt cold when they arrived. Clay lingered, offered to build a fire in the cookstove, heat up some coffee, but Kelsey said no, so he finally went upstairs. She stood at the doorway of her bedroom for a long moment, listening to the sound of his boots on the staircase, the creak of his bedroom door, and then, finally, the silence.

Could anyone look at her and tell what she'd done? Would it be obvious? Was she now a marked woman?

Kelsey stepped into the busy kitchen, where the air was thick with the scent of frying bacon. She'd dressed in a black skirt and a dark green blouse with a high collar, and styled her hair in the same severe coif she'd seen Miss Chalmers wear, hoping to cast no suspicion on herself for her actions last night. But, despite her effort, would she find herself the talk of Eldon this morning?

Etta Mae turned back from the stove, dripping oatmeal on the floor. "Why, good morning. I didn't expect to find you here until later in the day."

Sue Ellen Parker looked up from the dough she was rolling on the sideboard. "I thought you were staying at the Morgans' all night."

"I decided not to." She edged toward the pantry, avoiding their gazes.

Etta Mae gave her a knowing look. "I heard there was quite the goings-on there last night. Hmm?"

Kelsey swallowed hard. "I—I don't know what you mean."

"That fancy eastern lady getting her jewelry stolen."

Sue Ellen waved the rolling pin. "And right under everybody's nose, too."

"Mr. Morgan must have been fit to be tied. Hmm?" Etta Mae nodded wisely.

"Oh. That. I didn't hear much about it." Kelsey pulled an apron from the drawer by the sink and held her breath. "What else did you hear?"

"Estelle Duncan left in a snit," Sue Ellen reported. "And Miss Mallory was seen dancing with nearly every young man at the party."

"I heard that she was partial to that young man over at the express office. Hmm?" Etta Mae bobbed her brows at Kelsey.

She tied the apron around her waist. "Ernie? No, I don't think so."

Sue Ellen nodded slowly. "I heard the young man was quite taken with you."

Kelsey couldn't deny the attention Ernie had lavished on her last night, but he'd seemed more enthralled with her bosoms than by the rest of her. "We danced a time or two, that's all. Did you hear anything else? Anything at all?"

The two women looked at each other and shook their heads.

"That's about it." Sue Ellen turned back to her biscuits.

Etta Mae's brows bobbed. "Was there something else?"

"No," Kelsey said quickly. She hurried toward the door. "I'll go check on the dining room."

She breathed a sigh of relief as she passed through the hallway into the lobby. If Etta Mae and Sue Ellen hadn't heard about her torrid moment with Clay, hopefully no one else in town had, either. No one would understand. They'd think it some cheap, tawdry encounter and brand her a harlot of the worst sort. And to Kelsey, it had been nothing but beautiful. She was glad she'd shared it with Clay.

But the possibility of a baby growing inside her this morning lurked in the back of her head. It was the first thing—no, the second thing—that had popped into her mind when she woke. And if it were true? Well, like all the other situations in her life—her father's illness, her brother in prison, her financial problems—she'd deal with it as best she could.

When she glanced into the crowded dining room and saw that Clay wasn't there, she was thankful. The proper etiquette for the morning after was quite beyond her.

At the front desk she glanced over the register and noted that a new guest had checked in this morning. Kelsey allowed herself a small smile. Maybe this would be a good day, after all. She looked closer at the name scrawled in bold letters across the register. Harlan Winthrope.

Kelsey gasped aloud as she realized that this was *Judge* Harlan Winthrope. A judge. Staying at her hotel. A federal marshal wasn't enough—she had to have a judge, too? Why didn't every law-enforcement official in the whole state just move in with her?

Kelsey pushed the register away, and the hope that this may be a good day faded fast, then disappeared completely, when Ernie bounded into the lobby.

"Good morning, Miss Kelsey." His gaze swept her face momentarily, then settled on her bosoms.

Kelsey's shoulders sagged. "Ernie, good morning."

He slicked his hair down and leaned against the front desk. "I—ah—I had a good time with you last night."

She busied herself with the register. "It was a very nice party."

Ernie tugged on his suspenders. "Mr. Bean says I'm sure to make senior agent in no time."

She managed a small smile. "That's nice."

"The express office is the place to be." He nodded wisely. "Fact is, there's big stuff happening over there right now."

It occurred to her to wonder, if Ernie really was so important, and big things really were happening at the express office, then why was he here with her? She thought the answer lay in her bustline. "Is that so?"

"Mr. Morgan is over there this very minute, making plans to send out his payroll again." Ernie thumped his chest. "I heard them taking myself."

Kelsey's heart slammed against her ribs. She smiled sweetly, doing her best to mimic Mallory. "Well, my, Ernie, it must be very exciting sending the payroll out on one of your very own stagecoaches."

Ernie leaned closer. "That's the big plan, Miss Kelsey. It's not going out on the stage this time. That's why Mr. Morgan is over at the express office right now. He's checking the schedule so he can send the payroll out after the last stage run. Mr. Morgan's got his own wagon and two guards to get his payroll through."

Kelsey gripped the edge of the desk. "A wagon and two guards? All for the payroll to the mines? I guess Mr. Morgan is taking no chances."

"You can say that again." Ernie glanced around, and lowered his voice. "He's sending three months' payroll this time. I tell you, big business over at the express office."

Breath left her in a tiny puff. "Three months? Oh, my."

"Mr. Morgan needs to talk to the marshal." Ernie pulled an envelope from his pocket. "See that Marshal Chandler gets this, will you? Mr. Morgan wants to talk to him right away, so they can make plans for this afternoon."

Kelsey took the envelope. "Don't worry, Ernie. I'll see the marshal gets it. Now don't let me keep you from your work. I know you have to get back."

He nodded wisely. "Real busy over there."

Ernie backed across the lobby, gave her breasts a final look and left the hotel.

Kelsey tapped the envelope against her palm. Reading a hotel guest's mail was unthinkable. But, on the other hand, Clay was more than a guest. She'd seen him naked, for heaven's sake. And if you'd seen a man naked, surely it entitled you to read his mail.

She glanced around the lobby, then opened the envelope. The note gave no details, just said that Mr. Morgan wanted Clay to meet him as soon as possible. That could only mean that he wanted Clay to guard the payroll. Well, she could prevent that easily enough. She slid the letter into her pocket.

Ernie said the wagon carrying the payroll would leave after the last stage run this afternoon, and that left little time for preparation. There'd be two guards to deal with, but only two, now that she'd prevented Clay learning of the plan. And there'd be no passengers for the guards to consider and to keep from trying to be heroes. Kelsey paced behind the front desk. Risky. Very risky.

But three months' payroll was a lot of money. So much that this could be their last robbery. Kelsey's spirits soared. If they could pull this off, she could pay all the mortgages on her family's holdings. Holly could get her baby back. The chance was too good to pass up.

Her mind whirling, she hurried down the hall and into the kitchen. She had a lot to do in a very short time. Kelsey ducked into her bedroom, wishing she felt better. She hadn't slept a wink all night.

He'd slept like a rock.

Clay set his Stetson at a rakish angle and bounded down the staircase whistling as he crossed the lobby. Morning sunlight shone through the windows. What a beautiful day.

He smiled and nodded pleasantly to the other diners as he made his way to the table in the back of the dining room and sat down. The kitchen door swung open, and the serving girl came in, carrying a coffee-pot.

It wasn't Kelsey, but Clay was only mildly disappointed. No doubt she was still asleep. He shifted on the chair. After last night, who could blame her?

"Good morning, Marshal." Sue Ellen poured coffee into his cup. "You're looking in good spirits today."

"Yes, ma'am, I guess you could say that."

She grinned. "I've never seen a smile that big on a man before."

Was it that obvious? He didn't care. "I'm starved. Bring me a steak, rare. And anything else you've got in the kitchen, too."

A short while later, she brought out his breakfast, and he ate every bite of it, then finished it off with a hot cinnamon roll and another cup of coffee. Satisfied, Clay sat back and patted his belly. Now he needed to see Kelsey.

Etta Mae looked up from the stove when he walked into the kitchen. "Good morning, Marshal."

"I came to see Kelsey. Can you get her up?" Though he'd rather handle that little detail himself—seeing her snuggled in bed, exhausted after their love-making—he didn't think she would appreciate all the prying eyes on them.

"Hmm? Oh, yes, well, Kelsey's not here."

"Sure she is." He'd overslept. Certainly Kelsey had, too.

Etta Mae smiled and waved a dripping spoon around the room. "She was up and gone early this morning—hours ago."

"She was?" Clay scratched his head. "Where'd she go?"

"Hmm? Home, I suppose. That's where she usually goes."

Clay walked back to the lobby. The sunlight didn't look as bright as it had a while ago. Then it occurred to him that he could ride out to Kelsey's house and see her. The day brightened again, and he crossed the lobby whistling. After all, he had nothing else to do this morning.

Deuce.

Clay stopped and turned back to the lobby. Where was Deuce? He'd talked to him outside the jail just last night. The boy was supposed to meet him here first thing this morning so that they could go talk to Miss Wilder about that job.

He checked the dining room and peeped into the cubbyholes behind the front desk, hoping for a note from the boy, but found nothing. Clay stepped out onto the boardwalk and stroked his chin.

Where could Deuce be? What could he be doing?

Chapter Twelve

Clay saw Jack Morgan across the street at the same moment the man spotted him. They glared at each other as horses and wagons passed between them. The line of Clay's mouth hardened, and he folded his arms over his wide chest. Finally Morgan crossed the street.

"Didn't you get my message?" he growled.

Clay straightened. "What message?"

"Look, Chandler, I've got a lot of money going out on that wagon today. Those investors last night were mighty concerned with the law in this town, and I intend to change their minds before they leave here and take their money with them. I want my payroll protected. The governor—"

"Yeah, yeah, I know. He's a personal friend of yours." Clay pulled his Stetson lower on his forehead. "I'll go talk to the sheriff about it."

"Save your breath. I just went by the jailhouse, and it's locked up tight."

Clay tensed. "Where's the sheriff? Where's that deputy of his? There's prisoners inside."

"The sheriff is eating somewhere, I guess. Billy got drunk on his butt last night. He's sleeping it off at my place." Morgan slid his finger over his thin mustache. "Besides, I've already got a plan, Chandler. I told my men to shoot first and ask questions later. I don't care if those outlaws are a bunch of kids—"

"Hold it, right there." Clay planted his fists on his hips. "I'm running this, not you. The last plan you came up with nearly got me killed."

"Now see here, Chandler—"

"No, you see here." Clay tapped the badge on his chest. "I'll get your payroll through—my way."

Clay pushed past him. Damn fool businessman, thought he knew how outlaws think. The Schoolyard Boys might be kids, but they'd robbed the stage and made a clean getaway five times already. Outlaws that successful needed a special touch. And Clay knew just what to do.

At the thought of boys and outlaws, Deuce came into his mind again. Clay turned the corner and walked to the livery stable. Morgan and his payroll could wait.

Ben stood in the paddock, watching a bay mare prance across the ring, trying out her new shoes.

"Morning, Ben." Clay rested his arms on the top rail of the fence.

He flung his hammer into the wooden tool box at his feet. "Marshal..."

He looked like a bear coming out of winter hibernation, and sounded just as grumpy. "I'm looking for Deuce."

Ben pointed a big, meaty finger at him. "When you find that boy, tell him I've got a strap waiting for him, and he'll be lucky to have an inch of hide left when I get done with him."

Clay tensed. "What happened?"

"The boy didn't come home last night."

"You haven't seen him this morning, either?"

"If I had, you'd have heard the yelping by now." Ben pulled at his neck. "When I get my hands on that boy…"

"I'll find him." Clay pushed away from the fence and headed for town. He had to get to Deuce before Ben did.

A knot twisted in his belly as he walked down the boardwalk, and his gaze settled on the jailhouse. He froze in his tracks. Luther.

"Damn it…" Clay's chest tightened. He should have thought of it sooner. He should have kept a closer eye on Deuce.

He mumbled another curse and crossed the street in front of Braden's Dry Goods Store. He stopped, then, on a hunch, turned down the alley. At the rear of the store, in a maze of wooden crates and barrels, he saw the top of a light brown head.

At that moment, he understood Ben's concern for the boy, and was tempted to give him a swat on the seat of his pants for worrying him. But knowing what else Ben had planned, he didn't seriously consider it.

Clay wound his way through the crates and barrels. Deuce looked up at him. The bruise around his eye had darkened, and he looked tired and drawn. Fear shone in his eyes as he rose from the bench. He looked guilty as hell over something.

"Sit down." Clay put a hand on his shoulder, and they sat down on the bench.

Deuce squirmed and shifted and chewed his lip before finally looking up at Clay. "I know I was supposed to meet you at the hotel this morning."

"I was worried about you."

His brows bobbed up. "You were?"

"Sure. Where have you been?"

"I had some thinking to do." Deuce's gaze fell to the ground.

A long moment passed. "And?"

Reluctantly, Deuce looked up at him. "I decided not to leave."

Clay leaned closer. "Luther is trying to talk you into breaking him out of jail, isn't he?"

Deuce shifted, but didn't reply.

"You brought him that bottle of whiskey, didn't you?"

His gaze came up quickly. "How did you know?"

He shrugged. "A hunch."

The line of Deuce's mouth tightened. "I thought hard about leaving, about going with Luther and never coming back. I thought a long time about it. Then I remembered what you said, how the decisions in life keep getting harder. I knew it wouldn't be right for me to run away. I couldn't do it."

Clay put his arm around Deuce's shoulder and gave him a squeeze. The boy had so much heart, so much goodness in him. He could accomplish anything, if he had a little guidance. And all his pa wanted to do was take a strap to him.

He blew out a heavy breath. "You made a good decision, Deuce. I'm proud of you—damn proud."

"Yeah?" A little smile tugged at his lips.

"Are you still interested in that job over at Miss Wilder's place?"

"Yes, sir, but my pa—"

"Let's take one thing at a time." Clay rose. "Come on." He rested his hand on Deuce's shoulder as they walked away.

* * *

An ankle crossed over one knee, Clay sat back on the bench outside the barbershop, his Stetson covering his face. The warm rays of the midday sun seeped through him.

"Having some sweet dreams?"

Clay grabbed his hat and bolted to his feet.

"Sweet dreams about a certain young lady?"

He scowled at the sheriff's leering smirk and settled his Stetson in place. "What do you want?"

Sheriff Bottom patted his round belly as he laughed. "Hold on, now, don't go getting all in an uproar. You and your little lady's secret is safe with me."

Clay didn't want to be beholden to anybody—especially the sheriff—and was about to tell him so, but he didn't think Kelsey would appreciate his bravado. As with last night, he felt the overwhelming need to protect her. "I don't want to hear any more about her being one of the Schoolyard Boys."

"I've got bigger fish to fry right now."

Clay nodded his agreement. "Any idea who took the jewelry last night?"

"Nope. But somebody better come up with some ideas real soon. The last thing Mr. Morgan wants is those investors to turn tail and run—taking their money with them."

"Is Morgan in some kind of financial trouble?"

"You didn't hear it from me."

Clay shifted. He'd already heard it from several other sources.

Sheriff Bottom nodded wisely. "Looks like we'll put the Schoolyard Boys out of business this afternoon. If those kids come sniffing around Morgan's payroll, they're going to get themselves shot."

Clay snorted his disgust. "Morgan's plan is as

worthless as a milk bucket under a bull. Get Billy so-
bered up and have the two guards Morgan hired meet
me at the jail.''

"You got an idea on how this thing ought to be
handled?''

"Damn right.''

Sheriff nodded. "Good. You bring those kids in, and
we'll get them sent off to prison or have them dangling
from the hangman's noose real quick. Judge Winthrope
rode into town this morning.''

"Jesus…'' Clay pulled off his hat and plowed his
fingers through his hair. Harlan Winthrope. The last
man he wanted to see. Damn those Schoolyard Boys
for keeping him here.

Clay glanced through the barbershop window and
saw Deuce perched in the chair, getting his hair cut.
He lowered his voice. "Look, Sheriff. I need you to
go talk to the judge about Deuce. Get him to see the
boy just got caught up with the wrong bunch. I'd do it
myself, but I've got things to get handled before Morgan's payroll leaves here this afternoon. Take care of
it, will you?''

"Winthrope that sort of judge?''

Clay nodded. "He's fair. You give it to him straight
and he'll listen. He'll do what's right.''

"I'll go talk to him.'' Sheriff Bottom headed off
down the boardwalk.

Clay paced the boardwalk until Deuce came out of
the barbershop. He gave his fresh haircut a nod of approval. Deuce didn't look nearly so frail and spindly
in the new clothes they'd bought him, clothes that fit
properly. Though it was doubtful he'd ever be as big
as his pa or brother, the boy had more growing to do,
and he'd fill out eventually.

They walked across town to Miss Wilder's little house, and Clay knocked on the door.

"Nervous?"

Deuce sucked in a deep breath. "A little."

"Have you ever asked for a job before?"

"No, sir."

"Be polite and speak up. Tell her what you can do to handle the job."

He nodded and closed his eyes, seemingly rehearsing what he should say.

"Don't worry. She's a nice lady."

"Wasn't she the schoolmarm about a hundred years back?"

"About that."

The door opened, and Miss Wilder smiled brightly. "Why, good day, Marshal. What a pleasant surprise." She looked at Deuce. "And who have we here?"

Clay tipped his hat. "Miss Wilder, I'd like you to meet Dennis Tucker. I wonder if we could come inside?"

"Why, certainly. Come right in." She showed them to the parlor. "Just sit right down. I'll bring us some tea."

Deuce's gaze roamed the tiny room crowded with all sorts of odds and ends. "She's got money to pay somebody to catalog her books?"

Clay settled his big frame into a flower print chair. "Her nephew sent it."

Deuce rolled his eyes. "She ought to pay somebody to straighten up this room."

Clay chuckled. "Miss Wilder seems a little eccentric."

"She's fixing us tea? I never had tea before."

"Something tells me that if you get this job you'll be having it a lot."

Miss Wilder carried a tray into the room bearing a china tea service. She poured and passed tiny pink flowered cups to Clay and Deuce, then sat back on the settee with a cup of her own. She talked about the weather, her garden and her latest letter from her nephew, and finally sat her cup aside.

"Now, what brings you two nice boys over today?"

Clay returned his cup to the tray, and Deuce quickly did the same; he looked relieved he hadn't spilled any of it and had actually managed to keep the cup on the saucer.

"I recall that you were looking for somebody to catalog and pack your books, Miss Wilder. I think Dennis is the man for the job."

"Oh, really?" Miss Wilder turned her gaze on Deuce and eyed him for a moment. "Well, my, but you do look plenty strong to handle the crates and do the packing. Tell me, dear, how well do you read?"

Deuce cleared his throat and sat up straighter. "Well, ma'am, I'm a real good reader. Miss Chalmers said I was best in the class."

"Is that so?"

"Yes, ma'am. And I can write good, and I know all my ciphering."

"You certainly seem like a bright young man." Miss Wilder pushed aside the clutter from the table beside her chair and picked up a leather-bound book. "Would you mind reading a little for me, dear?"

Deuce opened the book and read four pages without faltering. Then he looked up at Clay, who nodded his approval.

"Well, Miss Wilder? What do you think?" Clay asked.

She folded her hands in her lap. "I think he'll do just splendidly."

Clay rose from his chair. "Good. How about if he starts tomorrow?"

"That would be wonderful. Thank you so much, Marshal, for taking time from your work. I know how busy you are."

"My pleasure."

They said goodbye and left the house with Deuce's promise to be there first thing in the morning.

Deuce stopped at the picket fence and looked back at the house. "She seems like a nice lady."

And somebody to be nice to him was just what Deuce needed. Clay nodded. "You'll get along here all right."

Deuce shoved his hands in his pockets. "Now I've got to tell Pa."

"Yeah." Clay didn't relish confronting Ben Tucker any more than Deuce did, but he didn't let it show.

"You're coming with me, aren't you?"

"You bet." He dropped his hand on Deuce's shoulder. "Let's get this over with."

When they reached the livery stable, Ben looked like a bull ready to charge. He grabbed for Deuce. The boy broke for the door. Clay stepped between them, planted his hand on Ben's chest and caught Deuce's arm.

"Now, just a minute, Ben. The boy's been with me. Settle down. We've got some talking to do."

Ben glared at Deuce, then backed up a step. "All right, Marshal, but just 'cause it's you that's asking."

Clay released Deuce's arm. "You go on outside for a minute while we talk."

When they were alone, Clay spoke. "Ben, I don't have any kids, and I can't pretend to know what it's like, but you said yourself that Deuce doesn't belong here at the livery. He's too small to do the work. And you've got a lot on you already, running a business, working hard, supporting a wife and children. You can't watch the boy every minute."

Ben grunted, but didn't say anything.

"So, I took it on myself to find him another job."

His frown deepened. "What kind of job?"

"Working for Miss Wilder—"

He squinted one eye closed. "The old school-marm?"

"He's cataloging her books and packing them off to her nephew."

"I should of knowed he'd end up doing something like that," he muttered.

"It's what he's good at, Ben. And it will keep him occupied."

"Yeah? For how long?"

"Should take a couple of weeks to get all those books cataloged and shipped."

"What happens after that?"

An idea had taken root in Clay's mind, and the more time he spent with Deuce, the more it blossomed. But he wasn't ready to spring it on Ben.

Clay pulled at his neck. "Well, Ben, I figure we'll worry about that when it gets here. So, what do you say?"

Ben fumed silently, then nodded. "All right. I guess he can do it."

Clay heaved a silent sigh of relief. "Deuce!"

He came inside and approached them cautiously. Clay pulled him closer. "Is it okay with you, Pa?"

"Yeah, I reckon." Ben pointed a finger at him. "But you'd better not get into no trouble. And you'd better be home in time for supper. You worry your ma again like you did last night and I'll—"

"He won't cause any trouble. Right, Deuce?"

"I won't, Pa. I promise."

Ben glared at him, then walked away.

"All right, listen up. Anybody have any questions?" Clay looked hard at the three men assembled across the sheriff's desk from him. "Will? Mackey? You two understand the plan?"

They looked at each other, then at Clay.

"Well, I don't know..." Will said.

Clay shifted in the chair, forcing down his temper. The two men Morgan had selected to help guard the payroll looked better suited to guarding an outhouse.

Mackey leaned forward. "So, if them outlaws try and stop us, you want us to shoot."

"No!" Clay thumped his fist on the desk. "Look, just do whatever they tell you. Understand?"

Will and Mackey looked at each other again.

"Is that gonna be all right with Mr. Morgan?" Will asked.

"You're not working for Morgan this afternoon. You're working for me." Clay glared at them until they lowered their gazes to the floor.

He turned to Billy, who was seated under the gun rack. His chin rested on his chest, and his eyes were closed. "Billy!"

He jerked upright, banged his head on the gun rack and spouted a filthy curse.

Oh, yeah. Bottom had done a great job sobering him up. "Billy, are you listening?" Clay demanded.

Gingerly he touched the top of his head. "I'm listening."

"You understand what you're supposed to do?"

"Yeah, yeah. I got it."

Clay shook his head slowly as he surveyed the three men. The plan he'd devised was a simple one, luckily. If they did as he'd instructed, no one would get hurt. Clay rose from his chair. "All right. Let's go."

Sheriff Bottom stepped through the door as Will, Mackey and Billy clambered from their chairs, guns in hand, and headed out. The sheriff stepped in front of Clay. "I talked to the judge like you asked."

Clay picked up his Winchester from behind the desk. "Good. It's all taken care of?"

"I explained to him about Deuce, like you said, and he seemed real understanding. Wanted to go light on the boy, give him another chance." Sheriff Bottom's eyes narrowed. "Then I told him you were involved."

Clay's belly clenched. "What happened?"

"Judge Winthrope turned nasty at the mention of your name. He said if you were in on it, that changed everything." Sheriff Bottom shook his head. "Looks like Deuce is going to prison."

Chapter Thirteen

"Damn it..." Clay yanked his own thoughts back to the road stretching out in front of him and chastised himself again for not concentrating on the job at hand. Beside him, Billy offered little distraction. He hadn't spoken two words since they left Eldon, and he actually looked as if he might fall from his horse at any minute. Up ahead about a half mile, just out of view, Morgan's payroll wagon lumbered toward the mine. Clay could only hope Will and Mackey weren't having as much trouble keeping their minds on business and would follow the plan he'd laid out for them.

Clay gazed at the sun slipping toward the horizon and acknowledged that he himself had more reason to find his thoughts wandering than the other men. And he had only himself to blame for it.

Kelsey. She'd been with him all day. First in his thoughts, as he'd recalled every moment with her last night. That had caused a reaction as predictable as the sunrise, and he'd felt her presence in the pressure behind his fly all day, too. She'd been in his arms, as well, and they felt empty without her, and against his chest, still tingling from the softness of her breasts against him.

But he hadn't expected to find her winding her way around his heart. The leather saddle creaked as Clay shifted. His chest felt heavy, and his belly hurt as it had after he spent the night at her home, with her family. A longing, deep and primitive, had claimed him, and had been with him since. It had only worsened after he held her in his arms and made love to her last night.

Maybe he should talk to Kelsey about it. Clay rubbed his chin. She could help him. After all, she'd made him feel better about Rebecca.

Clay touched his heels to the stallion's sides, urging it to a faster pace. He wanted to get this job finished and head back home to Kelsey.

"Hey, Chandler, you hear that?"

Jarred from his thoughts, Clay looked over at Billy. He strained to hear above the mild breeze and the birds chirping high in the treetops. "I don't hear anything."

"Yeah, I know." Billy looked over at him. "I don't hear that squeaking wagon wheel anymore."

Clay tensed in the saddle. He'd instructed Will and Mackey to stop the wagon at the first sign of trouble, toss down the payroll and move on quickly. Riding behind, he and Billy would come across the outlaws before they had time to open the strongboxes and make their getaway. Now, it seemed that someone had fallen into that trap.

Clay nodded at Billy. "Let's go."

He spurred his horse to a run, its long legs quickly chewing up the ground. Dense forest lined both sides of the road as it dipped into a shallow valley, then rose again into a long, slow curve. They rounded the bend, and Clay pulled back on the reins. Billy's horse pranced to a stop beside him. Just ahead were three boys wearing oversize hats, and red bandannas.

Clay's heart slammed against his chest. The Schoolyard Boys.

The strongboxes lay on the ground, surrounded by two of the outlaws. A third sat on horseback, holding a pistol, watching the road ahead of them; none of the boys had seen Clay and Billy approach from behind.

Clay pulled his rifle and fired a shot into the air. "Hold it right there! Federal marshal!"

Billy pulled his pistol and leveled it at the outlaws.

Two boys dived to the ground. The rider's horse pranced fitfully and tossed its head. The boy spotted Clay and raised his gun, pointing it square at his chest.

Clay whipped the rifle to his shoulder, finger on the trigger, and caught the boy in his sights. His hand froze. Between the brim of the floppy hat and the bandanna, he glimpsed green eyes. The green eyes that had cut the hangman's noose from his neck.

Clay's blood ran cold as the boy's gun bore down on him. Then, suddenly, the boy holstered his pistol and wheeled his horse around. He lunged into the trees.

"Hold those two!" He shoved his rifle into the scabbard.

Billy nodded as Clay dug his heels into his stallion and charged after the boy.

Kelsey bit down on her lip as she pushed her horse through the thick trees. Her heart pounded, stealing her breath. The reins slipped in her wet palms. Clay Chandler! Of all people! She thought she'd gotten rid of him by hiding Morgan's note. Kelsey cursed silently. She should have known better, where Clay was concerned.

Her horse jumped a fallen log and plunged down an

embankment. Kelsey crouched low in the saddle and stole a glance behind her. Clay. Hot on her trail.

She yanked the reins hard and nearly lost her seat as the mare turned sharply to the left. She had the advantage. She knew the lay of the land. She'd use it to her benefit.

She descended a steep hill, leaves and plants rustling under the pounding hooves, and reached the edge of the creek. Kelsey turned the horse again and disappeared behind a huge outcropping of rocks. Using them for cover, Kelsey urged the horse to a full run, then squeezed her knees tight and guided it into the creek.

Cold water splashed her boots as the horse galloped through the shallow creek. She chanced a look over her shoulder again. No sign of Clay. He wasn't far behind, though, and he wouldn't give up. But she only needed a few minutes. The creek had bought her that time.

She pressed farther downstream, around a steep bend, then turned left again and urged the horse up the creek bank. She pulled back on the reins and held her heaving breath. Water splashed in the distance. Clay was in the creek. He wouldn't know which way she'd gone. Just the delay she needed.

With a fleeting sigh of relief, Kelsey nudged the horses's sides and rode straight up the hill. She reached the road and slowed to a trot, not wanting to announce her arrival. Kelsey pulled her pistol as she rounded the bend.

Billy's back made a big target as he held his gun on Mallory and Holly, seated against the trunk of a big oak, their hands tied in front, hats and bandannas still in place. She pulled back the hammer as her horse danced to a stop.

"Drop it, lawman!"

He spun around and fired. The sound cracked like thunder in the still forest. Kelsey crouched low on the horse's neck and felt the bullet whiz past. She squeezed off a shot, and Billy's hat flew from his head.

She cocked the gun again. "I said drop it!"

Eyes wild, he raised his hands as he looked behind him for his hat. He tossed his pistol away.

Arm extended, she pointed her gun at his chest. "Hit the ground, lawman."

Billy dived facedown onto the forest floor.

Mallory and Holly scrambled to their feet as Kelsey guided her horse closer. In a swift motion, she holstered her gun and pulled her bowie knife, slicing through their ropes. They grabbed their guns and scrambled onto their horses.

Trees rustled, and Clay emerged from the woods. Kelsey's back stiffened. He'd doubled back. She hadn't counted on that.

Kelsey screamed at Mallory and Holly. "Ride!"

In a prearranged plan they'd never thought they'd need, Mallory and Holly took off in separate directions.

Kelsey's horse pawed anxiously at the soft ground; she held the reins taut. Across the road, Clay waited at the tree line. He didn't go for his gun. His gaze burned into her. She glanced toward the forest, where Holly had gone. No sign of her. She threw a glimpse the other way; Mallory had disappeared into the trees. A modicum of relief touched her.

On the ground at her feet, Billy poked his head up and lunged for his gun.

"No!" Clay shouted.

Terror surged through Kelsey. She kicked her horse hard, and it sprang forward. Down the road they raced. Kelsey bent low on the horse's neck. She glanced back.

Clay was right behind her. The mare beneath her was no match for his stallion on this long stretch of open road, and the thick trees made a quick escape into the forest impossible at this speed.

Kelsey kicked the horse again. A meadow opened off the road just up ahead. Her only chance. If she could make it that far, she could lose him in the hollows below.

Thundering hooves sounded behind her as Kelsey eased out on the reins. A few more yards. That was all she needed. She leaned forward, calling encouragement to the mare. From the corner of her eye, she saw Clay pull up on the right. A scream hung in her throat. She couldn't get caught. Not by Clay. He drew nearer. She nudged her horse again.

The tree line broke away, and a wide meadow opened. Kelsey leaned hard to the left and the mare cut sharply, jumping the small embankment. They raced across the field. She glanced back. Clay hadn't anticipated the move. Hope surged through her. She called to the mare again, her eyes trained on the forest and the hollows below, a hundred yards ahead.

Damn that kid. He knew the land too well. Clay pulled hard on the reins, sending his stallion up the embankment and into the meadow. If the boy made it into those woods, he'd never catch him. Clay touched his heels to the stallion's sides, and it lunged forward.

The big stallion stretched out, chewing up clods of earth and grass as it closed in on the mare and the outlaw boy clinging to its back. The woods lay just a hundred feet away. Clay leaned forward, urging the stallion on.

He guided his horse to the left side of the mare, drawing closer, closer, until he pulled alongside. Clay reached for the reins at the mare's mouth. The boy swung his arm and caught Clay across the face in a backhand slap, then cut his horse to the right. It stung just enough to make Clay mad.

He drove his heels into the stallion, and it lurched forward, bringing him alongside the mare in three quick strides. The boy swung at him again. Clay looped his arm around the boy's waist and yanked him off the mare.

Arms and legs flailing, the boy dangled from Clay's arm as he eased back on the reins. He felt tiny, much smaller than Clay had imagined. He tightened his grip, afraid the boy might fall, with all his thrashing around. He struggled harder, kicking and waving his arms wildly.

The horse bounced to a stop and Clay climbed down, hauling the boy with him. He held him securely around his waist, arms and legs dangling.

"Hold still!" Clay commanded.

Teeth sank into Clay's knee.

"Yeow!"

Clay dumped him on the ground and grabbed his knee. The boy scrambled to his feet, but Clay stuck out his leg and tripped him. He landed hard on his belly. Clay grasped the boy's boot and dragged him back, then rolled him over. He'd had his fill of the School-yard Boys long ago. He wasn't going to take any more.

Clay straddled the boy's hips and pinned him to the ground. "Hold still!" he snarled.

Flat on his back, the boy brought both hands up, palms open, and slapped them against Clay's ears.

"Jesus…" He reeled backward and covered his ears with his hands. Loud ringing echoed in his brain. He shook his head and looked down at the floppy hat and bandanna covering the boy. Kid or not, he'd had enough.

Clay grabbed a handful of the boy's baggy coat and drew back his fist.

The boy gasped and threw his hands up for protection. "No, don't. Please..."

Clay froze. Time stopped. The eyes between the hat brim and the bandanna softened.

That voice. The raspy croak that had instructed him to throw down his weapon at the last robbery, and had told him to eat dirt the day he nearly hanged. The voice had also moaned his name in the throes of passion only last night.

His belly tightened into a knot.

Clay yanked off the floppy hat and sent it sailing. A braid of light brown uncoiled. He pulled down the red bandanna. Full, soft lips.

Kelsey.

"Oh, God..." Clay shoved himself off her and stumbled away. His belly churned. Bitterness rose in the back of his throat.

He sank to his knees in the soft grass. God help him. He'd fallen in love with an outlaw.

Slowly, Kelsey got to her feet. Much of the sun had slipped behind the Ozarks, settling a pallor of gray over the meadow. She brushed the dirt from her clothes, watching Clay. He'd been sitting on the ground a few yards away, with his back to her, for a long time now. She couldn't venture a guess at his thoughts.

Finally, he stood and turned on her, shoulders rigid, jaw set, eyes a cold steel gray.

"What the hell were you thinking?" His long legs brought him in front of her in three strides. "How could you do this? How could you put yourself in this kind of danger?"

"I—"

"Billy could have shot you! *I* could have shot you!" Clay dragged his hand across his mouth. He thought he might really vomit now. "Of all the stupid, lame-brained, crazy fool things I ever heard, you have got to be—"

"Shut up! Just shut up!" Anger flamed her cheeks. "You don't know the whole story!"

He flung out his hands. "You robbed the goddamn payroll, Kelsey! Five times! What else do I need to know!"

"You think you can come riding in here with your fancy federal marshal's badge and know what's going on in this town? Well, lawman, you don't know spit! You hear me?"

He gripped his hips with his fists. "You think you've got some reason to justify what you've done?"

"Of course I have!"

Clay bent down until his angry face was even with hers. "Well, I'd sure as hell like to hear it!"

She jerked her thumb toward her chest. "I'm taking back what belongs to me and my family."

"Oh, Jesus…" Clay stalked away, pulled at his neck, paced back and forth, then turned to her again. "You're crazy, lady. Crazy as a mouse in a milk can!"

Kelsey's whole body stiffened. "It's my money!"

"It's Morgan's money! His payroll! That's why it was locked in a strongbox, with men guarding it!"

"It's mine!" Kelsey's hands curled into fists. "Morgan stole it from my father!"

"Of all the—" Breath left Clay in a loud huff. He stepped closer. "What did you say?"

Her chin went up a notch. "It belongs to my family. Morgan stole it."

Clay pulled off his Stetson and plowed his fingers through his hair. Morgan. The man's name popped up with every problem in Eldon.

He let out a heavy breath and settled his hat in place again. He walked over to Kelsey. The pants, coat and bandanna swallowed her, made her look tiny and vulnerable, despite the determined jut of her jaw. The knot in his gut softened, and he wanted to take her in his arms.

Clay stopped himself. No. He wouldn't do it. He was a federal marshal, and she was an outlaw, caught redhanded at attempted robbery. Once before, he'd let down his guard, gone with his instincts, and his sister had died because of it. Never again. He'd sworn it that day, and it never applied more than at this moment. Kelsey Rodgers was a criminal. Nothing else.

Clay pulled his hat low on his forehead. "If you have a statement to make concerning your attempted robbery, I'll listen to it."

An aura of aloofness settled over Clay, but Kelsey ignored it. She'd held the truth inside for too long. And Clay, of all people, should hear it.

She stepped back, needing some distance from his cold gray eyes. "My father started out in the fur trade years ago, and did quite well for himself. He met Jack Morgan and took a liking to him—for reasons I'll never understand—and they became partners. Their businesses flourished. Everything they touched made money. Then, a few years back, Morgan began branching out on his own. One venture after another failed, costing him a great deal of money. My papa, you see, was the brains in their partnership. Morgan couldn't stand admitting Papa knew more than he, couldn't bear losing the money. So, about a year ago, he lured Papa into a business deal he knew would fail.''

"A year ago? Wasn't that about the time your mama died, and your pa—''

"Yes, Papa's mind was failing considerably by then. And Morgan knew it. Papa mortgaged all his property—all the businesses, our home —to Morgan. He knew it was only a matter of time before Papa couldn't keep up the payments, or died, and it would all belong to him. He desperately needed Papa's money to shore up his own cash reserves.''

"How did you find out about all this?''

"Seth figured it out." The memory made her proud.

Clay nodded. "That was Morgan's motive for conspiring with Nate Duncan to send Seth to prison.''

"Exactly.''

"Why didn't you go to the law and put a stop to Morgan legally?''

Kelsey uttered a bitter laugh. "Such as who? The sheriff? Judge Kingsley? With Seth out of the way and Papa's health failing, there was no one to stand in Jack Morgan's way. Or so he thought.''

"Then you started robbing his payroll.''

"I was taking back my papa's money." Kelsey's spine stiffened. "I needed cash to make the mortgage payments and keep my family together.''

"Did you intend to keep committing robbery forever?''

"No. Just until Seth got out of prison, or the mortgages were paid off, whichever came first.''

Clay pulled at his neck and turned away. "That's a harebrained scheme if I ever heard one.''

Kelsey grabbed his arm and pulled him around to

face her. "Well, what else was I supposed to do? Seth was gone. Papa, too, for all intents and purposes. I couldn't go to the law. I had no way of earning that kind of money, no other family to turn to. Should I have just stood by and let Morgan take the house away from us? Have the church send Toby to live with some family in the next county? Lose the hotel?" Her gaze searched his. "Well? What else could I have done?"

He wanted to hold her. He wanted to sweep her into his arms and make everything all right. The desire to shield her and protect her nearly overwhelmed him.

Clay stepped back and hardened his heart. "You committed robbery. Nothing justifies that."

He'd never looked so cold before, but then, she didn't expect any sympathy from him. She'd known when she first hatched the plan to reclaim her family's money that one day this might happen. The possibility of prison had always hovered in the back of her thoughts.

The hardness in his heart melted with each second that passed, despite Clay's determination to hold on to it. She was no criminal, no Scully Dade. She hadn't hurt anyone. Hell, she hadn't even fired a shot until today. And how could he argue with her reasoning? Jack Morgan was a bastard. He deserved losing his payroll.

Clay stared at her, his mind and heart tugging against each other. He couldn't bear the thought of taking her to jail. He wanted to let her go.

Clay pulled at his neck. He'd make her swear, swear on Toby's life, that she'd stop the robberies. Make her promise never to do such a thing again.

Yes, he could make her swear. But could he make her stop?

He'd seen the determination on her face, the edge in her voice when she spoke of keeping her family together. Nothing—absolutely nothing—was more important to Kelsey than her family. The fact that she'd hatched this plan and carried it out proved where her loyalties lay. And her financial troubles weren't over. Even if he got her to promise to stop, what guarantee did he have that she'd keep her word?

What would happen then? She might get shot next time. And if not Kelsey, who? Some lawman? Some innocent bystander?

Somebody's sister?

Clay's gut churned feverishly. No, he couldn't let her go. He couldn't take the chance.

"Who are the others in the gang with you?"

For a second, she'd seen a flicker of lenience in his eye. Now it was gone. He was all business again. Kelsey shook her head. "I'll never tell you who they are."

"It will go better with the judge. He'll lighten your sentence." The words caused his belly to knot again.

She shrugged. "Maybe. If it comes to that."

His brows went up. "You don't think Judge Winthrope will hesitate to throw your sweet little fanny behind bars?"

"I'm a woman, for one thing. Judges don't like sending women to prison. Plus, I'm the daughter of one of the supposedly wealthiest, most respected businessmen in the state. I'll take my chances with the judge."

Clay shook his head. "That might have worked with Kingsley, but not Winthrope. He believes in justice. Tell me the names of the other gang members, Kelsey. Make it easy on yourself."

Determination hardened her face. "I'll take it to my grave, lawman."

"It may come to that." Clay's features hardened to match hers. "Harlan Winthrope is the only judge ever to send a woman to the gallows in this state."

Kelsey's courage faltered. She swallowed hard. "If we made a deal, could you guarantee—"

"I don't bargain with outlaws." He gave her a cold, hard look, and turned away.

Kelsey watched his big, broad shoulders as he headed toward his horse, grazing in the meadow, and for a fleeting second she wanted to run after him and beg for his help. She hadn't wanted that from any man in so long. And if anyone could come to her rescue, Clay Chandler was the man, and not because of the badge on his chest.

She sucked in a deep breath and pushed her braid back off her shoulder. So, the marshal wouldn't bargain with an outlaw? He hadn't heard her offer yet.

"Hey, lawman!" He turned and gave her a cold glare. "You want information?"

He hesitated a moment, then walked over. Clay braced his legs wide apart and stared down at her. "I'm listening."

Kelsey tucked a stray wisp of hair behind her ear. "I've got something you want."

"Yeah. The names of your accomplices."

She put her hand on her hip. "No. Something else."

His gaze raked her up and down. "I've already had that."

Her cheeks flamed.

With a final scathing look, he pivoted and walked away again.

"I'm talking about Scully Dade."

Clay turned back. "What?"

Kelsey took a step forward. "I'll give you Scully Dade. I know where his new hideout is."

He advanced on her and grabbed her upper arms. The horror of losing her consumed him. "What are you doing mixed up with the likes of Scully Dade, Kelsey? They're cold-blooded killers. They—"

He stopped himself and stepped away. Memories of Rebecca, and his monumentally poor judgment, flashed in his mind. He had to keep his distance. "All right, let me get this straight. You take me to Scully Dade and I let you go free. Is that your offer?"

"No. I'll take you to Scully Dade and you let my brother out of prison."

"Well, at least the payroll got through." Roy Bottom plopped down in the chair behind his desk and turned up the lantern flame against the closing darkness. "Both them boys got away from you, huh, Billy? Couldn't you get a good look at either of them?"

"I dang near got my head blowed off. See?" Billy yanked off his hat and pushed his finger through the gaping hole in the brim. "Yeah, them two got away, all right, 'cause I stayed with the payroll. I figured Morgan would rather have the money than their two scrawny hides."

"You did right, Billy." Sheriff Bottom reared back in his chair. "What about the one you chased, Chandler?"

In the shadows across the room, Clay leaned against the wall, arms folded over his chest. "He got away."

Sheriff Bottom sucked his gums. "Looks like this plan of yours didn't come to much."

"The payroll got through, didn't it?" Clay clamped his mouth shut. Damn fool sheriff thought those

Schoolyard Boys and Morgan's piddly-ass payroll caused the sun to rise and set. The Dade gang was in his grasp now, and telling the sheriff about Kelsey's involvement would only jeopardize the deal he'd made with her. He wasn't going to lose Scully Dade, not when he was this close.

Clay pushed away from the wall and walked to the door. "We've seen the last of those boys, anyway."

Across the street at the Watering Hole Saloon, music and laughter wafted from the open windows. He could sure as hell use a drink, but he walked the other way instead. Each step jarred his aching knee and reminded him of the slight ringing in his ears. Minor problems, considering what kind of a day he'd had. He was hungry, but his belly hurt too much for him to eat. Fatigue sapped his strength, and his will. Clay stepped up onto the boardwalk in front of the courthouse and forced himself inside the building.

Lanterns burned low in the deserted courtroom. Kelsey flashed in his mind. She'd be here in this room one day. Clay steeled his runaway emotions and crossed the room. He knocked on the closed door in the back. A muffled voiced summoned him, and he went inside.

Judge Harlan Winthrope looked up from behind the cherry desk and squinted at him in the dim light of the lanterns. He looked respectable and dignified in his black suit and cravat. Gray feathered the dark hair at his temples.

"I wondered if you'd be too stubborn to show your face in my chambers." Judge Winthrope reared back in his chair and crossed his arms over his barrel chest. "Or too scared."

Chapter Fourteen

Clay stiffened and glared at Judge Winthrope, then tossed his hat aside and sank into the leather chair across the desk from him. "Hell, I don't know, Uncle Harlan. Maybe a little of both."

Harlan chuckled. "I never thought I'd hear you admit to either. But it's been a long time since I saw you last."

Clay rubbed his forehead. "Yeah, yeah, I know."

"Your mother misses you."

He shifted uncomfortably.

"You broke her heart, Clay."

He shoved out of the chair. "I didn't come over here for a lecture."

Harlan's expression hardened, but he spoke in a slow, even voice. "If you thought you could face me after all this time and not discuss what you did to my sister, you're wrong."

They glared at each other for a long moment.

Clay drummed his fingers against his gun holster, then sat down again. "How's Pa?"

"Miserable." Harlan leaned forward on the desk.

"They're both miserable. They miss you...and Rebecca."

Clay winced.

"No one blames you for what happened to Rebecca. No one but yourself." Harlan softened his voice. "You shouldn't have run off, Clay."

"I'm going to get that bastard who killed her."

"Your folks needed you. They still need you. They weren't finished being parents. They have more love to give. Your father's got no one to argue points of law with. Your mother's got no one to drill on etiquette. They sit by themselves in the big, empty house and—"

Clay whipped out his pistol and slammed it down on the desk. "Just shoot me, will you? Right through the heart. It couldn't hurt any more than listening to you. But I'm not going back until I bring in Rebecca's murderer. I'm not."

Harlan pushed the gun at him and sat back in the chair. "What are you here for? That Tucker boy?"

Clay relaxed against the chair. "I don't want him going to prison, Uncle Harlan."

He chuckled deep in his chest. "I figured that would get you over here to see me. But I haven't decided yet. Attempted murder of a federal marshal is a serious offense."

"He's just a boy. He got caught up in a bad bunch. Besides, I've got something in mind for him." Clay looked across the desk. "I need your help on something else. I want a man let out of prison. His name's Seth Rodgers."

Harlan shrugged. "Never heard of him."

"Local trouble. He got sent up for attempted robbery

of the hardware store. Personally, I don't think he did it."

"Prison is full of innocent men."

"Kingsley gave him five years."

"Kingsley, huh..." Harlan rubbed his chin. "What's so special about this Rodgers fellow?"

"I have an informant willing to take me to the Dade gang in exchange for Rodgers's release."

Harlan folded his arms across his chest. "I'm not letting a convicted criminal go free without good cause. Who is this informant?"

He'd rather keep Kelsey out of it, but he couldn't expect Harlan's cooperation without all the facts. "A member of the Schoolyard Boys."

"An outlaw, huh? What's his connection to Rodgers?"

Clay cleared his throat. "He's her brother."

His brows rose. "*Her?* Your informant is a woman? A woman member of an outlaw gang?"

"Yes, sir." Clay watched as Harlan lapsed into thought, knowing that the whole story sounded crazy. Finally, Clay leaned forward on the desk. "I want Scully Dade, Uncle Harlan."

He sighed. "I'll see what I can do. But first, I want something from you."

"Morning, Marshal. Where have you been? I haven't seen you in a while." Deuce pushed open the door and stepped back.

Clay pulled off his Stetson and stepped inside Miss Wilder's house, unsure of how to describe the time that had passed since he'd last seen Deuce. "Business, that's all."

"Are you all right? You don't look so good."

He didn't feel so good, either. Kelsey had given her word that she'd stay at the hotel while he made the arrangements to hold up his end of their bargain, and he knew she wouldn't leave until Seth was safely released from prison. But he couldn't get her out of his mind, couldn't take his eyes off her. And he couldn't bring himself to talk to her, either, though he really wasn't sure why.

Clay shrugged. "How's things going here?"

"I started cataloging books, but haven't got much done. Miss Wilder likes me to read to her. Her eyes got old."

Clay glanced around the silent house. "Where is she?"

"In town, shopping." Deuce led the way into the parlor. "I try to clean up a little when she's not looking. My mama would have a conniption fit if she saw what this place looks like. Problem is, there's so much stuff, I can't find a place to put it all."

Miss Wilder exhibited all the signs of being a lifelong pack rat. Clay gazed around the room and nodded his understanding. "Do you like working here?"

"Sure. Miss Wilder is a real nice lady."

The job seemed to agree with him. He wore another new shirt, his hair was combed neatly in place, and his face and hands were scrubbed clean. "Good, because I've got another job for you. Judge Winthrope is in town. He needs somebody to clerk for him."

Deuce's eyes rounded. "A judge? You want me to work for a judge?"

"You'll do fine." Clay patted his shoulder. "But this is important, Deuce. You be over there first thing in the morning. Listen close and pay attention. I want

Judge Winthrope to know what kind of young man you are.''

''What am I supposed to do?'' Panic tinged his voice.

''The judge will explain it to you.''

He spread out his arms. ''But what about Miss Wilder?''

''You can still work for her in the afternoons.''

Deuce shifted uncomfortably. ''Okay, if you say so.''

''I'll be back to check on you in a few days. If you need anything, you let me know.''

Deuce followed Clay to the door, then wandered back into the parlor. He'd been with Miss Wilder nearly two weeks, and he'd just settled in. Now he was supposed to work for the judge? The judge—of all people?

Deuce shook his head. If the marshal thought he could do it, he'd try his best. Something about the marshal always made him do that.

''Yoo-hoo!''

Miss Wilder sang her greeting as she came through the front door and shuffled into the kitchen. In the parlor across the hall, Deuce watched as she lifted her big straw satchel onto the table and took off her shawl.

''What a morning, my goodness!'' She heaved a heavy sigh.

''Did you find what you were shopping for?'' Deuce asked.

''Not a thing,'' she called. ''Go on back into the library and I'll fix us some tea, dear. I'll be there in a minute.''

''Yes, ma'am.'' Deuce turned to leave, but stopped when Miss Wilder pulled her flowered handkerchief from her satchel and unwrapped a pepper shaker from it. The black spice sifted onto the table. Next she pulled out a thimble, and set them both amid the clutter atop the pie safe.

Suspicion rose like a lump in his throat. Deuce turned slowly and took in the parlor. Odds and ends, knicknacks, an assortment of objects, covered every surface of every piece of furniture in the room. Had it all come from Miss Wilder's daily shopping trips in town?

He walked to the mantel and gently fingered the worn measuring tape and half-filled saltshaker laying there. Strange items to purchase. As was the small satin bag propped up beside them. He lifted it from the other items and pulled open the draw strings. A tangle of rubies, pearls, diamonds and sapphires tumbled into his palm.

Deuce gulped hard and glanced back over his shoulder. Miss Wilder still puttered in the kitchen. He shoved the jewelry into the bag and tossed it back where he'd found it.

Clay Chandler undoubtedly was the most annoying man ever put on this earth. Kelsey grabbed the broom from the pantry and stalked across the kitchen, throwing a scathing look at him, seated at the table. He'd hovered around her for days now, giving her only brief respites when he ventured out for short periods. And he'd hardly spoken to her at all.

But he'd watched her. His gray eyes had followed every movement she made as she went about her work at the hotel. Kelsey swept the broom across the floor in front of the stove. She felt as if she were already in prison.

Harder and faster she swept, her annoyance with Clay growing as she cleaned her way to the table. She yanked out the chair beside him. "Move."

He leaned his head back and gave her an insolent glare. He didn't budge.

Kelsey jabbed the broom straws into his legs. "Move!"

He surged to his feet, towering over her. "Sorry, I don't hear like I used to. I've had this ringing in my ears lately."

From where she'd slapped him. Her palm itched to do the same again. "They why don't you go to the doctor—and leave me alone?"

She was wound tight enough to explode, and he wasn't far behind. Clay glared down at her. "I told you I'm keeping my eye on you until your brother gets here. Get used to it."

"Ahhh!" Kelsey whipped around, clenched the broom in her fist and flung it back into the pantry. He was doing this just to annoy her. She was certain of it.

Fired up and ready to blow, and all Clay could think of was claiming that emotion for himself. Desire surged though him, hot and unchecked, as he watched her stalk through the kitchen, slamming cabinet doors, tossing pots and pans. He wanted to hold her and kiss her and take her upstairs. He wanted to show her how much he loved her. Kelsey bent over and flung a skillet into the cabinet. His insides flamed. Harlan Winthrope better get Seth here soon. He didn't know how much longer he could hold out.

Kelsey stepped out the back door and lifted a tray of potatoes from the supply of vegetables that had been delivered earlier this morning. Clay crossed the room and reached for it. "I'll take this. It's too heavy for you."

She swung it away from him. Yes, it was heavy, but at the moment, the anger boiling inside her gave her twice her usual strength. "I've got it."

He grabbed the other end of the crate. "I'll take it."

She pulled it her way. "I can handle it."

He yanked it back. "Give it to me!"

"No!"

He leaned down until his nose was even with hers. "Would it kill you, Kelsey, to accept help from somebody? Would it?"

She glared at him, her fingers locked on the crate.

He softened his voice. "You don't have to do everything alone. Ease up on yourself. Let me help."

At that instant, she wanted nothing more than to throw up her hands and let him do everything. Let him worry about her brother, Holly, Holly's baby, Toby, her father, the bills, the mortgages, the hotel, Jack Morgan—all the things she'd carried alone for so long. She gazed into his eyes of warm blue and wanted to lose herself in them, in his arms, in him.

But where would Clay Chandler and all his good intentions be when they carted her off to prison? She'd be on her own then, as she had been for so long. And to change now would only do her more harm in the long run.

She tightened her hold on the crate. "I don't need you."

Clay released the crate and watched as she dumped the potatoes into the bin inside the pantry. He blocked most of the doorway to the alley and refused to move, forcing her to squeeze by him as she set the crate outside the back door again. A breeze carried her fragrance over him, soft, delicate, inviting. His insides churned fitfully. He wanted her so badly. And she stood only a few inches away. Clay steeled his feelings, coiling his hand into a fist, fighting for strength to hold himself in check. Then he kissed her.

He took her in his arms and locked her tight against his chest, covering her lips with a deep, demanding kiss. He expected vehement resistance—a slap, a bite, a kick in the shins. Instead, she moaned softly and leaned her head back, eagerly allowing his mouth to consume hers.

The fire smoldering low in his belly these past days ignited. He slid one hand down her spine and pressed her to him. She came willingly, curving her body to fit against him. Passion flamed as she slid her leg upward along his.

Kelsey coiled her arms around his neck, helpless in his embrace. His mouth on hers, his chest on hers, his obvious desire for her pressed intimately against her desire for him. With sweet abandon, she surrendered to him.

Heated passion grew to urgent demand. Clay pulled his lips from hers and rained hot kisses down her cheek and neck. She arched backward, urging him on. Memories of their past intimacy washed over her, robbing her of conscious thought. She wanted him. She wanted him to have her.

"Excuse me. I'll just be a minute."

Clay pulled his mouth from the fabric of her blouse and gazed at Harlan Winthrope, who was crossing from the service stairway to the stove. Logical thought escaped Clay. He froze, with Kelsey arched backward in his arms, his leg eased between the fabric of her skirt, his breathing quick and labored.

Harlan smiled, as though nothing were out of the ordinary. "I just wanted a cup of coffee."

"Help yourself..." Kelsey called lamely. She gestured at the pot with one hand, the other clamped in Clay's thick hair; her leg was wound around his.

Harlan poured, then saluted them with his steaming cup. "Well, good day." He disappeared up the stairs.

Kelsey looked up at Clay. Naked, hungry desire was etched in every curve, every line, of his face. She gasped. Was that how she looked, too?

"Let go of me." Mortified, she pushed him away. She'd behaved like a strumpet. And in front of Judge Winthrope, too. What must he think of her?

His body ached with need when she pulled away, and his heart swelled nearly to a stop at the embarrassed look on her face. "Kelsey—"

She ducked under his arm and grabbed her shawl from the peg beside the door. "I have errands."

Damn it, where was his brain? He shouldn't have put her in a compromising position in the middle of the kitchen, where anybody could walk in. Clay plowed his hand through his hair. "Wait, Kelsey—"

She darted out the door.

"Don't run. Damn it..." He was in no condition to run, but he pulled on his Stetson and hurried after her.

He caught her at the corner and took her elbow. She swung around to face him, her cheeks pink, her lips wet and swollen. God help him, he wanted to kiss her again.

Kelsey pulled her arm away. "What do you want?"

He couldn't tell her that. She'd slap him for sure— and he'd deserve it. "Where are you going?"

"I told you, I have an errand to run. And it's not someplace you would like to go."

"I'll decide that."

"Fine." Kelsey set a brisk pace down the boardwalk and arrived at Patterson's Dress Shop slightly winded, Clay at her heels.

His mouth curled down when he glanced through the glass window. "What are you going in here for?"

She saved the I-told-you-so that begged to be flaunted. "I promised Edwina a new dress."

"Oh, yeah, for the birthday party," he muttered.

"You could go someplace else."

And maybe he should. This store reminded him of Kelsey's bosoms spilling out of her bodice, and he didn't need any more distracting thoughts.

"Marshal Chandler!"

Deuce ran toward them. Thank God. Clay opened the door. "I'll be in after a while."

Kelsey stepped inside and closed the door behind her.

Breathing hard, Deuce stopped in front of Clay. "Marshal, I've got to talk to you. That lady's jewelry that got stolen from Mr. Morgan's party. Do you know who did it?"

"No, not yet." He frowned. "Why are you asking?"

Deuce drew in a deep breath. "Because, ah, because my mama talked about it last night, and I promised her I'd ask you. I guess that lady would be pretty happy to have her stuff back."

"No happier than Morgan. He got those men out here hoping to do some heavy investing. It looks pretty bad, having that jewelry stolen right out from under his nose."

"You think Mr. Morgan might give a reward?"

"I doubt it."

He nodded. "My mama says Mr. Morgan is as tight as bark on a beech tree."

"If he had it to spend, he might do it."

"Mr. Morgan is hard up for money?"

After what Kelsey had told him, Clay had no doubts. "He's feeling a pinch, I understand. But if these investors come through, that will take care of it."

"Well, let's say you found out who stole those jewels. What would happen to them?"

"Deuce, do you know something about those jewels?"

"No, sir."

He studied him for a moment, and Deuce squirmed a little. "I'd say whoever stole those jewels ought to come forward and turn them in."

"Will they have to go to jail?"

"Probably. And so will anybody else who had knowledge of the crime and didn't report it."

Deuce shifted uncomfortably. "Jail, huh?"

"Justice has to be served. That's what the law is all about." Clay leaned closer. "Is there something you want to tell me, son?"

"Well—" He chewed his bottom lip. "No, sir. I was just asking—for my ma. I got to go."

Clay watched him disappear down the boardwalk. For days now, he'd mulled over what ought to be done with Deuce. Now he knew for sure. As long as Harlan Winthrope didn't stand in the way.

Laughter brought Clay's attention back to the dress shop as Kelsey stepped outside along with Mallory Morgan. Mallory spotted him, giggled and flicked open her fan. "Why, Marshal Chandler, what a surprise to find you here." She tossed her head and batted her lashes. "Did you come all the way over here just to tell me goodbye?"

Clay tipped his hat cordially. "I wasn't aware you were going anywhere, Miss Morgan."

"I've been invited by Mr. and Mrs. Wilford Henry to accompany them back east for a visit." She tapped his chest with her fan. "I was just inside spending every cent of my papa's money I could before I leave town."

Clay grinned. "Do you intend to leave your father penniless?"

A slow, easy smile parted her lips. "Not to worry, Marshal. I have my own...nest egg."

Kelsey nearly groaned aloud. She'd tried to get Mallory to stay inside the dress shop, but, reckless as she was, nothing would suit her until she confronted Clay. Kelsey had deliberately stayed away from both Mallory and Holly since the failed robbery attempt, not wanting to give him any inclination that they were the other two Schoolyard Boys.

Mallory suddenly turned to Kelsey. "Say, have you seen Holly Duncan lately?"

"No, I haven't," she said evenly.

"She must be holed up inside her folks' store, because I haven't seen her in days." She touched her fan to her cheek. "I wonder why she won't come out?"

"Holly and I don't speak. Remember?"

"Well, whatever..." She rapped Clay's arm with her fan. "I'm leaving town in a few days. You be sure to come by the house."

"I have to get back to the hotel." Kelsey hurried away, not chancing a look at Clay.

Deuce hesitated a moment, then banged the brass knocker against the door. If Jack Morgan was really bordering on financial ruin, as the marshal had claimed, then he had to see the man at once.

A butler eyed him up and down when he opened the door. "Deliveries at the kitchen."

Deuce's courage faltered. "I'm here to see Mr. Morgan. It's a business matter. My name is Dennis—Dennis Tucker."

The butler brushed his hands together distastefully. "Wait here."

The door closed in his face, and fifteen minutes crawled by before the butler allowed him into the house. Deuce followed him through the marble foyer and down the hallway, and left him outside the study. Morgan sat bent over his cluttered desk, working feverishly.

He glanced up. "Yeah, what do you want?"

Deuce stopped in front of the desk and drew in a deep breath. "I came, Mr. Morgan, to bring to your attention that you overcharged my pa on his feed bills."

"Is that so?" Morgan tossed down his pencil.

"Yes, sir. I've got the bills right here. See?" Deuce's heart pounded as he fished the papers from his trouser pocket and handed them to Mr. Morgan.

"Well, let's have a look." Morgan sat back in his chair and studied each receipt. "I'd say you're exactly right."

Deuce relaxed. "The total is thirty-two dollars. I'd like it back, sir."

"Oh, you would, huh?" Morgan rose. "There's a hell of a lot of things I'd like in this world, too, boy, but I don't get them. Now get out of my house before I have you thrown out."

"But—you owe my pa."

"Your pa is nothing but a stupid, manure-shoveling fool. I don't owe him anything."

Panic clawed his belly. "I have those receipts."

"You mean these?" Morgan ripped them in half.

"Wait! You can't—"

He shredded them and tossed them in the waste can beside his desk. "Look, boy, you're no better than that idiot pa of yours. Worse, actually. You're already in trouble with the law. You're never going to amount to anything. Now get the hell out of here, before I see to it you spend the rest of your life in prison."

Stunned, Deuce stood there, mouth open.

"Get out, you idiot!"

He ran out of the house and halfway to Miss Wilder's place before he stopped in the middle of the street and turned back toward Morgan's home. Anger, hurt and humiliation boiled inside him.

"Bastard," he whispered.

Deuce trudged on to Miss Wilder's home and found her in the kitchen, fixing tea.

"There you are, dear. I woke from my nap and you were gone. Is everything all right?"

He paced the parlor, hands shoved deep in his trousers. "Yes, ma'am."

"You know, I was thinking," she called from the kitchen. "Maybe I should donate some of my books to the school."

"Yes, ma'am." He hardly heard her, with Jack Morgan's words echoing in his head.

"And maybe give a few to other people in Eldon. Miss Chalmers might enjoy several of my volumes, and Mr. Rodgers, as well. I think he has lots of time on his hands these days. That nice Mr. Bean over at the ex-

press office might like one, also. Can you think of anyone else you'd like to give something special to?''

Deuce raked both hands through his hair. ''No, Miss
Wilder, I—''

He froze. An idea blossomed in his mind.

Miss Wilder appeared in the doorway, holding a
sugar bowl. ''What did you say, dear?''

He nodded slowly. ''I said that Mr. Morgan would
like some of your books.''

''Oh, an excellent idea. Let's get them crated up
right away.'' She smiled proudly and disappeared into
the kitchen.

Deuce walked to the mantel and fingered the satin
bag nearly hidden among the clutter. Marshal Chandler
said decisions in life got harder, but this one was the
easiest he'd ever made.

''I'll deliver them personally, Miss Wilder. Don't
you worry. Just leave everything to me.''

''Come on.''

Kelsey tried to pull her arm away, but Clay held
tight. She waved a fistful of green beans under his nose.
''I'm fixing supper.''

''Kelsey will be back in a while,'' Clay called to
Etta Mae, at the cookstove.

''I don't know who you think you are, Clay Chandler, but I've had just about enough of your—''

He gave her a stern look that brooked no argument.

''Fine.'' Kelsey tossed the beans into the bowl,
yanked off her apron and stomped out the door ahead
of him.

''Where are we going?'' she demanded as they
walked through town. He didn't reply. That annoyed

her further. Kelsey clamped her mouth shut and walked alongside him without saying another word.

"Four minutes!" Otis Bean paced the boardwalk in front of the express office, clutching his pocket watch, as they approached. "Stage arrives in four minutes!"

Kelsey looked up at Clay, startled. "We're not going somewhere, are we? I can't leave town just like that."

He stopped at the door of the express office and braced his arm against the casing. "We're waiting for the stage."

What was this man thinking now? "Waiting for the stage? Why on earth would we be—"

Her heart tumbled. She grabbed Clay's arm. "Seth..." Tears pooled in her eyes. "It's Seth, isn't it."

He straightened and gazed down at her, seeing the elation in her expression. "Yes."

She threw her arms around him and buried her face against his shirt. Clay's knees went weak. He wrapped her in his arms and held her tight, tighter than he should have. She felt good against him, the joy in her heart touching his.

"Two minutes!" Otis looked at his schedule and consulted his pocket watch again. "Two minutes."

The big Concord coach swung into view in a cloud of dust. Up top, the driver hauled back on the reins and brought the coach to a stop in front of the express office.

Kelsey wiped away her tears as Otis opened the stagecoach door. She slid her hand into Clay's and squeezed. Another tear trickled down her cheek as she gazed up at him.

He put his arm around her shoulder and nodded toward the coach. "I believe that's your brother."

Threadbare clothes hung from his tall, thin frame as he stepped onto the boardwalk, and his green eyes were sunk deep in his chalky, gaunt face.

"Seth!"

Kelsey threw her arms around his waist and hugged him hard as tears flowed down her cheeks again. After a moment, he responded, in slow, measured movements, resting his hands on her shoulders.

She sniffed and wiped her eyes with her hands. "Oh, Seth, I'm so glad you're here."

He stared blankly at her, as if afraid to believe she was real. "Where's Holly?"

"At the store. I didn't tell her, Seth. I didn't want to get her hopes up, just in case."

"Where's the baby?"

"She's in Flint Valley. Holly saw her a few days ago, Seth. She's fine, except—" tears pooled in her eyes again "—except she needs her mama and papa."

Seth turned and saw Clay waiting at the entrance of the express office. He gazed at his badge and stopped dead in his tracks. Pain and hopelessness showed in his face.

"It's all right, Seth." Kelsey grasped his arm. "This is Clay Chandler. He's a friend of mine."

"Glad to know you." Clay offered his hand.

He eyed his badge.

"Clay helped arrange your release, Seth."

Finally, Seth grasped his outstretched hand and shook it slowly. "Thank you." His voice was a raspy whisper.

Seth turned and headed down the boardwalk, eyes forward.

Kelsey grasped Clay's arm. "What's wrong with

him? He's so different, as if he has no feelings in him anymore."

"Prison. It sucks the life out of a man." Clay patted her hand. "Give him some time. He'll come around."

"I hope you're right."

Clay caught her chin and tilted her face up. "This means you and Holly will have to stop your fighting. It won't do Seth any good seeing you two going at each other. Besides, you're family now."

For so long she'd thought nothing of lying to Clay about her true feelings for Holly. Now, though her conscience bore heavily on her, she had to continue the charade.

"You're right." She dipped her gaze contritely. "We won't fight anymore. I promise."

"Good." Clay shook his head. "I swear I know Holly from somewhere."

Kelsey steeled her feelings. "People always say that about Holly. I guess she just has one of those faces."

"Maybe...."

They followed Seth to Duncan's General Store. Kelsey tried to go in with him, but Clay held her back.

Behind the counter, Estelle gasped and clutched her throat. A bottle slipped from Nate's hand and crashed onto the floor. Seth riveted them both with a cold stare.

"Mama, I—" Holly walked in from the storage room and saw Seth. She threw out her arms. "Seth—"

He held up his hand. "Go pack your things."

She flew from the room, her footsteps echoing on the staircase. Seth glared at Nate and Estelle, but neither of them tried to stop her. Holly returned a moment later, her belongings stuffed into a carpetbag. Seth took her hand and led her out of the store. Neither looked back.

On the boardwalk, Seth turned to Holly. "We're getting married. Now. Tomorrow, we're getting the baby."

Holly began to cry, and that caused Kelsey to tear up again. "We'll all go," Kelsey said. "I'm dying to see my very first niece."

Holly clutched Seth's arm and they walked away. Clay dropped his hand on Kelsey's shoulder, halting her.

"You won't be going to Flint Valley tomorrow."

"But…" She glanced at Holly and Seth, then back at Clay. "Holly will need help with the baby. I want to be there when Seth sees her for the first time."

A coldness settled over him. "You'll be at Scully Dade's hideout tomorrow."

"You thought I would actually take you there myself?" Kelsey's eyes widened. "I'll make you a map. You can find it easily."

"Oh, no." He shook his head. "I'm not riding off on some wild-goose chase. You're taking me."

"And be alone with you out on the trail?"

"What do you think is going to happen—" his eyes raked her "—that hasn't already happened."

Her cheeks reddened. She drew herself up straighter. "All right. I'll take you."

"Good. I'll tell the sheriff this afternoon and have him round up a posse. We'll head out—"

"I'm not riding the trail with a bunch of strange men." She rolled her eyes, as if he were the biggest idiot she'd ever met. "I'll take you, nobody else."

He pulled his hat down to his brows. "And how am I supposed to arrest Dade's whole gang, alone, with you underfoot?"

She tossed her head. "I agreed to show you his hideout. Arresting him is your problem."

He grumbled under his breath. "All right. You show me the hideout and I'll ride back with a posse."

Kelsey jerked her chin. "Fine."

Clay stared hard at her. "Be ready. We ride at first light."

Chapter Fifteen

The closed bedroom door and what lay beyond taunted Clay as he poured himself another cup of coffee. He reminded himself—again—of the vow he'd made during last night's many sleepless hours. Kelsey was an outlaw. Her only purpose was to lead him to the Dade Gang. After that, he was duty-bound to arrest her and let justice take its course.

Clay glanced at the morning darkness through the kitchen window as her door opened. Kelsey came out wearing scuffed boots, a faded blue shirt, a red bandanna around her neck and baggy brown trousers held up by suspenders. Her outlaw clothes. Clay's belly tightened, though it would have been impossible from the fit to guess a woman inhabited those clothes. But he knew she was a woman, all woman, and seeing her without her petticoats, bustles and corsets was almost too much to bear.

Clay slammed his coffee cup down on the table. Damn, he was off to a good start.

"Shh! Do you want to wake the whole hotel?" Kelsey gave him a disapproving look and dropped her gear on the table.

"Aren't you ready yet?" he grumbled.

"Are you always this pleasant in the morning?"

She tossed her single braid over her shoulder and moved silently around the kitchen, gathering food in a sack, nibbling on last night's bread.

"I got you a horse from the livery. The ones in your stable belong to the hotel guests, don't they?"

She licked her fingers. "I usually take one of them."

His mouth sagged open. "You steal your guests' horses for your robberies?"

"I bring them back when I'm finished."

"Jesus..." Clay stalked out the back door.

Crisp, cool air greeted Kelsey as she stepped outside with her gear. The faintest light of dawn stretched up from the horizon.

"How far is it?" Clay threw her saddlebag over the back of the mare.

"A day's ride. We can get there and back, and you can take the posse tomorrow." Kelsey patted the sorrel mare Clay had gotten for her while Clay double-checked the cinch and bedroll, and tied her canteen and the food sack to her saddle. She eased up beside him and pulled her gun belt from the saddlebag.

"What the hell do you think you're doing?" He pulled it from her hands.

Stunned, she looked up at him in the dim morning light. "Give me my gun."

He laughed bitterly. "I saw the hole in Billy's hat."

She planted her hands on her hips. "I could have killed him if I'd wanted to. You know that."

"My point exactly. That's why I'm keeping the gun."

Kelsey fumed silently as she pulled on her oversize

coat, coiled her braid around her head and yanked on her hat.

"You ride beside me. I want to keep my eye on you," Clay told her as he climbed onto his stallion.

Kelsey pulled herself into the saddle and headed off down the alley.

They rode west out of town and followed the road through the hills. Sun rays warmed them, and Kelsey shrugged out of her coat. Clay stole a glance at her and instantly regretted his decision to have her ride beside him. The suspenders pulled her shirt taut, and he could see the outline of her breasts. Her bottom swayed and bounced in rhythm with the horse as her legs accommodated its girth. Until this moment, Clay had never felt envy for a saddle.

At midday, Kelsey shielded her eyes from the sun and looked skyward, judging the time. "I know a place to stop. Are you hungry?"

"My mouth's been watering all morning."

She led the way off the road a few hundred yards and slid off the mare in a clearing beside a small stream. She stretched and rubbed her back as the horse drank. Clay climbed down and dropped the reins as his stallion edged alongside the mare. He reached for his canteen and caught sight of Kelsey walking into the woods. He almost called to her, then remembered himself and walked the opposite way.

They met at the horses a few minutes later. Kelsey took the sack of food and settled onto a fallen log. Clay brought their canteens and sat down beside her.

"What have you got in there?" He peered over her shoulder.

She pulled a linen towel from the sack and spread it on the ground. "It's the best I could do on short notice.

I couldn't exactly ask Etta Mae to prepare a meal for two without explaining why."

Clay helped himself to a chicken leg. "Won't she wonder where you are?"

Kelsey pulled off her hat and shook out her braid. "She thinks I'm at home."

"Let me guess. Your family thinks you're at the hotel. Right?"

"Works perfectly." Kelsey slid onto the ground and rested her back against the log. She tilted her head up and let the sun rays filtering through the trees bathe her face.

"You'd better eat." Clay picked up another piece of chicken and bit into a chunk of bread.

"Is there anything you don't feel responsible for?"

His gaze clashed with hers and held for a long moment. He turned back to his food and ignored her.

Finally Kelsey nibbled on a piece of chicken, then took an apple and polished it against her shirt. "Seth and I used to ride through these hills together."

"So that's how you know the land so well." He crunched into an apple. "Is that when you started picking out prime spots for robberies?"

She laughed gently. "Stagecoach robbery is a career I stumbled upon much later on."

"And did you stumble upon Dade's hideout the same way?"

Kelsey coiled her legs under her. "After the first robbery, we were so scared we rode into the hills and hid out overnight. The next morning, we caught sight of the Dade gang riding out of a hollow near a cabin. We'd have never spotted them, except we happened to be on the ridge above them."

"So it was just dumb luck?"

"Yes. Just like the time we happened on Luther and Deuce trying to string you up." His eyes turned to soft blue as he gazed at her, but he didn't speak. Kelsey jerked her chin around. "No need to thank me, or anything."

"How did you know it was Dade?"

She bit into the apple. "Are you kidding? There's Wanted posters up for him all over the place."

Clay braced his elbows on his knees and looked down at her. "Then why didn't you turn him in? You could have used the reward money instead of Morgan's payroll money."

"The reward wasn't enough."

Clay laughed bitterly. "The boys have expensive tastes?"

"What boys?"

"The boys in the gang. Your accomplices."

"Oh...those boys." Kelsey cautioned herself to be careful. "Besides, how could I explain to the sheriff that I had discovered the location of the Dade hideout?"

Clay rose and stretched. He'd had enough of this conversation. Everything Kelsey said about her involvement with the robberies sounded so damn logical it made him mad.

They cleaned up and repacked the last of their food, and headed west again. Several miles farther on, they left the road, and Kelsey led them northwest through the wooded hills. Hours crept by as they traveled in silence. They stopped to water the horses at a wide, shallow creek as sun rays slanted through the towering trees.

Clay turned in the saddle, searching the woods. "This looks pretty good. We'll camp here tonight."

Kelsey perked up in the saddle. "Camp? We're not—"

Clay turned his horse from the stream, circled a large outcropping of rock and rode up the hill to a clearing.

"Wait!" Kelsey guided her mare up the hill after him. "I never said I was spending the night out here with you."

He climbed down from the stallion. "We're losing daylight."

"We can be there in an hour—maybe less."

Clay untied his bedroll from the saddle. "I'm not going up against the Dade gang after dark without any notion of the lay of the land. I won't give them the advantage. We'll ride in tomorrow, early."

Kelsey's anger rose. "This wasn't part of our deal. Look, lawman, you're on your own. I'm going back to town."

He grabbed the mare's bridle. "I make the rules out here, and I don't give a damn about our deal. Now get down off that horse, and let's make camp."

She glared at him, her anger growing.

He let go of the bridle. "Besides, if I were you, I wouldn't be so anxious to get back to town. Judge Winthrope is waiting. Remember?"

Fear tempered her anger, but only slightly. Kelsey slide from the horse and stomped across the clearing.

She gathered small branches and twigs and placed them inside a ring of small stones she'd found down by the creek. By the time Clay had tended their horses and brought over the last of their gear, Kelsey had a fire going. Orange flames licked the darkness as they sat on their blankets and ate their supper in tense silence.

Clay stood and brushed crumbs from his trousers. "We'd better turn in."

She ignored him and pulled her coat closer around her. The dew had fallen, and it was chilly now. She watched as Clay shrugged into his coat; it looked warmer than hers. But, of course, he was prepared for nights on the trail, and she wasn't. Kelsey's contempt for him doubled. He spread out his blanket across the campfire from her and stretched out, covering his face with his Stetson.

He was asleep. Already! Kelsey fumed silently as she spread out her own blanket and lay down on her side, facing the fire. He had his nerve. Dragging her out here, making her stay all night in the cold, then falling asleep as if nothing were wrong. She crossed her arms in front of her and curled up her knees, but even her anger couldn't keep her warm. She began to shiver.

He sat up suddenly and laid his hand on his pistol. Ears straining, he pushed his hat in place and swept the perimeter of the campsite. Finally he squinted at her through the flickering flames. "Are your teeth chattering?"

She clamped her jaws tight together, but couldn't keep them still. "N—n—no."

He got to his feet and rounded the campfire. She raised her head. "What are you doing?"

Clay grabbed the ends of her blanket and dragged it around the fire and alongside his. Then he picked up the side and rolled her onto his blanket.

"Hey! What are you—?"

"Just hush." He circled behind her and lay down, then spread the other blanket over them.

"You can't—"

Kelsey rolled onto her side, away from him, and tried to rise, but he looped one arm around her waist and slid the other under her neck. He opened the buttons of his coat and pulled her against his chest.

Sensations assaulted her as his thighs rubbed the back of her legs, his midsection curved against her bottom and his hands settled comfortably between her breasts.

"You have no right..."

"You're not cold anymore, are you?" He whispered the taunt softly against her ear.

She tried to wiggle away, but he held her snug against him. Angry, she butted him with her bottom, then realized her mistake as she felt his hardness press into her soft flesh. She stilled immediately. "You're not cold, either, apparently."

No, he sure as hell wasn't. A few other things, but not cold. "Go to sleep." He meant to sound gruff, but didn't.

He held her locked in his arms, feeling the softness of her body even through the layers of clothing that separated them, sniffing the sweet fragrance of her hair tucked under his chin. Finally, she relaxed, and he heard the even rhythm of her breathing as she fell asleep. Both aroused and contented, he drifted off.

When he awoke the next morning, she was gone. Clay got to his feet and stretched, his gaze searching the campsite. Early-morning sunlight sifted through the trees, bringing the forest to life. Both horses stood tethered where he'd left them. Wisps of smoke rose from the gray ashes of the fire.

He rubbed his eyes and decided she'd gone off into the woods for a moment of privacy. But when he'd done the same, built a fire and put on the coffee and she still wasn't back, he began to worry.

The forest grew before his eyes as he turned in a circle. The trees looked taller, the distances vaster. He cupped his hands around his mouth. "Kelsey!" Birds chirped a reply. Clay pulled out his pistol and spun the chamber. Fully loaded. He headed off down the hill, toward the creek.

He'd berated himself for bringing her into the woods, staying overnight and taking her gun away by the time he reached the large outcropping of rocks. He stepped around the dark gray stone and gazed at the small creek a few feet away. His heart tumbled.

Kelsey sat facing the rushing water on the creek bank. Her hair, free from the braid, tumbled in a thick mass down her bare back. She wore her trousers, rolled up to her thighs, but that was all. He caught a glimpse of her full, bare breasts as she dipped each dainty foot into the water.

Clay sagged against the rocks, unable to drag his eyes from her. The woman tempted him at every turn, without even trying. His knees went weak, while the rest of him took a predictable course. His body had never been so aroused for so long in his entire life.

Maybe if he hadn't made love to her, he wouldn't feel this way. Maybe if he didn't know the sweet joy of sharing himself with her, he'd feel differently. Clay shook his head slowly. The thought of simply being between some woman's legs held no appeal now. Kelsey was in his heart.

He squeezed his eyes shut and curled his hands into fists. An outlaw...an outlaw...an outlaw... She was an outlaw, and he would send her to prison. Somehow.

* * *

"How much farther?"

His voice sounded strange, given that those were the first words he'd spoken to her all day. Kelsey obliged him by stretching up in the stirrups and gazing at the hills and valleys below them. From their vantage point here on the ridge, she could see for miles.

"A little farther."

"Well, how far is that?" he barked.

"Much too far." She kicked her mare and rode ahead without him.

He seemed content to hang behind, and that suited her fine as she followed the narrow, rutted trail through the woods. He'd been a bear all morning, and while part of her wanted to head back to town and never lay eyes on Marshal Clay Chandler again, another part of her, a stronger part, wouldn't let her leave.

The creak of wagon wheels sounded in the stillness. Clay was in front of her in a heartbeat. He held up his hand for silence as he gazed through the trees alongside the winding road ahead of them.

A wagon rounded the curve, and the man holding the reins pulled the horses to a stop. As usual, Clay's badge attracted attention first.

"Morning, Marshal." He dipped his head and looked around Clay at Kelsey.

She tilted her chin, which brought the brim of her hat farther over her face, and shrank into the upturned collar of her coat. The gray-haired man looked harmless enough, but Kelsey was thankful—very thankful—that Clay stood between them.

"Morning, ah…Deputy." He looked at Clay again. "Mighty far out, Marshal. Trouble?"

"Have you seen anybody out this way lately?"

The old man stroked his chin. "Naw. I don't rightly recall seeing nobody around. That's what I like about it!"

"Do you live around here?"

He gestured back up the trail. "A few miles back. Got me a little cabin up there. I'm headed down to Harmonville for a few days to fetch some supplies. You're welcome to stop by my place, water the horses. Always glad to see a federal Marshal around."

"Much obliged." Clay urged his stallion up the trail. Kelsey hurried behind.

They passed the cabin, a neat little place a few yards off the trail, and rode a few more miles into the woods. Kelsey stopped her mare at the crest of the ridge and pointed at the hills below. "There. That's it."

Clay stopped beside her. "Where?"

"See those two big elms at the base of those rocks?"

His gaze followed her finger. "Near the pines?"

"That's it."

Clay's stomach knotted. "Dade's gang is back in there?"

"Go between those elms and behind those rocks and you'll find a series of hidden hollows and hills. You'd never know they were back there unless you went in through those elms. You can't see them from up here because of the trees."

Clay studied the ridges and valleys, the trees and rock formations, his face drawn in hard lines. Suddenly he turned his horse around. "Let's go."

They wound back down the trail, and Clay stopped his horse outside the cabin. He dismounted and looped the reins over the hitching post.

"Are we watering the horses before going back down?" Kelsey slid to the ground.

Clay walked onto the porch and kicked the door open.

"Clay! What are you doing?" Kelsey hurried into the cabin after him.

He took in the small one-room cabin with a quick turn. Brass bed in the corner, table and chairs by the cookstove, all neat and clean.

"You can't just kick somebody's door down and—" Kelsey froze as his hard, cold gaze impaled her. She'd never seen that look in his eyes before. It frightened her.

"You stay put. I'll be back later."

Fear sliced through her. She grabbed his arm. "You said you'd get a posse."

He glared at her, but she wasn't sure it was she he saw.

"You can't go back there by yourself, Clay. There's four of them. You could be—" Her stomach knotted. "Give me my gun. I'm going with you."

"Hell, no. You're staying here." He grasped her upper arms, his voice low, and pulled her up even with him. "If I have to get the rope and tie you here, I will. You can't come with me."

"It's too dangerous. Dade's a killer!"

"Don't you think I know that?" Hatred, strong and rancid, poured out with his words.

Kelsey felt the color drain from her face and her knees go weak as she gazed up at him. She swallowed a lump of emotion. "Rebecca..."

Clay released her and stalked out the door.

"It was Dade, wasn't it? He's the one who killed your sister." She ran onto the porch. "Clay, don't do this!"

He mounted his horse and rode away without looking back.

Kelsey paced the porch, her stomach churning. She had to do something. The sheriff at Eldon was too far away. Harmonville was closer, but still a day's ride.

She couldn't let Clay face Scully Dade alone. He wasn't thinking clearly. Memories of Rebecca controlled him now. He'd be lucky to get away with his life.

Kelsey scrambled onto her mare and headed up the trail. She couldn't let him get hurt—she loved him too much.

Chapter Sixteen

Gunfire echoed through the hollows as Kelsey urged her mare between the elms. Hope and fear tingled up her spine. If they were still shooting, Clay was still alive.

Ahead, just below the crest of the rise, she saw Clay's stallion tied to a pine. She wound through the trees and tethered her mare alongside his horse. Kelsey opened his saddlebag and strapped on her gun.

On hands and knees, she crept to the top of the rise. A long, wide valley stretched out below her, rimmed by a ridge of gray rocks and towering trees. On the far side of the valley, a ramshackle cabin squatted in the shadows of the ridge. Dade's hideout. Gunfire flashed from the window of the cabin and the corner of the woodshed nearby. Two men lay on the ground, lifeless. Kelsey's stomach pitched. Where was Clay?

Directly across the valley, separated by a sloping, grassy meadow, a large outcropping of rock jutted skyward. A hail of bullets from the cabin bounced off the rocks. Clay popped up suddenly, sighted his Winchester at the cabin and returned fire. Kelsey dropped to the ground, heart pounding. He was alone, and pinned down. Dade and the surviving member of his gang would work their way to Clay's position sooner or later. She had to do something—now.

Kelsey raised her head, surveying the forest separating her from Clay. Neither he nor the outlaws expected her. Kelsey made her move.

She drew her gun and crouched low, using the trees for cover as she picked her way around the ridge and darted to the rocks. She dived behind them and landed on her belly.

Clay spun and drew the rifle down on her.

"No! Wait! It's me!" Kelsey whipped off her hat.

He froze for an instant, then dropped his rifle. Absolute fury contorted his features. "What the hell are you doing here?"

Clay crept along the ground, grabbed the collar of her coat and dragged her to him. Bullets ricocheted off the rocks above their heads. He pushed her back against the cold stones.

"I told you to stay at the cabin!"

She holstered her gun. "I came to help you."

"Oh, God, no..." Fear overwhelmed him. Clay curled his fists into the front of her coat. "No, no, you shouldn't have come. It's too dangerous. You could get killed, Kelsey. I can't lose you, too."

"I'm not Rebecca!" She gazed at his face—it was twisted with fear and worry—and splayed her hand across his cheek. "Listen to me. I'm not going to freeze. I'm not going to just stand there and get shot. I'm not Rebecca."

He held her gaze for a long moment, lost in thought, lost in memories.

Finally, Kelsey turned away. "Besides, you're not

doing so well here, lawman. You look like you could use some help.''

"I'm doing all right.'' Clay eased upward. Bullets whizzed past his head. He dropped to the ground again.

"Did you tell them you're a federal marshal?''

"We didn't exactly take time out for introductions.''

"Did they see your badge?''

"Oh, yeah. They're using it for a target.'' He picked up his rifle. "They saw me ride up. I got two of them and made it here before the others figured out what happened.''

Kelsey drew her gun. "So, it's just the two of them left?''

"One of them's Scully.''

The one he was after. The one he'd ridden miles and waited years to capture. Kelsey nodded. "That's him in the cabin.''

He glanced down at her. "How'd you know?''

"Big as a grizzly. Pretty hard to miss.'' Kelsey drew her feet under her and crouched low. "What's your plan?''

"Can't sit here all day.'' Clay shoved cartridges into the Winchester. He nodded to the right. "I'll work my way around the ridge, go through those trees and come up on the woodshed.''

Kelsey nodded. "I'll cover you.''

"No, you won't. You keep your head down and stay put.''

"You're being stupid, lawman. They don't know I'm here. They'll think it's you shooting at them. You can make your way to the woodshed without them suspecting anything.''

He grasped her arm. "Have you ever shot a man before?''

She rolled her eyes. "I'm not going to really shoot anybody. I'm just going to shoot around them."

Clay pulled on his neck. "All right. But you keep low, and promise me you'll stay here."

"I promise." Kelsey drew in a quick breath, bobbed upward and squeezed off three shots. "Go!"

Bullets dug into the rocks beside her. She dropped to the ground again, heart pounding. Clay was gone. She'd never felt so alone in her life. She gathered her courage, rose and fired again.

In that brief second, she saw Scully in the cabin and the other outlaw crouched by the woodshed. Both had fired straight at her. Neither suspected Clay was working his way around the rim of the valley. Thank God.

The gun felt slippery in her wet palms as she ducked for cover and reloaded. Kelsey crept a few feet along the rocks, then emptied the gun in the direction of the cabin. Two pistol shots sounded, then a rifle, and she saw the outlaw collapse into the woodpile, just before she dropped behind the rocks again.

The firing stopped. The sound echoed through the hollows, then faded away. Kelsey loaded her gun again.

"Dade! Federal marshal! Give yourself up!"

She crept to the crest of the rocks and saw Clay take cover at the corner of the woodshed, rifle ready. The door to the cabin lay only a few yards away. She couldn't see Scully now.

"It's no use, Dade! Come on out of there!"

A long moment dragged by. Kelsey clung to the rocks. Vulnerable, Clay needed her help. She kept her gaze trained on the cabin. Where was Dade?

He appeared at the rear of the cabin, pistol drawn. Tall, with wide shoulders and a full frame, he crept silently toward the woodshed. From his position at the other corner, Clay couldn't see him. Kelsey's heart surged. She raised her gun and caught Dade's chest in her sights. With his attention focused on Clay at the woodshed, she could drop him easily. Kelsey pulled back the hammer.

Rebecca popped into her head. The memory of her death lived in Clay's mind, and would never be put to rest until he'd brought the man who killed her to justice. He'd waited years for this moment, made it a part of him, as if it were a living thing. Kelsey lowered her gun. She couldn't take this away from him.

"Rear of the cabin!" she screamed, with every ounce of breath she possessed.

Clay whipped around the corner and held his rifle pointed squarely at Dade's chest. "Hold it right there!"

The big man froze, then bent slowly and dropped his gun to the ground. Suddenly he surged upward and drove his shoulder into Clay's stomach. His rifle flew from his hands as Dade pounded him against the woodshed.

Kelsey gasped and scrambled higher on the rocks. The two men struggled, trading punches, until they'd fought their way to the open meadow. Dade tripped and pulled Clay with him, sending them both tumbling down the hill. Dade got to his feet first and slammed his fist into Clay.

Frantic, Kelsey raised her gun. She couldn't get off a clear shot. Clay was a big man, but Dade was bigger. And he was desperate. That gave him the advantage.

Kelsey pressed her lips together. She had to do something. She couldn't stand by and watch Clay get beaten to death, or let him get killed with his own pistol if Dade managed to pull it from Clay's holster. If only she had a way to distract Dade. If only she had something that would draw his attention, even for a second. But she was just a woman. What could a woman do to intervene?

Clay hit hard on the ground, but scrambled to his feet and slugged Dade in the face. He reeled back, but didn't fall. Clay swung at him again. Dade blocked his arm and threw a punch at his nose. Clay ducked and drove his fist into Dade's stomach. He doubled over, then looked up at Clay, hatred in his eyes. He charged forward, grabbed Clay's shirtfront and drew back his fist. Clay braced himself.

A sharp, high-pitched whistle sounded. Looking past Clay, Dade froze. His jaw dropped.

Clay turned. Atop the rocks stood Kelsey. Hair loose and flowing, hand on her hips, she was naked to the waist, her face turned skyward as her bare breasts shone white and creamy in the afternoon sunlight.

Stunned, Clay ogled her, but he recovered before Dade. He pulled his pistol. Dade turned, grabbed his wrist and drove him backward to the ground. Clay pulled him down. They wrestled. A shot rang out. Clay tensed, waiting for the hot, searing pain, the warm rush of his blood. Neither came.

Clay pushed Dade off him and struggled to his feet. A wide red circle was growing in Dade's chest. Clay stared down at him. Scully Dade was dead.

"Why don't you lie down?" Kelsey lifted his empty plate from the table and glanced at the brass bed in the corner. "You look like you could use some rest."

Clay sat back and pushed his fingers through his hair. He blew out a heavy breath. "I don't know...."

Kelsey carried the dirty dishes to the sideboard and pumped water into the basin. He'd had little to say since they left Dade's hideout, not even to fuss at her for interfering, and certainly not to thank her. But she understood his silence. Finally, after so long, he'd brought down the man who'd killed his sister. He needed time to come to terms with it.

He'd gone back to the hideout with a shovel and buried the outlaws while Kelsey found her way around the cabin and prepared their meal. Thankfully, the place was neat as a pin and absolutely spotless, a pleasant surprise, considering the man who lived here. When he returned from Harmonville in a few days, he'd likely be surprised to realize they had made themselves at home in his place. But Kelsey was of no mind to camp out in the open tonight; she'd be sure Clay left money to compensate for the supplies they used.

The chair scraped across the floor, and Clay ambled to the sink. "You want some help?"

She rolled back the sleeves of her shirt. "No, thanks."

He stood beside her for a long time, then rubbed his eyes. "Maybe I'll lie down for a while."

Aside from the emotional upheaval he'd suffered today, he'd also sustained more than a few bumps and bruises in his fight with Dade. Kelsey nodded. "I found fresh linens in the cupboard and put them on the bed. Lie down. You need some rest."

"Don't let me sleep long. If we ride hard, we can get back to town tonight before it's too late."

Kelsey began washing the dishes and, after a moment, heard his deep, even breathing. She worked quietly, then stepped onto the back porch. A mild, refreshing breeze cooled her face.

She sat down on the wide wooden swing that hung from the roof of the porch and stretched out her legs.

Below the cabin, heavily wooded hollows spread out for miles. This quiet, isolated spot felt right to her—just what she needed.

Somewhere amid the day's turmoil, she'd discovered that she loved Clay. She'd loved him all along, but she hadn't realized it until she faced the possibility of losing him. Now, she knew she never wanted to be apart from him again.

But that presented a problem. Kelsey dropped one foot to the porch's plank floor and set the swing in motion. First and foremost, Clay Chandler was a lawman. He hadn't expressed any feelings of love for her, hadn't even hinted at it. All he'd said was that when they returned to Eldon, he'd turn her in. As a good lawman would.

Kelsey rose from the swing and leaned against the roof's support column. Maybe she wouldn't have forever, but she had today.

He came awake slowly and sat up on the edge of the bed. Clay rubbed his eyes. A tiny flame burned in the lantern on the table, a circle of light in the dark cabin; moonlight brightened the windows. He pushed himself to his feet, and stiff, achy muscles reminded him of the fight he'd been in this afternoon. Reminded him, too, of Scully Dade.

At the washstand beside the bed, Clay splashed water on his face. For an instant, he thought the whole incident had been a dream. God knew, he'd lived it in his sleep enough times. But now, for the first time in years, the weight bearing down on him had disappeared, gone when he'd thrown the last shovel full of dirt on Scully's grave. Clay stretched up on his toes reaching toward the ceiling, and yawned. Yes, the load seemed lighter.

A little grin pulled at his lips. Kelsey. A tiny outlaw who'd helped bring down the infamous Scully Dade. He reveled in the mental image of her standing on the rocks—a hell of a way to win a fight.

Clay chuckled aloud in the dark cabin, then turned quickly. Where was she? She'd proved she could handle herself at the Dade hideout today, but worry coiled in his belly just the same. Clay pulled on his boots and strapped his gun belt low on his hips. At the back door, he picked up his rifle and stepped outside.

Bright moonlight illuminated the hollows below the cabin. He listened hard at the still night, but heard nothing more than the night song of the insects and animals in the woods. A comfortable breeze stirred the air.

He followed the path through the trees to the barn. Kelsey was supposed to awaken him long ago. Had she gone back to Eldon without him? She shouldn't be out on the trail by herself. Worry lengthened his strides.

At the corral, he found both horses content. Clay rested his hand on his pistol and gazed through the trees. Nothing. He continued down the path, deeper into the woods.

A twig snapped behind him. Clay tensed and drew his gun, but a sharp object jabbed into his lower back before he could turn. Clay froze.

"Drop 'em, lawman."

The gentle breeze brought a delicate scent that even the raspy voice couldn't disguise. Clay laid his rifle and pistol on the ground, straightened and raised his hands.

"No. I meant these." Fingers tugged at the waistband of his trousers.

Clay turned. She was naked, the soft moonlight bathing her. Tiny droplets of water shimmered on her skin. Her hair, wet and slicked back off her face, fell to her waist. Clay swallowed hard.

Kelsey giggled playfully and ran away from him, down the path into the woods. Mesmerized as he was by the sight of her, a moment passed before Clay came to his senses. He ran after her.

At the end of the path, huge gray rocks formed a natural pool, catching the clear creek on the ridge above, which spilled over the rocks in a gentle waterfall. Clay stepped up onto the rocks in time to see Kelsey's head bob to the surface in the center of the pond. Intense desire surged through him.

She swam toward him, her body moving fluidly through the crystal water. She looked up at him, her arms and legs churning to keep her afloat in the deep water. "How do you like this place? I found it this afternoon while you were sleeping. Pretty, huh?"

Clay licked his dry lips. "If I'd known the scenery was this spectacular, I'd have gotten up hours ago."

She giggled and dipped her lashes coyly. "The water feels good. Want to try it out?"

His heart slammed against his ribs. "Sure."

"Okay." Kelsey floated onto her back and kicked furiously, splashing water on him. She laughed wildly. "Like it?"

Clay jumped back. He couldn't resist her challenge. Quickly he shucked off his clothes and dived into the pond. Kelsey squealed and swam away.

He surfaced near her just as she turned to splash water in his face. Clay swiped his hand across the pond, sending a wave over her. She laughed and screamed, shoveling water back at him. She was no match for his big hands. Kelsey rolled onto her back and kicked wildly, creating more whitecaps than the waterfall behind her.

Laughter rumbled deep in his chest as he grabbed her ankle and pulled her toward him. She squealed and tried to swim away, but he held her easily. Clay dived under, pulling her down with him.

Beneath the cool water, they struggled playfully, until Clay released her and they both swam to the surface. In a spray of water, they both gasped for air, laughing and giggling.

"You tried to drown me!" Kelsey cried accusingly.

Clay ran both hands through his hair, slicking it off his face. "If I'd wanted to drown you, I'd have done *this!*"

He planted his hand atop her hair and dunked her. Arms and legs flailing, Kelsey fought her way to the surface. Coughing and wheezing, she said, "See how you like it!"

She grasped both his shoulders and pushed him down. But he didn't move. Like a giant rock, he stayed atop the water. She pushed harder, then burst out laughing, though she meant to sound mean. "That's not fair!"

Clay laughed, low and menacing, and she knew what he intended. He reached for her shoulders, but Kelsey wasn't going down alone. Quickly she threw her arms around his neck, ready to pull him under.

But instead, they both froze. Her breasts tantalized his chest. They stared at each other in the golden moonlight as the sound of the splashing waterfall echoed through the trees. A long moment slipped by, their playfulness rippling away with the churning water.

Clay slid his arms around her and pulled her close. Heat seared their flesh as the cool water swirled like silk between them. He lowered his head and covered her lips with a hungry kiss. Kelsey coiled her arms around his neck and met his desire with hunger of her own.

Passion, strong and unchecked, coursed through Clay as he kissed a hot trail down her neck. She arched back, welcoming him. He slid his tongue downward and lifted her higher until her breast crested the water. Then he claimed it with his lips, suckling and teasing until it tightened. Kelsey thrust her fingers into his wet hair and moaned.

Clay lifted his head. His hand took up the task his lips enjoyed as he cupped her breasts and circled the crest with his thumb. He claimed her lips again in a deep, demanding kiss.

Comfort, excitement and a sense of belonging swelled inside Kelsey. Being locked in Clay's embrace, drinking in his kiss and his caress, brought a desire to stay here always, to please him, to hold him, to love him.

Kelsey shifted beneath the water and slid her leg across him. She circled his hips, settling against him intimately.

Clay groaned. Almost overwhelmed by the need to claim her fully, he willed himself to hold back. Slowly, he slid his hands down her spine, over the curve of her hips, and captured her soft roundness with his palms. Buoyed by the water, he explored her thoroughly, seeking, finding and stroking until urgency claimed her.

Clay pushed against the bottom of the pond. Kelsey clung to him as they glided to the smooth round stones behind the waterfall. The cool liquid splashed against his back and slid down his spine as he found his footing and positioned Kelsey against the rocks. He lifted her hips, pausing for a moment at her threshold, to delight in the feel, then drove himself inside her.

Sensations assailed her as he worked his magic, stroking her desire until it flamed. She grasped a fistful of his wet hair as she arched to meet his demands. Her breasts felt full against his chest, fueling her need. Passion throbbed deep within her, growing, swelling with his unrelenting thrusts until finally it exploded. Great tremors of pleasure pulsed through her over and over again as she pulled at his hair and devoured his mouth with hers.

Clay moaned as her tongue assaulted him and her body undulated with release. Aching with need, he plunged deep within her. Again and again he plied her. Desire, want, passion, drove him until pleasure so exquisite it hurt broke over him. Wonderful, giant waves engulfed him, drained him, until he sagged against Kelsey, sated.

Long moments passed before Clay lifted his head from the rocks. Gently he kissed Kelsey's shoulder, then her throat. Still twined intimately with her, he reveled in the feel of her. Clay drew his hand down her cheek and cupped her chin. "You're beautiful."

Kelsey gazed up at him. A teasing grin parted her lips. "I'll bet you say that to all the outlaws."

Clay chuckled. "Let's go."

They swam across the pond and climbed out onto the rocks. Kelsey pulled her hair over her shoulder and squeezed; water cascaded over her breasts. She reached for her clothes, piled nearby, but Clay laid a hand on her.

"You're not going to need them." Clay lifted her into his arms and headed down the path.

* * *

Gray shafts of dawn slanted through the cabin windows as Kelsey pushed herself up on one elbow. She didn't have to look to know she was alone in bed. Clay's presence there beside her all night had left an indelible mark on her.

She collapsed onto the pillow and stared at the ceiling. They'd made love last night in the small brass bed, but there had been no talk of love. Clay had taken her to the heights of ecstasy. He'd held her. He'd whispered endearments. He'd shared himself with her.

But he hadn't spoken.

Kelsey dragged herself from bed and threw the quilt around her shoulders. She held it together and crossed to the back door, the wooden floor cold on her bare feet.

Today they would return to Eldon. He'd be a lawman once more, and she'd be an outlaw. Clay would do his duty. He'd see justice was served. He'd turn her in. And tonight, she'd sleep in Sheriff Bottom's jail.

The back door squeaked as Kelsey stepped outside. Clay stood at the opposite end of the porch. His back to her, he braced his arm against the roof's support column as he gazed into the hollows below the cabin. He was naked.

She'd never seen him like this in the daylight before. He was lean, with strong, corded muscles. His legs were long, his hips narrow. His wide back rippled when he moved. He turned when she approached. Dark stubble shadowed his jaw.

Clay jerked his chin toward the hollows. "Looks like it might rain."

Fog lay between the ridges and valleys, cold and gray, like the sky. Kelsey stepped closer. "It might."

He cleared his throat. "I wouldn't want to get caught on the trail in a storm."

She stopped in front of him. "I brought my rain gear." She was certain he had, too. She knew what he really wanted, but couldn't—wouldn't—make it easy for him. If they were to delay their return to Eldon, it had to come from Clay.

He threaded his fingers through his hair. His gaze riveted her for a long moment. Finally, he heaved a heavy breath. "I want to stay here today."

Clay caught the fabric of the quilt and opened it; she didn't protest as he leisurely looked her up and down. He spread it on the porch swing, sat down and pulled her onto his lap. She curled against his chest as he wrapped the quilt around them.

One foot planted firmly on the porch, Clay set the swing in motion and rested his chin atop her hair. He snuggled her close against him and sighed.

For all the passion they'd shared last night, having Kelsey in his arms now brought only feelings of comfort and contentment. Her body against his, the familiar scent that wafted around her, left a calmness about him.

"You did good yesterday." Clay rubbed his cheek against the top of her head. "At Dade's hideout. You did real good."

"See? It wasn't like Rebecca."

"Thank God." He whispered the words and kissed the top of her head.

Kelsey softened her voice. "You don't have to be responsible for everything and everybody, Clay."

He drew in a deep breath. "Maybe not."

"I was scared yesterday," she admitted.

"Me too."

She leaned her head back on his shoulder to get a look at his face. "I'm glad it's over."

Clay nodded. "It's finally over. All of it."

"Maybe now you can write to your family. They miss you."

"How do you know?"

"Because I know what kind of person you are, and if you were my brother, I'd miss you a lot."

Clay chuckled and ran his finger down her cheek. "Honey, the last thing I want to be is your brother."

She giggled. "You should write to them."

His uncle had said these same things to him only days ago. "I guess you're right. Maybe I'll go see them. My pa is a lawyer, you know. He wanted me to do the same."

"And you didn't want to?"

Clay shrugged. "Went to college and got a law degree, but never used it. Being tied down to one place never appealed to me." *Until now*, he almost added.

They sat together in each other's arms, rocking gently in the porch swing, content in the silence. Kelsey combed her fingers through the dark hair of his chest. He strummed his thumb across her bare back. Finally, Kelsey lifted her head from his shoulder. "Hungry?"

Clay nuzzled his nose against the sweet flesh at her throat. He sighed, deep and low in his chest, a sign Kelsey had already learned to interpret. She turned her head and nibbled at his ear. "I'll make you some breakfast," she offered, though she knew his response.

"In a minute..." Clay covered her lips with his. He rose from the swing, trailing the quilt, and carried her inside the cabin. He laid her on the bed. "I need a shave."

It seemed an odd moment to be concerned with facial hair, since his desire for her was readily apparent. But Kelsey pulled the quilt up around her and leaned back against the headboard, watching as he dumped the contents of his saddlebag on the table and quickly scraped the dark whiskers from his face at the washstand.

He perched beside her on the edge of the bed and splayed her palm across his cheek. "Smooth?"

He felt wet and slick. "Yes."

"Good." Clay rose above her and kissed an enticing path the length of her. Kelsey moaned and twisted the pillow in her fist as his mouth touched places he'd missed the night before, places she'd never imagined would be kissed. Yet, with Clay, it felt loving and right.

Need built swiftly, demanding fulfillment. Sensing her desire, Clay settled himself deep within her. She whimpered and locked her arms around him. He moved with her, and their passion rose until their union crested in waves of pleasure and they collapsed in each other's arms.

Clay levered himself above her and rolled onto his side, panting. "Okay, I'm hungry."

Kelsey's hand fell to her forehead, and she rolled her head back. "You're going to have to fix it yourself, now."

Clay chuckled and snuggled against her. Finally he got out of bed. "I'll be back." He left the cabin.

Kelsey pushed her tangled hair off her shoulder and climbed out of bed, draping the linen sheet around her and tying it under her arms. It dragged on the floor as she searched the pantry and assembled food on the sideboard.

A moment later, Clay stepped through the back door,

his trousers pulled on. He carried his rifle, his gun belt and the clothing they'd abandoned by the pond last night.

"I thought you might want to put on..." His voice faded away as he took in the sight of the sheet tied in the cleft of her breasts, swinging open as she cooked. He tossed the clothing out the back door. "Never mind."

They put fresh coffee on the stove, prepared eggs and bacon and sat together at the table eating and talking.

"So how come you haven't married?" Clay asked as he helped himself to the strawberry preserves they'd found in the pantry. Pretty, funny, daughter of a wealthy businessman, she'd be a prime catch for any man, and she should have married years ago.

Kelsey batted her lashes. "I attribute my luck to good clean living."

Clay chuckled. "You don't want to marry?"

"I haven't found the right man, but never sought one, either. I figured that one day I'd look up and there he'd be." As Clay had been. She grew serious. "And, besides, my mother was ill for a very long time. I couldn't accept any suitors, with her to care for."

"Didn't she want you to find a husband? That was one of my mama's big wants for Rebecca."

"Of course. It was one of the things we always talked about, since I was her oldest daughter." A sad smile pulled at her lips. "We had the wedding all planned. But now..."

But now she'd go to prison. Clay took another bite of eggs. Maybe it was better her mother wasn't around.

They cleaned the kitchen together, and Clay pulled on his boots and shirt and left to take care of the horses.

The day grew cooler, without a single shaft of sunlight finding its way through the clouds, so Kelsey laid a fire and sat on the rug in front of the hearth.

"Cold?" Clay asked when he came through the back door.

She rubbed her bare arms. "A little."

He shrugged out of his shirt and draped it over her shoulders, then sat down behind her and pulled her against his chest, circling her with his arms. They spent the afternoon there, whispering, sharing secrets, gossiping about the people in Eldon. They discussed the world, politics, their families. They talked of everything but the future.

The cabin grew dim and the fire faded.

"Put another log on the fire, would you, Clay?" Kelsey snuggled nearer.

"If I do that, you won't need to sit so close."

"You put out a lot of heat, all right." Kelsey turned and sat up on her knees in front of him. "I'll just have to make sure you keep up the good work."

A grin tugged at his lips. "What did you have in mind?"

Kelsey braced her palms on his shoulders and leaned forward, covering his mouth with hers. He sighed contentedly as she worked her lips over his, then moaned as he untied the sheet from around her and let it slide down to her hips. He cupped both breasts in his hands, kneading them gently.

Kelsey broke off their kiss, but denied him nothing else. "I never thanked you for letting Seth out of prison."

Exquisite urgency had already claimed him, and he couldn't form a logical thought. Instead, he got to his feet and pulled Kelsey up with him, tracing his palms over her soft curves. Quickly he pulled off his boots and trousers and tried to lift her in his arms. She splayed her hand over his chest, instead, and urged him backward into the bed.

As he had shown her, Kelsey kissed him, finding new and different places that made him writhe and groan with delight. She plied him until she knew him completely, then slid her knee across his hip and settled herself around him.

"Oh, God..." Clay grabbed a feather pillow above his head and locked his fists into the fabric. Muscles straining, he pushed himself into her. She moved with him, in sweet, erotic torture, tempering his eagerness in knowing ways, then urging him on with her boldness. Her hands encouraged him, driving his desire to a higher level, until she became caught in the moment herself and arched against him. He thrust deep inside her. Groaning aloud, his muscles contracted, ripping the fabric of the pillow. A storm of white feathers showered them as great waves of pleasure racked them both.

Kelsey eased herself onto his chest and stretched out atop him as he muttered incoherently.

"I suppose that means you're pleased," she whispered against his ear.

Clay wrapped his arms around her.

"Thank you." She kissed him on the cheek. "Thank you for getting my brother out of prison."

He gave her a big, goofy grin.

"I hope my thank-you was adequate." She threaded her fingers through his hair, plucking the chicken feathers away from his damp brow.

"Oh, yeah. In fact, do you have any other relatives behind bars? Any at all? They don't even have to be relatives, just people you've met, or heard of. Anybody.''

Kelsey smiled and snuggled close to him. They fell asleep tangled in each other's arms.

Kelsey woke at dawn to the sound of horses out front. She made her way to the window, dragging the quilt, and pulled back the curtain. Both horses were there, saddled. Clay stood between them, checking the gear.

Through the glass, Kelsey saw the lines of his face, drawn in deep, determined lines. His lawman's face. She dropped the curtain and fell against the wall.

There'd be no reprieve today. Clay was taking her in.

Chapter Seventeen

The mare pawed the dirt in the darkened alley. Kelsey held the reins firmly and waited as, up ahead, Clay realized she was no longer riding beside him. He turned in the saddle. His eyes held no warmth; they'd been that way all day.

Fear and dread tightened her stomach. She nodded at the jailhouse down the alley. "Aren't we supposed to go here?"

He didn't answer, just touched his heels to the stallion's flanks and rode on. Kelsey swallowed hard and followed.

He rode to the rear of the hotel. She stopped her horse beside his and slid to the ground. The ride back to Eldon today had been long. Each mile, each step, had brought her closer to the inevitable—her trial, her humiliation, her family disgrace and, finally, her sentence. She'd always known getting caught and going to prison was a possibility, but it had never seemed real. But the mental images had tortured her all day. Now she felt sick from thinking about it.

Clay dismounted and took the mare's reins. "You

have to give me your word you won't try to leave town.''

Not an ounce of compassion warmed his voice. If her situation wasn't so dire, she might have been angry at him. Seemingly, the intimate moments they'd shared, when her own heart was so full of love, meant nothing to him. Maybe she deserved that, too.

Kelsey pulled off her hat. "I want to go home and see Seth and the baby.''

His expression hardened. "You'd rather I take you over to the jail tonight?''

Her stomach twisted. "No.''

"Then stay in the hotel until tomorrow. Judge Winthrope will see you right after lunch. Don't be late. And wear something pretty. Fix your hair up. Put a flower in it, or something.''

"A flower?'' It seemed an odd thing to wear to a trial.

"You don't want him thinking you're some old maid who's got nothing to look forward to.'' Clay turned the reins over in his hands. "I've got to get these horses over to the livery. Good luck tomorrow.''

Kelsey's heart lurched. Instinctively she latched on to his arm. It was hard and strong beneath his shirt-sleeve. "Aren't you going to be there?''

His gaze searched her face in the dim light, as if he were looking for something. Kelsey held her breath. Finally, he said, "No.''

Clay mounted his stallion and rode away, leading the little mare. He didn't look back.

Heartsick, Kelsey ran into the hotel and slammed the door.

"Well, I guess that's that.'' Sheriff Bottom pushed the report across his desk and reared back in his chair.

"To tell you the truth, Chandler, I didn't think you'd do it. I guess what everybody says about you is true."

Clay sipped from the blue-speckled cup and set it on the edge of the sheriff's desk; the coffee was as tasteless as everything else he'd eaten this morning. "The Dade gang is gone. That's all I care about."

"So, who're you trailing next?"

Clay walked to the window and gazed at the Eldon Hotel, down the street. "Another outlaw."

The chair creaked as Sheriff Bottom got to his feet. He chuckled. "Well, whoever it is, they don't stand a chance against the likes of you."

"I don't know," Clay mumbled. "This one is pretty elusive."

"By the way, that Judge Winthrope gave Luther a stiff sentence for trying to hang you."

Clay turned away from the window. "I know. I saw the judge first thing this morning."

"Did he say what he's going to do about the Tucker boy?"

Clay shrugged, unwilling to discuss Deuce's future with the sheriff. Explaining it to Ben Tucker this morning had been enough for one day; of all the errands he'd run this morning, that had been the toughest. Besides, he still had to break the news to Deuce.

"Too bad nobody ever claimed that reward for ol' Scully. That was a nice bit of coin." Sheriff Bottom pulled Dade's Wanted poster from the wall and crumpled it into a ball. "You know, I could put that money to use myself."

The jailhouse door came open, and Deuce bounded inside. "Sheriff, I—" He spotted Clay in the corner and fell back a step. "Oh, Marshal, I didn't know you were back in town."

The boy had the worst poker face Clay had ever seen. Guilt etched every line of his expression. Obviously he hadn't expected to find Clay in town, and that heightened Clay's suspicion.

"What are you up to, Deuce?"

"I, ah, I came to talk to the sheriff about... something."

Sheriff Bottom sank into his chair. "Spit it out, boy."

"You remember the jewelry that was stolen from Mr. Morgan's party?" He glanced nervously at Clay. "I, ah, I found it. I know who took it."

"What?" The sheriff lunged to his feet.

Clay eyed him cautiously. "How did you find out?"

Deuce swiped the back of his hand across his lips, and he swallowed hard. "Miss Wilder decided to give some of her books away to folks here in town. So I packed them up and delivered them. That's how I found the jewelry."

The sheriff's eyes narrowed. "What do you mean, boy?"

Deuce drew in a deep breath, avoiding Clay's gaze. "I found them hidden in the bookcase in Mr. Morgan's house. He stole them."

Clay pounded his fist on the front door. At his side, Sheriff Bottom winced.

"Jack Morgan is a big man in Eldon. We can't just go busting into his place, accusing him of something like this."

"Yeah. Why worry about justice, when your pension is on the line?"

Sheriff Bottom ducked his head at Clay's sarcasm and didn't say anything else as the butler answered the door.

Clay pushed his way inside. "Where's Morgan?"

Indignant, the butler replied, "He's in the study with—Wait! You can't go in there!"

Chester Higgins-Smythe and Wilford Henry, the coveted eastern investors were sitting across the desk from Jack Morgan when Clay and Sheriff Bottom entered the study.

"What the devil's going on?" Morgan rose from his chair.

"It's probably nothing," Sheriff Bottom said, hedging. "Sorry to interrupt you fellas."

Wilford Henry pushed aside the stack of papers and laid down his pen. "Is there a problem, Marshal?"

Clay's gaze swept the room. "Could be."

Chester Higgins-Smythe folded his long hands in his lap. "We were about to conclude an important business deal."

"I want an explanation, Chandler." Anger twisted Morgan's face.

"We got a report that Mr. Henry's wife's jewelry had been found."

Morgan sank into his chair, his demeanor now relaxed. "Great. That's great." He looked across the desk at the two other men. "See? You're making the right decision."

Relieved, Wilford Henry said, "Good work, Marshal. So, where is my wife's jewelry?"

"And, more importantly," Mr. Higgins-Smythe said, "who is responsible for the theft?"

Clay crossed to the bookcase on the opposite wall. Fifth row up, on the right. He pulled out the handsome leather-bound volume and, as Deuce had said he would, spotted the small satin bag. He dumped the contents in his hands. "Is this your wife's jewelry, Mr. Henry?"

Stunned, he exchanged a look with his business partner and nodded. "Yes, Marshal, it is."

All eyes turned to Morgan.

"Now—now hold on here." He came to his feet slowly. "I don't know how that jewelry got there. You don't think that I..."

Sheriff Bottom stepped forward. "Maybe we'd better go down to the jail and talk about it."

Morgan jerked away from him. "No! This is a mistake. I don't know anything about that jewelry. I swear!"

Mr. Higgins-Smythe stood and squared his shoulders. "We knew you were in need of capital, Morgan, but frankly, we didn't think you were desperate enough to steal from us."

"No, no, you're wrong!"

"It appears my wife was right about this place."

Mr. Henry nodded solemnly. "I'm glad now we sent them back home ahead of us. I wouldn't want Abigail to see this."

"Thank you, Marshal." Mr. Higgins-Smythe rose and gave Clay a stiff bow.

Mr. Henry accepted the satin bag and dropped it in his pocket. Both men shot Morgan contemptuous looks and left.

"Wait!" Morgan collapsed into the chair.

Sheriff Bottom shrugged helplessly at Clay.

He waved him away. "You bring him down to the jail. I need some air."

Clay left by the front door and stepped into the warm

morning sun. He spotted Deuce standing behind a big elm across the road, watching the house. He ducked behind the tree when he saw Clay heading his way, but didn't run.

Clay stopped in front of him and folded his arms across his chest. "We found the jewelry, just like you said."

Deuce glanced at the house. "What's going to happen to Mr. Morgan?"

"The sheriff's taking him down to the jail to question him. Either way, he's pretty much washed up. Those investors are hightailing it out of town now."

Deuce's expression hardened. "That's what he gets for being greedy."

Clay hung his thumbs in his gun belt. "So you just happened on that jewelry when you were delivering Miss Wilder's books. Is that right?"

A long moment dragged by. Deuce lifted his gaze and looked Clay straight in the eye. "Yes, sir."

"I'd say that was pretty lucky."

Deuce shook his head. "I'd say it was justice."

Knuckles white, Kelsey clutched the broom handle as she swept her way across the kitchen floor. Not only did her hands tremble, but her head hurt, her knees wobbled, and her stomach was coiled tighter than a hangman's noose. She glanced out the window. The sun was high overhead. Noon. She gripped the broom tighter and thought she might faint.

How could she have been so stupid? Forming a gang of outlaws, jeopardizing the lives of her friends, robbing the stage, stealing money. What had she been thinking? Kelsey leaned heavily on the broom as the sins of her past assailed her.

Clay was right. She knew that now—she believed it with all her heart. She should have tried other ways. She should have gone to the law. She should have trusted someone.

Kelsey drew in a ragged breath. None of that mattered now, though. In a few minutes, she'd face Judge Winthrope, and with the overwhelming evidence against her, she'd surely go to prison—or even hang.

If only Clay were here. If she could just see him one last time before she went to the courthouse. But he'd left early this morning. He hadn't even come in for breakfast. Kelsey pressed her hand to her lips.

"You're mighty dressed up today."

Kelsey turned to face Etta Mae, coming through the back door, and ran her hand down the skirt of her pink dress. It was the prettiest thing she had with her at the hotel, so she'd put it on, as Clay had instructed. She hoped it was the judge's favorite color.

"I felt like fixing up today." Kelsey turned back to her sweeping.

Etta Mae hooked her shawl on the peg by the door and tied on an apron. "Something special going on? Hmm?"

Kelsey's knees nearly gave out. "No. No, nothing."

"I didn't think so, what with your friend leaving, and all. The whole town's talking."

Kelsey touched her hand to her forehead. "What?"

"Hmm? Oh, your friend Miss Mallory, leaving town yesterday with them uppity eastern ladies." Etta fetched a sack from the pantry and plopped it on the sideboard; flour billowed around her and settled onto the floor.

"Mallory left?"

"Oh, well, yes. But you were out at your pa's place yesterday, weren't you? You didn't know."

So Mallory had gone back east with Mrs. Henry after all. Kelsey slumped against the broom. It was the only relief she'd felt in two days. As outrageous as she was, Mallory might have blurted out the truth of her involvement with the Schoolyard Boys—just to spite her father—and implicate Holly as well. At least now, the two of them were safe. Kelsey alone would pay the price for what they'd all done, as she should, since it had been her idea in the first place.

"Estelle Duncan has been crying for two days." Etta Mae took a bowl from the cupboard. "That's what Polly Lincoln said. Said, too, that Nate had sent for the doctor. Hmm?"

Seth's appearing in town suddenly, marrying Holly on the spot, and the two of them claiming a baby that wasn't supposed to exist, was scandal enough to make anyone's mother cry. But Kelsey felt little sympathy for Estelle Duncan, after all the pain she'd caused.

"She should cry," Kelsey said. "I doubt she'll show her face in public again, with the town talking about Holly and everything."

"Hmm? Oh, no." Etta Mae nodded wisely. "She's crying for the loss of her daughter and that new baby. Remorse. It's eating her up inside."

Kelsey turned quickly and dropped the broom in the pantry. Remorse of her own weighed her down like an anchor. Though she'd prefer other company, she knew how Estelle Duncan felt.

Her heart fluttered as she looked out the back door. The bright sun overhead told time accurately enough to convince her she could put off her departure for the courthouse no longer. "I have to run a few errands, Etta Mae. I'll be back in—" What? Eight to ten years?

Etta Mae waved her away as she splashed water down the sideboard and onto the floor.

Kelsey drew in a deep breath and stepped outside. She told herself to be brave, to be strong. It didn't help. She thought she might actually become sick.

Suddenly, Clay stepped around the corner. Kelsey's heart soared. She ran to him and curled her fists in the front of his shirt. "Oh, Clay. Where have you been? I'm just sick with worry."

He tensed and backed away as far as he could, with her clinging to his shirt. "I was over talking to Deuce."

No compassion showed in his face, no warmth gleamed in his eyes. She didn't care. He knew she was an outlaw, he'd seen her naked. Why shouldn't he know she was afraid?

Tears pooled in her eyes. "I'm so scared. I need you, Clay. Please come with me to the courthouse. Please."

He stared down at her. "You want me with you?"

"Oh, yes." She tugged on his shirt. "I don't know why I did such an idiotic thing in the first place, robbing the stage. You were right, Clay, I should have tried another way. Please don't make me see the judge alone. I need you with me."

"Oh, God…" Clay pulled her tight against him and wrapped both arms around her. The lawman in him needed to hear her remorse for what she'd done. The rest of him needed to hear that she wanted help, that she wanted him. She trembled in his arms, and his heart melted.

She looked up at him, and her bottom lip quivered. "You'll go with me, won't you?"

"Sure, honey." He released her from his embrace. "I'll be back in a minute."

"Where—where are you going?" She watched as he jogged down the boardwalk toward the hotel.

"I've got to change my shirt."

"What?" She'd poured out her heart, begged for his help at the most vulnerable point in her life, and he wanted to put on a fresh shirt?

"Stay there. I'll be back."

She heard his footsteps run up the service stairway, and a short while later he bounded out the back door again. He wore a crisp white shirt now, but that wasn't all he'd changed. He sported a dark vest with threads of gold through it, and a black coat. He'd put on different trousers, too, and wiped the dust from his boots; a string tie dangled around his neck. He looked devilishly handsome, though for the life of her, Kelsey couldn't imagine why he'd need to impress the judge.

"We'd better hurry." Clay fumbled with his tie all the way to the courthouse. At the doorway, he gave up. "Do something with this thing, will you?"

"Good thing I have brothers, huh?" Kelsey stretched up and expertly fashioned his tie into a presentable bow.

Clay closed his hands over both of hers. "Nervous?"

She wasn't nearly as nervous now that he was with her. Kelsey managed a small smile. "A little."

"Yeah, me too."

What was he nervous about? "Clay, I—"

"Now listen, when you talk to Judge Winthrope, tell him the truth. Understand?" She nodded, and Clay drew in a big breath. "Okay. Let's go."

He opened the door, and Kelsey stepped into the

courtroom. The chairs were all empty, and the bench was vacant.

"Shouldn't people be here for the trial?"

Clay pulled off his Stetson and ran his hand through his hair. "This, ah, this isn't a trial. It's a—a hearing. Yeah, that's what it is, a hearing. Come on."

"But, Clay—"

"Did you want the whole town here to witness this?"

Kelsey shuddered. "Of course not."

She followed him across the room and stood in silence as he knocked on the door of the judge's chamber. Her stomach tightened when the gruff voice answered.

Judge Harlan Winthrope lifted his wide girth from his chair behind his desk as they walked into the room. He eyed her sharply, and Kelsey sank into one of the leather wingback chairs as her knees threatened to give out.

Clay tossed his Stetson on the edge of the desk. "Judge Winthrope, this is Miss Kelsey Rodgers."

He nodded cordially. "Yes, Miss Rodgers, I'm staying at your hotel. Your hospitality has been most enjoyable."

Kelsey wanted to sink into the floor. The judge had caught her in the kitchen, locked in Clay's arms, his knee wedged between her legs, kissing him like a half-eagle whore. He probably wondered when he'd get his share of her hospitality.

Kelsey clasped her hands in her lap. "Thank you, sir."

"Well, let's get on with this." Judge Winthrope lowered himself into his chair and settled his spectacles into place. He picked up several sheaves of paper and looked over them.

Beside her, Clay took the other chair and caught her eye. He winked. Despite herself, Kelsey relaxed a little.

"The charges against you are very serious, Miss Rodgers. Five stagecoach robberies, one attempted robbery, assault on a deputy sheriff, assault on a federal marshal." The judge laid the papers down and looked directly at her. "What do you have to say for yourself, young lady?"

Kelsey twisted her fingers together. "Well, Your Honor, as far as assaulting Deputy Elder is concerned, it wasn't him I shot. It was his hat."

The judge sat back in his chair. "His hat?"

"Yes, sir. And I don't think assault on a hat is a crime. Is it?"

His brows rose. He glanced at Clay, then shrugged. "I know of no statute on the books protecting the rights of headgear." He picked up his pen and drew a line through a portion of the charges on the pages in front of him.

Kelsey fidgeted. "I did attempt to rob the payroll, like you said, but I didn't get a cent. I don't think that one should be held against me, Your Honor."

"You don't?"

Clay cringed and rubbed his forehead.

"No, sir. I don't."

Judge Winthrope shrugged. "Makes sense." He struck through another portion of the charges.

Kelsey pressed her lips together. She nodded toward Clay. "I did assault a federal marshal. But he started it."

Judge Winthrope reared back in his chair and

pressed his fingers to his lips, his eyes dancing. "Is that right, Marshal? Did you start it?"

Indignant, Clay sat up. "No, I did not."

Kelsey's spine stiffened. "If you hadn't been chasing me, I wouldn't have been forced to bite your leg."

"I was arresting you!"

The judge leaned forward. "He was chasing you?"

"Yes, sir, he was."

"Did you bite him?"

"Yes," she admitted. "But not as hard as I could have."

"Probably deserved to be bit. We'll dismiss that charge, too." He took up his pen and crossed it off the paper.

"Thank you, Your Honor."

Clay rolled his eyes and sank back in his chair.

The judge drew in a deep breath. "We still have the more serious charges to contend with. Stagecoach robbery, five counts."

Clay leaned forward. "There are some extenuating circumstances, Your Honor."

Kelsey eyed him sharply. "Well, it's about time you spoke up. I've saved your life twice already, for heaven's sake. You could at least put in a good word for me."

Judge Winthrope eyed Clay sharply. "Miss Rodgers saved your life? Twice?"

Clay shifted in the chair. "Yes, Your Honor. Miss Rodgers's gang of outlaws intervened on my behalf when two other outlaws attempted to hang me."

His brows rose. "Is that so?"

Kelsey dipped her lashes. "It was my idea. My friends said to let him hang. They said, how good a marshal could he be, if he got captured by that 'ol coot Luther McGraw and the little Tucker boy.''

"I was ambushed!"

Kelsey patted his arm. "Yes, dear. I'm sure you were."

"Now just a goddamn minute—"

"Anyway—" Kelsey turned back to the judge "—I had to stop the hanging, no matter what they said. It just wasn't right."

Judge Winthrope nodded slowly. "You said you'd saved his life on two occasions?"

"Yes, sir. The other time was at the—" Kelsey clamped her mouth shut, and her cheeks reddened. She'd nearly told the judge that she'd saved Clay's life at the hideout of Scully Dade. But that would have revealed that she'd been alone with Clay on the trail for days.

"Well, Miss Rodgers?"

She bit down on her bottom lip and cast a look at Clay. He read her concern easily.

"It was in connection with the Dade gang," Clay said. The finality in his tone allowed for no further questions.

Judge Winthrope nodded. "I see. Well, Miss Rodgers, is there anything else you'd like to say on your behalf?"

She sat up straighter. "Yes, Your Honor. I know now that I was wrong in committing those robberies. At the time, it seemed like the only way out of a very big problem. But Clay—I mean, Marshal Chandler—has shown me that taking the law into my own hands is not the right thing to do."

The judge glanced back and forth between the two of them. "He showed you that?"

"Yes, sir." Kelsey gazed at Clay. "And he showed me that it's all right to open my heart and trust someone else, and not try to do everything myself."

Clay grinned and took her hand. He gave her fingers a little squeeze.

Judge Winthrope rested both arms on his desk and sighed heavily. "This is not an easy case, by any means. As I understand from Marshal Chandler's report, Miss Rodgers, you felt the law had failed you and that you were recovering your own money in those robberies. Also, you did stop the attempted murder of a federal marshal, and you were instrumental in bringing down the Dade gang, a band of cutthroats who'd committed atrocities far worse than anything the Schoolyard Boys had done."

Kelsey felt Clay's hand tighten around hers, and for an instant she allowed herself to think Judge Winthrope might spare her. She held her breath.

"I've taken into account your background, Miss Rodgers, and I've also had occasion to observe you and Marshal Chandler together, and I believe there's only one course of action appropriate here." Judge Winthrope looked solemnly at Kelsey. "I'm going to recommend a life sentence."

Chapter Eighteen

The breath went out of Kelsey in a strangled cry. A life sentence? Her head spun. Her whole body went numb. No, no, it couldn't be true.

Clay pulled her to her feet and held her upper arms. "As my wife, Kelsey."

She stared blankly up at him. "What?"

"A life sentence as my wife." He looked deeply into her eyes. "I want you to marry me."

"Marry you?" She blinked, and the feeling came back into her limbs. Kelsey looked at the judge. "You're not sending me to prison?"

"No, dear." He smiled.

"Can you do that? I mean, is it legal?"

"I'm the circuit-court judge. I can do whatever I want." He softened his voice. "My recommendation stands."

"Kelsey, will you marry me?"

"Do—do you love me?"

"Oh, God, yes." Clay crushed her against him. "I love you so much, you're making me half-crazy."

Joyous laughter bubbled in Kelsey as she clung to him. Her heart soared. "I love you, too."

He set her away from him. "Then you'll marry me?"

"Oh, yes!"

She threw her arms around him, and he covered her lips with a deep, satisfying kiss.

Judge Winthrope chuckled as he gathered the papers on his desk. "Assault on a hat... That's a good one. Did she really bite you, Clay?"

He held Kelsey close against him. "She did, Uncle Harlan."

He shook his head. "She's a jewel, all right. Your folks are going to love her."

Clay beamed proudly, content with Kelsey in his arms.

Suddenly she stiffened and pushed herself away.

"'Uncle Harlan'?" She pointed an accusing finger at the judge as her gaze bored into Clay. "This man is your uncle?"

Clay held up both hands. "Calm down, honey. I can explain."

She advanced on him. "You let me think I was going to prison? And all along you knew I wasn't?"

He backed up. "There's a very good reason for that. If you'll just listen—"

"You let me worry myself sick! I was scared half out of my mind!"

Judge Winthrope's voice rose above hers. "Do you still want to go through with this, Clay?"

He looked down at her blazing green eyes, her pinkened cheeks, her tight angry lips and her determined jaw. He wanted that passion. For himself. For always.

Clay took both her hands. "Up until today, there was no room for me in your life. I had to know you wanted me, Kelsey. I had to know you needed me."

"And I," Judge Winthrope said, "had to know you were sorry for what you'd done. I had to hear it from you myself."

Clay lifted her hands and nibbled little kisses across her knuckles. He smiled gently. "Please marry me."

Kelsey stretched up on her toes and threw her arms around his neck. Her anger dissolved. "Don't forget— this life sentence works both ways."

His lips covered hers hungrily.

Judge Winthrope's throat-clearing interrupted them. "All right, you two. There's plenty of time for that later. Let's get on with it. I've got to catch the stage in an hour."

Kelsey turned as the judge pulled a worn Bible from his desk. She looked up at Clay. "We're getting married? Now? But my dress..." She realized then the reason Clay had instructed her to wear something pretty for the judge today, and why he'd put on a coat and tie for the occasion. She couldn't hold back her smile. "You had this whole thing planned all along, didn't you?"

He nodded. "Hold on. There's more. I rode out to your house this morning, and— Well, you'll see."

Clay crossed the room and opened the door. Holly stepped into the judge's chamber, followed by Seth. In his arms was their baby, snuggled in a delicate pink blanket.

Holly squealed with delight as she embraced Kelsey. "I'm so happy for you. And what a surprise! Why, when Marshal Chandler told us the news this morning I could hardly believe it. I only hope you two can be as happy as Seth and me."

Kelsey turned to her brother. The empty, haunted look she'd seen in his eyes the day he arrived on the stage was gone. He smiled and slid his arm around her shoulders.

"I want you to meet somebody, sis." Seth pushed the blanket from the baby's face. "This is Evelyn Estelle Rodgers."

Tears burned Kelsey's eyes as she gazed at the dark-haired child sleeping in his arms. "You named her after Mama. Oh, Seth, she's beautiful." She looked up at him suddenly. "You named her after Holly's mother, also?"

Holly slid her arm through his. "It was Seth's idea. He said we could go by and see my folks this afternoon."

He nodded. "I spent too long in prison, Kelsey, to let hatred steal from my future."

Kelsey kissed his cheek. "I'm glad, Seth."

"Excuse me," the judge called, "but I've got a stage to catch."

"Here." Seth dug in his shirt pocket and passed Clay a gold wedding band.

Clay pulled Kelsey into his embrace. "It's your mama's. I figured it was a way to have part of her with you today."

Kelsey blinked back tears. "It's perfect."

"You want to get married?" He grinned down at her.

"I sure do."

"Looks like Deuce made his decision," Kelsey said as they stepped onto the boardwalk in front of the express office. "I'll go talk to him."

Clay lifted her hand and kissed it softly; it was the first time he'd turned her loose since the judge pronounced them husband and wife, a few minutes ago. "He looks like he could use a kind word."

Judge Winthrope watched as Kelsey eased onto the bench beside Deuce; a worn, threadbare carpetbag sat at his feet. "He's a good boy, Clay. If you hadn't sent him over to clerk for me, I wouldn't have known that. You're doing the right thing."

Clay shook his head slowly. Even wearing his newest trousers and shirt, Deuce looked unkempt. "I should have bought him a proper suit to make the trip in."

"And spoil all your ma's fun? She'll dress him up, teach him manners and polish him until he shines. And your pa will take that bright mind of his and make it even better. He'll have him ready for college by fall." Judge Winthrope nodded slowly. "Your folks will be good for him. And he'll be good for them."

"I think you're right."

"But having Dennis with them won't make up for not having you," he pointed out sternly.

"I know, I know." Clay gazed at Kelsey again. "I'm taking her away from this place for a long honeymoon. We'll go see Ma and Pa in a month or so, after Deuce has gotten settled. With Seth back, he can handle things here, look after the family. Kelsey needs to get away."

"Did you tell her about the reward?"

Clay shook his head. "Are you sure you want her to have it?"

"She led you to the Dade gang. She deserves the reward. Besides, from what you tell me, her family can use the cash."

Otis Bean stuck his head through the door of the

express office. "Ten minutes! Stage arrives in ten minutes!"

Clay crossed the boardwalk and looked down at Deuce. Kelsey left them alone and joined the judge.

"All set to go?"

Deuce got to his feet. "Yes, sir. I guess so."

"Nervous?"

"No." His shoulders sagged. "Yes."

Clay patted his back. "You just stick beside Judge Winthrope. He'll get you to my folks' house safe and sound."

"The judge said your pa is a lawyer."

"That's right. He's the best lawyer around."

"Was he a good pa?"

Clay grinned at the sudden onslaught of memories. "Yes, he was."

"Then how come you left?" Deuce looked up at him. "He didn't...hit you, did he?"

Clay cringed. The wounds Ben Tucker had inflicted on Deuce had healed, but the scars would never fade. "No, Deuce. My pa never laid a hand on me. He won't hit you, either." The look in Deuce's eye told Clay he understood the words but the concept eluded him. It would take time to undo what Ben Tucker had done.

Deuce glanced toward Kelsey and Judge Winthrope, talking together at the edge of the boardwalk. "Miss Kelsey told me you two got married."

A big grin broke over Clay's face. "I'm a lucky man."

Deuce nodded. "My ma said you and Miss Kelsey would be good together."

How did Deuce's mother know everything that went on in town? Clay shook his head in wonder. "Is your family coming over to see you off?"

"I told Ma and the girls goodbye at the house. Ma cried. Then I went over to the livery and told Jared I was leaving." His gaze fell to the ground. "I tried to tell Pa, but he just walked away."

The hurt and rejection mirrored on Deuce's face hurt Clay nearly as much, but he tried to make the boy feel better. "It's hard on your pa, seeing you leave."

Deuce shrugged, as if he doubted it. "I guess."

"Eight minutes! Stage arrives in eight minutes!" Otis Bean's announcement rang out from the doorway.

"Yoo-hoo! Dennis!" Miss Wilder shuffled across the boardwalk toward them, straw satchel in hand, shawl clutched around her. "Oh, dear me, Dennis, I'm so glad I didn't miss you."

Clay tipped his hat. "Good day, Miss Wilder."

"Yes, Marshal, good day to you, too." She turned to Deuce. "I just wanted to tell you, Dennis, how much I appreciate all the work you did for me, and how proud we all are that you're going off to college."

He grinned. "Thank you, Miss Wilder."

"Yes, now, I'm going inside and see how Mr. Bean liked his books." Miss Wilder shuffled her satchel higher on her arm. "You be sure to write to me, Dennis."

"Yes, ma'am. I promise."

She touched her hat and went into the express office.

"She's a sweet old lady," Clay said as she went inside.

"Deuce?"

Ben Tucker stepped from around the corner of the express office, his bulky frame nearly blocking out the sun.

Deuce froze, and instinctively Clay stepped in front of him.

Ben walked over. He eyed Clay sharply. "I want to talk to my boy, Marshal."

Clay hesitated, then moved aside. Deuce seemed to shrink beneath his father's glower. Then Ben pulled off his hat and his face softened.

"I come to tell you, Deuce, that I'm gonna miss you." He twisted his hat in his hands. "You were always special, son, and sometimes, well, sometimes I just didn't know what to do with you. But I'm proud of you for what you're doing. Damn proud. Come here."

Ben wrapped Deuce in a bear hug so tight it pulled him off his feet. He held him and rocked him and kissed the top of his head before he set him down again.

Ben sniffed. "Now, you listen to me, son. Marshal Chandler's folks are good people—I wouldn't have agreed to let you go if they weren't. But if you don't like it there, or if anything bad happens, or if you decide you want to come home, you let me know and I'll come get you. No matter what, no matter when, I'll come after you. Understand?"

Deuce dragged his sleeve across his eyes. "Yes, sir."

Ben turned to Clay and offered his hand. "Thanks again, Marshal, for what you're doing for my boy."

He shook his hand. "He's a fine boy, Ben. He'll make us both proud."

"That he will." Ben nodded at Deuce and walked away.

Clay put his arm around Deuce's shoulder. "You still want to go?"

Deuce sniffed and watched his father until he disappeared around the corner. "Yes, sir."

"If you—"

"It's gone! It's gone!"

Shrill, frantic screams emanated from the express office. Otis Bean dashed out onto the boardwalk.

"My timepiece! It's gone! I can't find it!" He looked down the street in horror and pointed a long, thin finger. "And here comes the stage!"

Otis splayed his palms across his cheeks and ran back inside.

Deuce gasped and turned in time to see Miss Wilder disappear around the corner. He covered his eyes with his hand and turned away.

Clay followed the boy's line of vision, then looked down at him. "Deuce, what's going on?"

He drew in a deep breath and dragged his hand across his mouth. "Nothing."

With a creak of leather and a straining of wood, the stagecoach stopped in front of the express office. Dust settled around it as the horses tossed their heads and pawed at the street. Clay passed the baggage up to the driver.

Judge Winthrope cornered Clay and Kelsey at the door. "All right now, you two be good to each other. And I expect to see you both in a few weeks."

Clay slid his arm around Kelsey's waist. "I'll take her home and show her off, Uncle Harlan. But I want her to myself for a while."

Kelsey blushed and slapped him playfully on the chest.

Judge Winthrope gave her a hug and shook Clay's hand and climbed up into the stagecoach.

"Good luck, Deuce." Kelsey gave him a peck on the cheek. "We'll see you soon."

He blushed and grinned, then turned to Clay. "Thanks, Marshal, for everything."

Clay gave him a hug. "Don't worry about anything, Deuce. You'll do fine."

"I'll try my best." Deuce turned to board the stage, then stopped. He glanced around, then crooked his finger at Clay. He bent down. "I think maybe you should go over to Miss Wilder's place," Deuce whispered. "She needs to move down to her nephew's. You've got to tell her that."

"Why is that, Deuce?"

He glanced at Otis Bean through the window of the express office. The agent was tossing papers, logbooks, searching frantically. "Take a close look around her place. You'll see."

Otis Bean wailed inside the express office.

Clay nodded. "All right. I'll go over there."

Deuce climbed into the stage. Clay looped his arm around Kelsey. They waved as the coach pulled away.

Kelsey turned in his arms and splayed her hands across his chest. "It was a good thing you did for Deuce."

"Do you think so?" Clay nuzzled her neck. "Well, I've got a few things in mind for you, too."

"Clay, please, we're on a public street." She giggled her protest.

He touched his lips gently to hers. "Then we'll continue this at home."

She wrapped her arms around his waist. "We don't have a home."

"Oh, yeah." He kissed her again. "We'll worry about that when we get back from our honeymoon. If I decide to bring you back."

"Clay, you know I have to live here, near my family."

He nibbled at her cheek. "I'm your family, now."

Kelsey snuggled closer. "The sheriff is retiring this fall, you know. Or you could put your law degree to use."

Clay traced his finger along the line of her jaw and tilted her face up to his. "Kelsey, we have the whole world and our whole lives open to us. We don't have to decide right this minute."

She smiled. "You're right. And I like that idea of you and I being a family. Of course, we'll need some children. You do want children, don't you?"

"Oh, hell, yes." Clay kissed her again. "In fact, I'm thinking we ought to get to work on that right away."

Kelsey laughed low in her throat. "I believe—"

"Chandler! Marshal Chandler!"

Sheriff Bottom hurried across the street and stepped up onto the boardwalk, huffing and puffing. "Chandler, you've got to saddle up. We've got to hit the trail."

He kept Kelsey locked securely in his arms. "I'm kind of busy right now, Sheriff."

"It's Morgan. He's gone."

"Gone?" Clay lifted his head from Kelsey's neck. "Didn't you lock him up?"

Sheriff Bottom shifted uncomfortably. "Well, no. Him being such a big man in town and all, I didn't think I should. He promised he'd come over to the jail. But when he didn't show up, I went out to his place, and he's gone. That butler fella of his said Morgan threw a few belongings in a sack and hightailed it out of town. Said Morgan didn't say where he was going or if he'd ever be back."

Kelsey's eyes rounded. "Jack Morgan is gone? For good?"

Clay lifted a shoulder. "Looks like it."

"Come on, Chandler, we've got to go find him," Sheriff Bottom insisted.

"Nope." Clay shook his head. "As far as I'm concerned, Jack Morgan can stay gone. If you think he's worth the trouble, you go get him."

"Damn..." Sheriff Bottom grumbled and walked away.

Kelsey heaved a sigh. "Jack Morgan is gone? What wonderful news for my family."

Clay snuggled her deeper into his arms. "A lot of good things happened today."

"Was justice served enough to suit you, Marshal?"

He mulled it over. "I'd say you got what you deserve—a federal marshal for a husband."

"And you got what you deserve. An outlaw for a wife." Kelsey grinned up at him. "Is that justice?"

He planted a sweet kiss on her lips and whispered, "No, honey, that's love."

* * * * *

A clandestine night of passion
An undisclosed identity
A hidden child

RITA Award nominee

presents...

Available in April,
wherever Harlequin Historicals are sold.

BIGB97-5

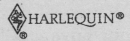

Not The Same Old Story!

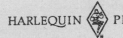 Exciting, emotionally intense romance stories that take readers around the world.

 Vibrant stories of captivating women and irresistible men experiencing the magic of falling in love!

 Temptation Bold and adventurous— Temptation is strong women, bad boys, great sex!

HARLEQUIN SUPERROMANCE® Provocative, passionate, contemporary stories that celebrate life and love.

 Romantic adventure where anything is possible and where dreams come true.

HARLEQUIN® INTRIGUE® Heart-stopping, suspenseful adventures that combine the best of romance and mystery.

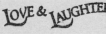 Entertaining and fun, humorous and romantic—stories that capture the lighter side of love.

LOVE *or* MONEY?
Why not Love *and* Money!
After all, millionaires
need love, too!

Suzanne Forster,
Muriel Jensen
and
Judith Arnold
bring you three original stories
about finding that one-in-a million man!

Harlequin also brings you
a million-dollar sweepstakes—enter
for your chance to win a fortune!

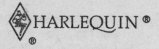 HARLEQUIN ®

It's hot...and it's out of control!

Beginning this spring, Temptation turns up the
heat. Look for these bold, provocative,
*ultra*sexy books!

#629 OUTRAGEOUS
by Lori Foster (April 1997)

#639 RESTLESS NIGHTS
by Tiffany White (June 1997)

#649 NIGHT RHYTHMS
by Elda Minger (Sept. 1997)

BLAZE: Red-hot reads—only from

Harlequin Romance ®

Delightful

Affectionate

Romantic

Emotional

Tender

Original

Daring

Riveting

Enchanting

Adventurous

Moving

Harlequin Romance—the
series that has it all!

HROM-G